The CAPTAIN

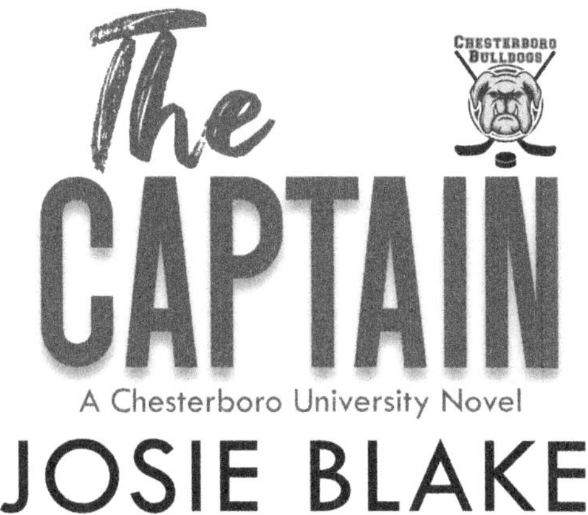
Chesterboro
Bulldogs
The
CAPTAIN
A Chesterboro University Novel
JOSIE BLAKE

This is a work of fiction. Names, characters, businesses, places, events and incidents are either the product of the author's imagination or used in a fictitious manner. Any resemblance to actual persons, living or dead, or actual events is purely coincidental.

Content edits provided by Jessica Ruddick.

Line editing suggestions provided by Red Adept Editing.

ISBN: 978-1-955887-00-7

Contents

For my family. You always have my back as I find my way.
Also, for the readers.
Thank you.

Captain (noun) - the leader of a team, especially in sports.

Hannah

THERE'S GOING TO BE a fight. As sure as "Sweet Home Alabama" will play between sets and as sure as there will be an argument at the pool table, someone's going to get a beating. I just don't know who it is yet.

The Pig's Tail doesn't attract the sophisticated set. It's fifteen miles from my elite college, Chesterboro University, in eastern Pennsylvania. The usual clientele is truck drivers, bikers, and the occasional locals who enjoy the dive bar atmosphere.

Of course, Ronnie, the guy who coordinates my singing gigs, isn't here. Who knows what hole he's currently lost in. He isn't ever around when things could get messy—or ever, really. He still insists on a percentage of my earnings, though.

I sigh. Someday, I'll look back on this time singing at dive bars like the Pig and laugh. But that day isn't today. Today, I need the money, and this pays the bills.

I peek out from the side of the Pig's stage, trying to determine where the tension is coming from.

"You ready?" Josh asks from behind me. He and I went to high school together. Burly and bald, Josh doesn't incite people to open up to him. Strange he would own a bar and be its primary bartender.

"Yeah." I smile over my shoulder. "I just had to get some water."

Not one to mince words, Josh nods and walks away.

"Hey, Josh," I call. He turns, raising an eyebrow. "Be careful tonight. Something's brewing in the air out there."

"Yeah." He snorts. "Bunch of college kids here for a twenty-first." He rolls his eyes and heads back to his post behind the bar.

Damn. Well, that explains it. Stepping farther onto the worn stage, I scan the crowd before spotting the group of seven or ten guys—more like a huddle of linebackers—at the bar. They're tall and built. With my outdated contacts prescription, I can't make out faces from here, but I can definitely admire all the chiseled shoulders. They tower over everyone else in the place, and in their expensive clothes, they stick out like sore thumbs. My bet is they're from Chesterboro.

Double damn.

I adjust my wig. It's late, after midnight. These guys have definitely been out partying for a while. They aren't going to recognize me. Even if they do, I doubt they'd care that the acclaimed classical composer of the Chesterboro University music department's senior class is singing at this hole in the wall. Hell, they might not even know there is a star in the music department. Not a lot of jocks in my classes. They probably ended up at the Pig last because it stayed open an hour later than everywhere else. They have the vibe of a bunch of fourth-graders on a field trip to the zoo, more interested in sightseeing the local color than anything else. Generally, though, the local color isn't interested in being watched.

I send up a quick prayer that the bar will close without anything eventful happening.

The jukebox goes silent, and the lights on the stage go up. In a place like the Pig, acts are generally greeted with sometimes good-natured and often not-so-good-natured receptions, but the room stays relatively quiet as I take the stage. Over the past year, I've sung all over the place, but this is only my second time singing here. Maybe people are starting to recognize me.

The only noise wafts from the Neanderthals at the bar.

As soon as I step on stage, though, none of that matters. Everything fades away. There's no drunken addict mother, no dead father, no messed-up childhood that requires escape. There are no bills I can barely pay or dreams that feel out of reach.

I smile, gripping the microphone. "How are you all doing tonight?" There are a few cheers and some claps, and I wink. "Sounds like we all could use a few songs, then."

I wait patiently for my music to cue up. The first few bars of an old Fleetwood Mac ballad begin. I love Fleetwood Mac in general and Stevie Nicks in particular. I open my mouth, and I'm lost.

It's always like this. I can't explain the joy that washes over me—no, through me—when I sing or play. Standing in front of these people makes me feel like there is nothing else, nothing but the breath in my lungs and the music in my bones. It's heaven.

After the first song, I have everyone's attention. I listen to the applause, louder now than before. "There you all are," I tease. "Let's try something more upbeat, then." I reach for the tablet that controls my set list. With a tap, I cue up my next song. My voice isn't the typical pop-music fare, so I favor more classic rock and country, some alternative. Next is Journey's "Don't Stop Believin'."

Before long, people are swaying, and some have made it to the dance floor. Stupid old contacts mean I can't see their faces, but I can definitely hear them belting out the lyrics along with me. I laugh, the cheerful off-key singing in front of me lifting my own spirits. God, there is nothing better than this. When I'm up here, leading a crowd, it's like we are all in it together. We are sad in the slow love songs, and we bounce around with the joyful ones. Here, on this stage, I can feel the things that are universal among us. When we all leave this place, we're different. Different races and creeds, different classes. We have different jobs and come from different backgrounds. But in the middle of a song, we all feel it together.

I wind us through song after song. The place gets hot. Sweat runs down the sides of my head and moistens the small of my back. It trickles between my breasts. It's more crowded than any of the other nights I've sung at the Pig, and that's great. Bigger crowds mean more money, and money is my ticket out of this godforsaken town.

My first set lasts an hour, and the place is buzzing with energy. Still, the birthday party group is by far the rowdiest bunch here. In the middle of my second set, the patrons around them get fed up.

I'm singing Kelsea Ballerini's latest hit, and the birthday boy—or who I assume is the birthday boy, based on his level of wobbly intoxication—must have bumped into the table behind him. I squint, making out a pitcher of beer spilled everywhere. I can definitely see two of the men at the table stand up. That's when the shoving starts.

Then one of them throws the first punch.

Things are going to get out of hand. As the half dozen guys with the birthday party try to hold the birthday boy back, I reach for the tablet and pause my music. With all the strength in my voice, I bellow into the microphone, "Did someone say to play 'Free Bird'?"

I wave my hands, doing what I can to regain everyone's attention. If the universal sing-along Lynryd Skynyrd song can't stop a fight, nothing can. "Everyone on your feet," I yell, laughing.

If I can get everyone up, then no one will mind the shoving. Or so I hope.

"There's a birthday party in the house. Why don't those guys come on up here and help me do this?"A couple of patrons grumble in front of me, but as the first strains of the melody waft through the speakers, the crowd parts. There are some additional shoves between the drunken man of the hour and whomever he pissed off, but his friends are big and burly, and they muscle him along, dragging him to the stage stairs.

Across the bar, I can see Josh's silhouette behind the bar, his arms folded over his chest, disapproval radiating off of him. Not happy I'm calling the guys onstage, probably. I ignore him, keeping the smile plastered on my face. It's hard, though, because as they shuffle closer to me, I recognize the entire group to be the top line of the Chesterboro University ice hockey team. They are gods on campus, and even I know who they are—especially the one bringing up the rear, the team captain, Cord Spellman. He is the god of all the gods.

"Damn" doesn't cover this situation.

It's too late, though. I've already invited them up, and I need to ride it out, no matter what happens.

I run a hand over my wig, though, making sure it's still in place. The long caramel strands cover my own pale waves. Thanks to the contacts, I don't have my glasses on either. With the stage makeup I'm wearing, I barely recognize myself in the mirror. No way these guys who didn't see me before would notice me now.

"Damn" might not do the situation justice, but it definitely describes this crew. As in damn, these guys are hot. They radiate male virility like only athletes at the top of their game can. But it isn't only that. The track team is in shape. So are the swimmers. But the hockey players…they're blatantly masculine with a whole lot of extra swagger.

I let that settle in my stomach as they ramble up onstage, making what already feels like a small space feel even more crowded. They shove and jostle one another. The only one not joining in is Cord, who leans against the side wall, all wide shoulders and hot body. But he isn't wearing his usual confident, easy smile. I don't have time to figure out what bug he has up his ass, though, because I'm too busy pretending not to notice him and trying to defuse the hostility his group has already wreaked in my audience.

I lean into the microphone and start the song.

Cord

FUCKING DORSEY. THIS WHOLE night has gone to shit because of him.

Mikey said he wanted a low-key twenty-first. Most of our remaining games are tough, and playoffs are just over a month away. Now isn't the time to get crazy. All of us should be refraining, but a guy only turns twenty-one once, so we're out. It's Friday, and we have a rare weekend off. Lots of time to recover. But the plan was to keep it mellow, go out for some beers, get some food.

Mikey definitely didn't say anything about shots and nothing about ending up in some rural dive bar outside of town.

We started out fine at Fat Eddie's, our local spot. We ate enough wings to set our mouths on fire. I nursed a beer. If they let loose, I keep an eye on them. I'm team captain, after all.

But then Rachel, my cheating ex, and a few of her sorority sisters showed up. I spent the whole time avoiding her not-too-subtle advances and watching out for my boys. Then Dorsey brought up some singer. He sighed, looking like the stupid heart-eye emoji, and called her soulful.

Dumbass. He's a hockey player, not a poet.

He only mentioned her after he plied Mikey with a couple of shots. The next thing I knew, we were waiting for an Uber to take us out to nowhere to listen to her.

I've never been to this place, the Pig's Tail. What kind of name is that, anyway?

When we got inside, I steered us into a corner near the bar, out of the flow of traffic. We're bulky in regular places, and in crowded spaces, we definitely get in the way, especially after a few drinks.

Dorsey bought most of the drinks earlier, so the rest of the guys jumped in, doing shots with Mikey. Then they all did some shots together. It devolved from there. Now, I basically have a herd of drunken gorillas on my hands.

When Dorsey's singer takes the stage, she doesn't look like much. Tall, slight, long hair. She's wearing jeans, some kind of bohemian flowing shirt, and stilettos. And she hobbles on the heels as if she isn't used to walking in them.

I sip my beer. This doesn't look hopeful.

Then she opens her mouth and launches into Fleetwood Mac's "Landslide" in a way that raises the hair on my arms. It's an old song, one my parents loved when I was a kid. Hell, they might still love it. Just separately now, since they've been divorced for almost a decade.

The lyrics are haunting on their own, but this woman…it's as if the words come from deep inside her slim body, as if she lived them or wrote them herself. She makes them her own, either way. Something about the nostalgia of the song and the way she sings it… I can't look away. I don't want to.

She finishes, and there's a moment of silence before the place bursts into applause. I didn't realize how quiet it had gotten until it's loud again. I glance around, and everyone in the bar looks like they are half in love with this wispy girl.

And I get it. I really do.

She laughs, and it's its own kind of music. I want to hear more of that. Instead, she dives into "Don't Stop Believin'," and everyone in the room is on board. She sways and dances along as she sings, as if the music has taken her, is moving her. Her mouth tilts into an enigmatic smile, and the energy courses through the room as her voice fills it. The place vibrates with it because of her.

She winds her way through her first set. A mix of classic rock, heavy on Fleetwood Mac and the Eagles, female singers with big voices, and current country hits. When she's upbeat, the room bounces along. The dance floor is packed. When she sings things slow, it's as if our hearts break along with it. Some slow dance, and others just stand, listening to her. A woman in front covers her mouth, tears in her eyes.

I've been to a lot of concerts, but they're always at huge venues. Big-name musicians. But this space is intimate. It's like she's singing especially for me.

They play the jukebox between her sets, but the crowd gets antsy. We know she's coming back, and we're impatient for her return. When she does, her joy is so intense that I can feel it—I really can. She dives right into "Baby Can I Hold You" by Tracy Chapman, a song I haven't heard since the first girl I dated in high school played it for me. I only listened then because I wanted to get laid. But when this girl sings it? Totally different.

Next up is Miranda Lambert.

The guys keep drinking, and they holler their appreciation for her, completely enthralled.

Then Mikey loses his balance. He's hooting his approval and bumps into the table in front of us. Their pitcher of beer tilts, spilling everywhere. The two men at the table stumble to their feet, all beards and black leather.

Damn it. "Sorry, guys." I say, sliding into the mix, offering them a classic Spellman grin, the one that says that everything is fine and generally defuses conflict. "Let me buy you all another pitcher."

One of them buries his fist in Mikey's face.

Guess he doesn't want a free round.

As the other guy attempts to push in, though, I step between them and dodge that guy's fist. Some things from hockey carry into real life, like not doubling up in a fight. And Mikey is seriously fucked up right now, so no one is going to take shots at him on my watch.

Just when shit looks like it's going to get out of hand and I worry I'll be dragging my defensemen off a couple of busted-up townies, the singer calls our whole party up with the promise of "Free Bird." Whatever magic she holds works, because suddenly, they're all swaying together, arms joined, drowning out the singer's angelic voice with their intoxicated warbling.

It's a damn shame, to be honest. She's stopped singing, her eyes closed, holding the microphone out to the guys.

Now, only five or six feet from her, I can't look away. Something about her feels vaguely familiar. It's the curve of her face, the angle of her chin and jaw. But her mouth… her lips are full, completely kissable.

Everything tightens in me. *What the fuck? So I'm some dive bar singer's groupie now?*

If she wants, my gut says.

As the song fades into the instrumental at the end, the guys all break into air guitar. The singer—Hannah, if the sign can be believed—steps to the side to let them at it. Only then, when the attention isn't on her, does her face change.

Tension tightens her features. I have no idea why, but I don't like it. Whatever is bothering her, well, it bothers me. I shift closer, trying to smooth things over. "Thanks. It's my friend's birthday."

She doesn't make eye contact when she nods, and her mouth is pressed into a line. Her response surprises me. I mean, not to brag, but I'm not usually ignorable. First, I'm huge. I'm six-three and a wall of solid muscle. Three years ago, I went in the first round of the draft, just like my dad before me. I'm also pretty likable, blessed with a charm that has been able to get me out of most trouble.

I'm not bad to look at, either, or so I've been told.

Even when I was dating Rachel and everyone on campus knew it, girls would come on to me. Now that I'm single, it's worse and more complicated because Rachel hasn't accepted that we're over either. Since we broke up last summer, between her increasing attention and the others trying to fill her role, this year has been a mess.

But Hannah doesn't seem to notice me at all. I don't like being invisible to her.

She leans in, holding the microphone away from her, keeping her face down. Her voice cuts through the air. "You need to get them out of here before things get bad."

What? Dragging my gaze away from her, I catch sight of my guys. They're hugging, laughing. They're all in varying states of intoxication. Glassy-eyed, sappy smiles, slapping one another on the back. I roll my eyes, glad they're enjoying themselves.

"Look at the audience, Cord." Her head stays tilted away, obscuring her face. But she's close enough that I can smell her. Lavender and something with a citrus tang, but not quite…

"You know who I am." I smile, trying to catch her eye, but she doesn't make eye contact. I knew she looked familiar, though.

Her mouth firms, and an edge of steel laces her beautiful voice. "Yeah. You guys play hockey. Big shots. I get it. But you have to get them out of here. This might be fun for you guys, hanging with the locals, but the locals aren't amused."

My temper flares. We have as much right to be here as anyone else. But then my gaze strays to the people standing on the dance floor. They don't look happy. They came to hear her sing, not listen to my guys warble off-key.

Worse, some of them look downright pissed.

We're headed for the playoffs. The last thing my team needs—I need—is bad publicity right now, and nothing would be worse than a brawl at a dive bar.

She's right. It's time to go. I pull my phone from my pocket and hit up the Uber app, cursing myself for not bringing my own car. With a few taps, Ralph with his Prius and Tamika with her Corolla are on their way to get my crew.

I hold up my hands to Hannah, showing her that we're ten minutes out, and she nods. She picks up her tablet and flicks her finger over it. Lifting the microphone to that luscious mouth, she says, "I think you all know this one too."

The next song on the speakers is the karaoke sing-along magic for a boy from the South like me, "Two Pina Coladas" by Garth Brooks.

She starts and encourages everyone to join in. It doesn't take much to get the whole place, including my guys, to get into it. She leads them all along, dancing and singing with them, allowing the momentum to take the crowd. She stays a safe distance away from me, too, I notice.

I lean against the wall on the opposite side of the stage from her, giving her some space and acting like her distance doesn't bother me at all as the rest of my guys goof off between us.

The last strains of the song ring through the speakers, and the whole place erupts. I set my empty beer bottle on the ground against the wall and spread my arms, stepping between my drunk-hugging, high-fiving teammates and the people in front of us. "Time to go, boys," I call. "I ordered the cars. Drinks at my place when we get back."

The suggestion that we can keep going strikes a chord with them, and they hoot and holler. I smother a grin. So predictable. That sounds good now, but after a twenty-minute ride home, it might be a different story.

"We can listen to the last songs from the back," I say, herding them off stage. I take a quick glance at Hannah and see relief on her features. It softens that mouth…well, it changes her face into something extraordinary.

I wait, watching her longer than appropriate. She catches me staring, and I meet her eyes. Brown. Pretty. Sharp. I wink. Quickly, she glances away. I immediately miss the contact.

Everything in me wants to stay, to smooth things over, to talk with her. But there's no way to do that now. I need to make sure Mikey gets home okay, and she's in the middle of singing. So I do the only thing I can and follow my guys off the back stairs.

As we sweep through the side exit and I hear the beginning strains of Maren Morris's "Bones," I feel like I do when I miss a big goal on the hockey rink.

Disappointed.

Hannah

I FINISH MY SET and even do an encore. With the crowd still yelling, I snag my weathered leather bag and toss the tablet that had been hooked up to the sound system inside. After hopping down the stairs, I pause behind the stage. I sweep out the back door, tugging my oversized beanie over the wig and tucking the strands inside it. The rock salt makes me wobble in my heels, and I keep my head down in the parking lot as I slowly make my way to my car, gripping my keys between my knuckles, my pepper spray keychain at the ready.

When I'm safely inside with all the doors locked, I send a text to Josh. *Ronnie will want his money, but you can Venmo me the rest of my take. And if I can pack the place like that, you guys need to pay me more next time.* I include a smiley face, but it isn't a joke. My boss at the truck stop has been cutting my hours, and my on-campus job doesn't go far, so I need the money. No reason to be shy about asking for it, and I'm right. I've never seen so many cars in this parking lot.

I drop my phone into my bag and start the car, sighing at the sick rumble of the muffler. That expense has to wait. It's right behind having enough electricity for heat and enough hot water for a shower.

I kick up the heat and wait for it to warm up. No way I would drive my girl, Cherry, when she's cold. And no way I can drive her in these heels.

They're the first to go. I toss them into the backseat, grab my pink Converse from the passenger side floor, and slide my feet in. Then I snag my camel-colored peacoat off the passenger seat and slip into it, shivering against the cold lining. I'd tucked my scarf into the sleeve earlier, so I pull it out and wrap it around my neck before I button the coat under my chin. I remove my hat, yank the wig off, and shove it into the bag on the floor of the passenger's side. Running my hands through my straw-colored waves, I groan. I hate that wig. It's itchy and hot, but my hair isn't as thick and glamorous. After a glance at the mirror on the visor, I cringe and tuck my hair back under the beanie. Waves plus sweat plus wig make me look a bit like Medusa. Scary.

I grab the generic makeup-removing-wipe container and pull one out, swiping off the thick foundation and mascara I wear on stage. I bought the wipes after my first time singing last summer. Mascara makes my eyes sting, and the foundation feels like war paint.

Digging around in my bag, I pull out my contacts case and my glasses case. In two pinches, I have the thin pieces of plastic out. I douse my eyes in saline, blinking in relief. I haven't been able to afford a new prescription in a long time, so the world always looks blurry.

I slip my glasses on and feel more like myself. I shift into drive and start out of the parking lot. Only one of my headlights works, so I squint as I head down the gravel drive away from the Pig's Tail. I turn on the radio, pressing buttons until the local country station fills the speakers. I inhale, stretching my neck from side to side, still buzzing from being on stage as I pull onto the main road. Music is my everything.

How much I love singing came as a surprise, though. I don't have a classical voice, so I've only ever messed around with vocals. My father, who first taught me piano, and my music teachers always seemed more interested in my instrumental work. I play classical piano, guitar, and violin, and I love them all. But there is something raw and intense about singing, especially singing popular music. Most of the time, I play music for people who are into classical. They're subdued, mostly quiet, and sort of stuffy sometimes. These strangers that I sing to don't care if I see their emotion. They sing along, dance, laugh, even cry. It's wonderful.

When I graduate, though, I'll have a double major with degrees in classical music composition and business. I plan to go to graduate school, but even if I don't, maybe I'll teach lessons or run a music school. If I'm lucky, I'll be able to play in an orchestra somewhere. It might not be huge money, but it's been my dream since I was young and my father's dream for me.

Singing is just paying the bills.

I signal, exiting from the main road onto the two-lane one that will take me into town and back to campus. Not that I live on campus. I can't afford that. I can barely afford the books and fees from attending Chesterboro University. No, the trailer I share with my mother is on the other side of town. Not sure "share" is the right word. She's hardly ever there.

In my car's single beam, I catch the silhouette of three figures walking in the shoulder of the road. Well, two of them are walking better than that other one, but it's hard to tell because the two on the sides are practically carrying the one in the middle. I would recognize the most upright one anywhere, though, with his wide shoulders and confident swagger.

Cord.

In the split second that I approach them, I weigh my options. I can keep driving. Maybe they won't recognize my car. Then again, my car is pretty distinguishable on campus, one of the most decrepit at a school full of rich kids. Cherry and I have been through a lot together, but she's not pretty.

On the other hand, none of them know me. The jocks don't spend much time in the fine arts building, especially the music wing. Mostly, I only see them crossing campus. Cord's in Pierce's music theory class, the one I'm an assistant in. But chances that he's noticed me there are pretty slim. I'm not like the girls he would notice. I shop at thrift stores for my preferred vintage and funky clothes. Those girls shop in New York. They're high heels, and I'm Converse. And makeup? *Please.* It's hard for me to keep from looking like a clown for my shows. No way would I wear that stuff every day.

Besides, the jocks at CU are annoying. The school isn't large, but it's known for hockey, football, and its fine arts programs. The fine arts kids and the jocks don't interact much. We stay in our state-of-the-art facilities, and they stay in theirs.

But if these guys are out here alone in the freezing cold, it's not because they want to be.

I slow down. It's still a few miles into town, and if that's Mikey Dischenski, the birthday boy, that the other two are carrying, then those few miles would feel like they were dragging a boulder up Mount Everest. The guy is humongous.

I pull off the road in front of them and hit my hazards, hoping all of those lights still work. In my rearview mirror, I watch Cord saunter toward the driver's side, illuminated red in the brake lights, all sexy and gorgeous. Turning the window's hand crank, I grimace as the mechanism in the door squeals in protest. *Thanks for that, Cherry.*

He leans down so he's at my eye level, an easygoing grin on his handsome face. "Hi."

The guy is on the side of the road in the freezing cold at two in the morning. *How does he look so laid-back? And why does it—and everything else about him—rub me the wrong way?* Maybe it's that he always seems to get his way with that charming smile. Or maybe it's because his dad is some famous hockey player and he's stupid rich. Or it could be that everything seems to come so damn easy to him. Everyone likes him in every situation. Girls sigh when they talk about him. He drives a great car and wears the best clothes. Seriously, how can one life be so perfect?

"Hello." Even as I greet him, I wish the sight of him didn't hit me with a curl of heat in the stomach, but it does. There's no denying how hot he is. Like everything else about him… perfect.

"I'm Cord Spellman. You look familiar. You go to CU?" He cocks his head, studying me.

"Yeah." It doesn't surprise me that he hasn't noticed me in his music class. And at a smallish school like Chesterboro, he's a celebrity. Everyone knows him, who he hangs out with, who he dates. And I'm nothing like Rachel Murray, his latest ex-girlfriend, or any of the girls he's been linked to before that. "I'm Hannah Marshall."

"Hey. Today is my friend Mikey's birthday," he says, waving toward the back of my car.

"Happy birthday, Mikey," I say, glancing in the rearview. I can only see the top of Mikey's head because he's hunched over at the waist. Definitely doesn't look the happiest.

Linc Reynolds is patting his back with one hand, the other gripping the back of his shirt, holding him up. Seeing him mothering his friend is actually pretty funny.

"We're on our way back to CU from the Pig's Tail, some dive bar the next town over, but he got sick in the car." Cord shrugs. "That got me a bad Uber review."

"I bet." Already, I regret stopping.

"Yeah, and now no one will pick me up, apparently." He checks his guys then his phone. "Linc's not having any luck either." His mouth tightens, and he sighs. "Listen...we're in a bind here. It's cold, and Mikey isn't in great shape. Any way you could help us out and give us a ride into town, to campus?" The side of his mouth tilts up. "You'd have my eternal gratitude."

"Just what I always wanted." Poor Mikey looks like a ghost in my brake lights. I can't leave them here. "Come on. I'll get you back to campus. Shepherd?" I mention the house where most of the undergraduate hockey players live and the team hangs out.

"You know where that is?"

"Yeah."

"Great, thanks." He straightens, and I close my window, keeping the heat in. I watch him tell the guys they scored a ride. My knuckles whiten as I grip the steering wheel and take deep breaths. It's only a few miles. I'll have them all back at Shepherd Hall in less than ten minutes. It's the right thing to do.

The back door swings open, and Mikey's voice vibrates through my decrepit sedan. "So, this is the party bus?" He follows that with a whoop, and if I hadn't already regretted stopping, I definitely do now.

"Shut it, douche." Linc shoves his friend's shoulder. "She didn't have to stop." He gives me an apologetic smile, a dimple in his left cheek. I flash a wan smile in return. "I'm Linc. It's Hannah, right? I think you know my friend, Shea Carmichael."

At that, I grin for real. "I do. We worked together on *Guys and Dolls* last semester." That had been the fall drama production. "She was in charge of the art sets." I did a lot of the instrumental work for the play, so I'd been able to put it on my graduate applications. I don't know Shea well, though, because she spends a lot of time driving back and forth to State, where her boyfriend goes to school. We never hung out socially.

Not that I go out much. I work all the time, and I don't drink. But still.

"I thought so. I saw the play. You guys did great."

"Thanks," I say.

"I don't get why Shea dates that preppy toolbag at State. I mean, there are plenty of better-looking guys—hockey-playing guys—here at Chesterboro." Mikey's voice booms in the car. "Like me," he offers, a roguish grin on his face.

"Yeah, you're a real catch right now, Dizz." Cord slides into the passenger's seat, filling up the space in my compact car.

Mikey's nod says he missed the sarcasm. "Right?"

Cord tosses me an eye roll, and I lift my eyebrows, amused in spite of myself. Maybe he isn't so bad. He definitely isn't bad to look at.

"There's a trash bag at your feet, in case he needs it," I tell Cord. He salutes.

As I signal and pull back onto the road, Mikey keeps up a steady stream of drunken rambling, enumerating all the ways that CU is better than State in general and Shea's boyfriend, Peterson, in particular. Linc offers a few contradictory remarks, but none of them sound convincing. Mikey isn't paying him any attention, so Linc settles into his seat, his arms folded and a scowl on his face.

Maybe he's counting the minutes for this car ride too.

"So, where are you coming from at two in the morning?" Cord asks.

"Nowhere." Obviously, he doesn't recognize me from the Pig. Not that I want him to. But for some reason, it stings.

"Hot date?"

Nevermind. Cord's a jerk. "No."

There's awkward silence. Even Mikey has gone quiet.

"I was joking." His smile is strained. "Just trying to start conversation."

"That I might be on a date is a joke?" I grit my teeth. Fine, he doesn't recognize me from the bar or from class. And I don't date much. Or at all, really. As if I have time for that. But that doesn't mean that the thought of me dating is funny.

"No. I mean…" He runs his hand in his hair. "I'm sorry. I didn't mean to upset you."

"I'm not upset."

"Right. Great. Glad to hear it." Now he's glaring at me.

We lapse into strained silence. I sigh. I'm tired, grouchy, and probably not being fair. I search for something to smooth over the tension, and a moan comes from the back seat.

"I feel sick," Mikey says.

Alarm snakes through me. I point at the floor of the passenger seat. "The trash bag at your feet."

Cord's eyes go wide in the passing streetlights. He holds up my purse.

"Really? No." I motion again as Mikey starts gagging, and my own stomach pitches in sympathy. I search for a place to pull over. We're in downtown Chesterboro, though. On-street parking is packed. "Trash bag."

It sounds like things are getting close in the back, and I listen as Linc pep talks Mikey, telling him to beast up, that he can hold it.

Cord throws a plastic bag over the seat as I whip the car into an alley and wrench it into park.

Too late. I scurry out just in time to watch Mikey Dischenski, prize winger for the Chesterboro Bulldogs, throw up in the bag where I'd tossed my wig earlier.

Cord

WE DRIVE THE LAST five blocks to Shepherd with the windows down.

In the driver's seat, Hannah looks pissed. Worse, she looks like she might cry. I didn't get a good view of the back seat, but it's not good if the steady string of curses coming from Linc is any indication. "Dizz, I fucking hate you right now. I'm never letting you live this down. I thought that time you farted in the locker room after burritos was bad. This is worse. You're the worst."

For his part, Mikey just groans.

This is a nightmare.

As Shepherd comes into view at the end of the block, I take stock of the situation. I have a drunken teammate, one that's pissed off, a backseat in need of hazmat containment, and a girl who looks on the verge of yelling at me or bursting into tears.

Not good.

Well, I'm the one who convinced her to drive us home. Sure, she stopped, but she didn't need to pick us up. It's my job to fix this.

The second we double-park in front of the huge old house, I start damage control. "Linc. Go round up whoever is around. We need help getting Mikey out of the car." His room is here, since he's only a sophomore. Linc and I live off campus.

Still clearly pissed, Linc nods. "Thanks for the ride, Hannah," he says before he bounds up the stairs to go inside, obviously in a hurry to get away from the smell of Mikey, which is valid.

I glance into the backseat. Mikey is curled into the fetal position. It looks like he made it mostly into the bag, which is a relief, but still…

I reach in, grabbing the bag he used. Strands of brown hair hang over the side. "What the…"

Glancing up, I meet Hannah's gaze. Everything clicks. *The singer at the Pig's Tail.* Hannah looked familiar, and now, I know why. That jaw, the shape of her eyes…and her fucking mouth. Sure, she put glasses on and removed the makeup and what was apparently a wig, but… "You're the singer."

She blows out a shaky breath, glancing away, but not quickly enough for me to miss the sheen of moisture in her eyes. The sight of it—of tears swimming, ready to fall—hits me right in the stomach.

"I can't really sing." She rolls her eyes. "I mean, I can. Anyone can sing. But it's not what I need to be focusing on." She swipes at her eyes, suddenly furious. "You know, it doesn't matter. I shouldn't have helped you guys. This isn't your business…" She swallows. "And that wig…" She glares at me. "It cost me a lot of money, and I can't afford to replace it, and it's you and your jackass teammate's fault."

The angry glint in her eyes is a welcome change from the tears. I hold up my hands, taking a deep breath. I'm losing control of this situation. “You can definitely sing, baby.”

“Don’t call me baby.”

“Right.” I grin, happy to see her mad. If she’s pissed, she isn’t crying. “You can definitely sing, beautiful.”

Her nose scrunches up, and I want to laugh. I don’t, though, because I have some restraint and because I’m sure that won’t help my cause. But without her tears, I’m on steadier ground. I quickly regroup. “You were amazing tonight. In fact, that was the best concert I’ve been to.” It’s a sincere confession, and I hope she can hear the truth in my words.

I expect her to preen or to smile. Something. Most of the girls I know become puddles at my feet with a few compliments, and I can’t remember the last time I’ve been sincere in giving them. Instead, she only glares at me, her mouth pursed like she’s…uncomfortable. *How is it possible that this woman with the killer voice and musical talent could struggle with a compliment?*

Crossing her arms over her chest, she exhales with a puff. “I don’t sing.”

“Well, I think you do.” I grin at her.

She rolls her eyes, exhaling as she meets my gaze. “I’m going to graduate school in the fall for music composition. I’m only singing at dive bars in bumfuck, Pennsylvania because I need the money.”

Hearing her curse is so adorable, I smother a grin and fake gasp, widening my eyes and flattening a palm against my chest. “Miss Marshall. Language.”

I’m not sure, but I think she growls at me.

Three freshmen stumble out of the house, shoving one another. Linc’s reinforcements. “Rookies,” I call. “Dizz is tired this evening. You guys want to help him up to bed?”

They all look at Mikey and exchange glances. The center guy, a winger with a lot of talent, grins, shrugging. "Sure, Cap."

Without another word, they coax Mikey out of the back seat. Two of them get under his arms, propping him up. In no time, they have him staggering up the front steps. This definitely isn't the first time any of them has helped someone onto their feet after a wild night.

"Don't forget to put him on his side. And get a trash can next to his bed."

They all call out in agreement.

As they drag Mikey inside, Hannah's brow drops. "You don't haze, do you?"

"God, no." I snort. As if I have to. These guys want to play, to get on well with the team. There's no reason to haze. They're eager enough to please the older guys on their own.

I glance at her beat-up red car and then at the bag of spoiled hair in my hands. Mikey's sorted. He'll sleep it off. He might be miserable for a while, and he's going to be embarrassed tomorrow, knowing him. But he probably won't remember most of it. Hannah, though? She definitely will.

I can fix this.

"Listen," she says, exhaustion leaking into her voice. "It's been…" She glances at her car, grimacing. "Yeah. Well, I've got to get home."

"No way."

"Stop me." She narrows her eyes. "This has been awful, Cord. All I want to do is go home, shower off the stink, and go to bed."

As she heads toward the driver's seat, I catch her arm. "Wait. Come on." I give her my most charming grin. "You can't drive that home. It's disgusting in there. Let me take you."

She glances down at where my hand grips her arm, and the air tightens around us. When she lifts her eyes, they're wide behind her glasses, unguarded. Maybe it's because she's tired or upset. I don't know. But this girl with the vulnerable eyes… I'm not about to let her down.

As fast as the open expression is there, though, it's gone. She pulls her arm from my grasp and tilts her head up. "I'm not interested."

I cock my head. "In a ride home?"

"In whatever you're offering." She crosses her arms over her chest, her eyes narrowing. "Come on. Why would you offer me a ride?"

"Because I'm a nice guy?" *What the hell is this about?*

She scowls, skepticism dripping from her.

It must be later than I realize because it takes too long for things to click into place. "You think I'm hitting on you."

"You aren't?" She drops her arms and gazes up at me, her brow an endearing wrinkle. I try not to notice how pretty her brown eyes look in the streetlight.

Am I hitting on her? "No." She doesn't need to know that I considered it back at the Pig. That was before she made it clear that she wasn't interested. "Not at all."

She studies me a moment longer. "Oh. Okay. Good. Because you're not my type."

Is she relieved? Talk about a blow to the ego. "Your type?"

"Yeah. I don't like hockey guys." She shrugs.

Tough crowd. I sigh, running my hand over my hair. "Come on. Let me take you home."

She looks at her car, clearly torn. “I can’t leave my car here. I live off campus too. I don’t have anything to do this weekend, but I can’t get to my eight o’clock on Monday without it.”

“Who schedules eight o’clock classes?” I ask.

She offers me a withering look.

“Right. Well, we can get you where you need to go until we get your car cleaned up.” I study the car with its rusted paint. I swear, the thing barely got us back to campus. A detailing isn’t going to fix this car. It needs a complete makeover. Or better, it needs to be put out to pasture.

My brain twists with possibilities. Even before Mikey’s gastrointestinal antics in her car, the night had been for shit. After finding out she cheated, I cut things off with Rachel in the summer, but she keeps showing up everywhere, doing what she can to try to get back together. If it isn’t her, it’s other girls now that I’m single, sneaking into my room at night, sending me naked texts, even one who ambushed me in the bathroom at Shepherd at a party last weekend.

It’s downright distracting.

My eighteen-year-old self might have gotten off on it. But now, after everything that happened with Rachel, it all leaves me cold. I just want them to leave me alone.

I need to focus on my career, and I have to be completely present in the lead-up to the playoffs. New Jersey, the team that drafted me, still hasn’t made me a contract offer. This is the last chance I have to make an impression, and I need it to be flawless.

Hannah could be the answer to those problems. She needs something—for this car to run—and she isn’t interested in me. She’s perfect.

“I have a proposal for you.” I check out her car again, hoping I’m not biting off more than I can chew. “And hear me out, okay?”

She scowls. “What?”

“I want you to pretend to be my girlfriend.” Even as the words leave my mouth, they sound crazy.

Her eyes widen, and she blinks then bursts out laughing. “I’m sorry, what?”

“All you need to do is let me drive you around. Maybe show up a few places together. We’ll tell people we’re together. Only for a few weeks. Until playoffs. Then we can break up or whatever pretend relationships do. In exchange, I’ll get your car fixed.”

Her eyes narrow again. “My car is fine.”

“Seriously?” I step away, walking around the car. It’s at least a decade old. “Your muffler sounds like you belong in NASCAR. And I bet it hasn’t had an oil change or a tune-up in a long time. Whatever it comes back with, I’ll fix it.” The car really is in bad shape. It doesn’t even look reliable.

“You think insulting my car is going to help your case?” She folds her arms over her chest, glaring. “Or maybe this is how you convince all the girls to go out with you.”

I’d never really had to convince anyone to go out with me. I lift my hands. “Not for real…”

“Right. Fake going out.” She makes quotation marks with her fingers. “Why in the world would you want to pretend to be my boyfriend?” She waves her arms, encompassing herself.

I take her in, from her oversized cream beanie to the gold-rimmed glasses covering her wide eyes, the worn peacoat with the bright scarf, and the beat-up pink Converse on her feet. I can’t find a single thing wrong. She rolls her eyes.

“I’m me. And I just told you I wasn’t interested.”

I try to pretend that doesn’t sting. “I know. That’s why you’re perfect for this.”

“Are you drunk?”

“What?” I snort. “No, I’m not drunk.”

“Huh.” She folds her arms over her chest. “Still, no.”

“I’m serious.” I exhale. “I need your help. And this car needs mine.” I step closer, dropping a hand to her shoulder. She isn’t a short girl—probably five-seven or so—but I’m big. Under my fingers, her bones are small, slight. I ignore how good it feels to hold her. “It’s almost the playoffs, and I need to focus. But my ex-girlfriend…”

“Rachel Murray.”

I shouldn’t be surprised Hannah knows who she is. Chesterboro isn’t that big. “Yeah. She wants to get back together. I’ve told her every way I can think of that it isn’t happening.” I stop. I’ve kept the details of what Rachel did quiet because that’s our business, and maybe she’s a jerk, but I’m not. I shrug. “If I start dating someone, maybe she’ll get the idea. Neither of us tells anyone.” I can’t even imagine what the guys would say if they found out I faked a relationship. Me, with all the girls bugging me right now. I would never hear the end of it.

“No thanks.” She snorts, waving a hand over me. “There’s probably a cheerleading squad full of girls who would go out with you. Why don’t you ask one of them?” She sounds almost pissed.

“No need to insult the cheerleaders, Marshall. It was just an idea.”

We stand there, staring each other down, and I’m completely out of my depth. What the hell had I been thinking, anyway?

She said straight up that she wasn't interested. Why would that lead me to think that she'd want to spend even more time with me?

Finally, I nod. "You know what? You're absolutely right. It was a crazy idea."

"It was. I mean, I'm sure hanging out with the hockey team would be fun or whatever," she finally offers as if trying to make me feel better.

If I didn't already feel stupid about asking, that makes my balls shrivel even more.

"But I work a lot. It doesn't leave much time for fun. And I'm applying to grad school, so I really need the money—"

I stop her. "We're good." I grin, and I think it feels almost convincing. "I totally get it." I don't really. I've never had a real job in my life. "Let me get you home, and I'll have Mikey clean your car. Serves him right."

"My Monday eight o'clock…" She scowls at her car, as if she blames it for being a mess.

"Seriously, though, who schedules eight o'clock classes?" When she glares at me, I hurry on. "Right. Well, if it's not done by Monday, I said I'd drive you, so I'll drive you." I sound defensive. But damn…most girls fall over themselves wanting to ride with me.

"All right." She sighs as if resigned and sets off ahead of me like she's doing me a favor. *Christ.* I barely keep from rolling my eyes. I never thought I had a huge ego, but this girl is really testing it.

"After you, baby girl," I can't help but say.

She doesn't even turn back. "I told you not to call me baby."

Hannah

"YOU CAN LET ME out here."

Dreamland Homes, the trailer park where I've lived for almost a decade, is far from a gated community. The only thing that marks the entrance is a crumbling brick sign that pronounces it a "family-friendly neighborhood."

Hysterical.

Next to me, Cord lowers his brows as he slows his BMW near the turn. "What? No."

I roll my eyes. Cord never struck me as the chivalrous type, but I guess people are full of surprises.

"Seriously. I'm only a few houses in. I can walk from here. No need to wake everyone up." There is nothing about Cord or his car that fits in at Dreamland. They are shiny, beautiful, clean, and whole. This place is a mishmash of broken things—broken dreams and broken lives, all piled together in a broken-down place.

Ignoring me, he pulls in. "I would never leave a girl in the middle of the road. Tell me which one."

I glance at him, taking in his set jaw. Yielding, I point at the right, and he turns the low-slung coupe along the pothole-filled gravel road toward my house.

A glow in the living room window of the Murphys' place says that Mr. Murphy is still up, probably watching westerns. He doesn't sleep much, as far as I can tell, or do much of anything. With a silent prayer, I hope he doesn't bother to get up and investigate. The one thing Mr. Murphy does excel at is giving his unpleasant opinion any time he can.

This night has already been crazy enough. I don't need his help.

The next singlewide is dark. It's rented out to a young couple, maybe fresh out of high school. They moved in last year and have the cutest baby girl. They're saving money and dreaming of buying their own place someday.

My place is the last one on this lane. I breathe a sigh of relief. The windows are dark, as they have been for the past few weeks, and there aren't any cars in the driveway. Mom isn't here.

"This is mine." I reach down and grab my purse, not making eye contact. I hate how defensive I sound, because I don't care what he thinks of my home, and I certainly don't need him to confirm how out of place it is. Chesterboro is a wealthy town, with all the genteel sophistication of academia oozing all over it. It's the county seat, so plenty of doctors and lawyers are mixed in with the professors at the college. Dreamland is a few miles out, tucked behind a bunch of overgrown trees. Unless someone grew up in Chesterboro, they probably wouldn't know where to find it.

I hadn't known about it until my dad died eight years ago. Before that, my family lived in a three-bedroom ranch on the other side of town. My mom cleaned at the college, and my dad ran a lumber yard. We weren't rich, but I'd had everything

I needed. I still marvel at the path that led me to this slice of heaven.

"Students rent here?"

Reluctantly, I squint at the house, trying to see it through his eyes. The fact that he's only getting the view through the headlights is probably good. Since I've been the one who's done the upkeep over the past three years, I've kept it as straightforward as possible. There isn't any fussy landscaping. I ripped out anything that required me to have a green thumb because I couldn't keep any of it alive. There is a minuscule patch of grass that I push a manual mower over in the summer.

I had the roof patched twice when it started to leak, but that is the extent of exterior work I've been able to afford. One of the shutters that had probably been meant to be cheerful came loose last year, so I just took it down. Now there's a dark spot on the faded siding where it used to be.

I glance at Cord. His skeptical expression highlights the stark differences between us. It wouldn't even occur to him, someone who's grown up rich and been handed everything, that one of the people he goes to school with was raised in a place like this.

I've been on welfare and went without electricity for a few days during the winter a couple years back. I wouldn't be able to afford Chesterboro if not for scholarships, and some of those I only get because the head of financial aid knew my mom and felt bad for me.

Bottom line: we might all go to the same classes, but the world he lives in is completely different from mine. There's no way someone like Cord would ever get that. Especially him—he's the brightest of them and as far from me as a person can get.

"I own it. I grew up here," I say. "At least for the past eight years. Thanks for the ride home."

"Wait," he calls, and I pause on my way out the door. "Give me your phone."

"Why?"

"So I can get your number. That way, you can text if you need anything this weekend." He cocks his head. "And remember? Your ridiculously early Monday class?"

"Lots of people take eight o'clocks."

"Right." He holds out his hand.

I sigh. "You're taking this too far. I'll call an Uber." Internally, I balk at the hit a car service would take to my savings, but anything has to be better than the pity I see in his eyes.

"No. I told you I'd help you out, and I will." He stares at me expectantly. "We'll have your car cleaned up soon."

I grab my phone from my pocket, slapping it into his outstretched palm. "Fine."

"Fine." He taps the face of it for a moment, a lock of dark hair falling onto his forehead. *Why does he have to be so hot?*

A faint vibration sounds, and he lifts up so he can reach into his pocket. When he pulls out his phone, he shows me the screen.

"'Hi, hot stuff'?" I read. "Really?"

He grins, offering me a salute. "See you later, Marshall."

I close the door on his smug face, throw my purse over my shoulder, and scurry up the front steps. I hadn't left the light on, not wanting to waste electricity, so it takes me a couple of extra tries to get my keys in the lock. I notice he stays in the driveway until I close the door behind me.

I lean back against the door, tilting my head up to the cheap drop ceiling.

Fake girlfriend. I still wasn't sure it had happened. One moment, I'm telling him that I'm not interested in him—that I don't even like jocks—and in the next, he's asking me to pretend to date him.

I'd heard playing hard to get could pique a guy's interest, but that was ridiculous. *Except…why am I considering it, then, if it's so crazy?*

Because honestly, hanging out with the hockey boys sounds fun. I can't remember the last time I went to a party. Definitely not since freshman year. That was when Mom's disappearances became more frequent, when she stopped leaving money to help with the trailer and signed the title over to me.

I didn't miss going to parties. Or I didn't have time to miss parties. But with only a semester left in my senior year, I can't help wondering if I've been missing out. I don't usually have time to think about that because I don't have much time in general. But now, when offered the chance for some fun, it's tempting.

Especially because I wasn't kidding. There can't be anything between Cord and me. Not because I'm not attracted to him. I doubt there's a red-blooded girl in the tri-state area that isn't attracted to him. But we don't fit. We're like lemonade and brownies or sauerkraut and jellybeans.

Plus, he said he would fix my car. I have no idea how a hockey player would get that done on his own, but I have to admit that Cherry needs work. I've been putting it off because I'm saving every penny to go to grad school next year. Even if I manage to get financial aid, I'll need as much in savings as I can get. My car hasn't been a priority. So until I can get another waitressing job, get more hours at the truck stop, or book some more singing gigs, she has to wait.

I can't let him pay. But maybe he knows someone who would give us a deal, someone who would do it for reduced labor or just for the cost of parts…

I shake my head as I push away from the door, blowing out a snort. Seriously, if I didn't have any free time for fun before, I definitely don't now. Why did he even have to make that stupid offer so I'm standing here thinking about it? I'm not wrong—there are loads of girls who would be happy to play the part of his girlfriend and who would be his girlfriend for real if he asked. *Why would he bring me into it?*

Though the logical part of me isn't interested, my body definitely is. When he put his hand on my shoulders, I couldn't breathe right. The hair on my neck tingled, and I stared into his gray eyes and got lost for a second. His whole body was big and warm in front of me, with wide shoulders and slim hips. I'd even caught a few inches of forearm peeking out from his fleece. I've always been a forearm girl.

I don't know what his motives are, but I do know one thing for sure: Cord Spellman is a distraction I don't need.

Cord

I TEXT HANNAH A few times over the weekend. I don't want to leave her with no transportation. But most of it isn't received well.

Me: *Checking in. You need anything?*

Her: *A milkshake.*

Me: *Seriously?*

Her: *No.*

And:

Me: *Running out. Need food?*

Her: *Tootsie Rolls and a KitKat.*

Me: *Tootsie Rolls are nasty.*

Her: *Take your invalid opinions elsewhere.*

Then I started to have fun with it.

Me: *Champagne with your caviar?*

Her: *Bubbles make my nose hurt.*

Me: *I can let it get flat first?*

Or:

Me: *Making soup. Do you want some?*

Her: *You cook?*

Me: *The can has a pull tab.*

By Monday morning, I must be excited to see her because I pull up to her place five minutes early. In the morning light, the place looks like even more of a dump than it did on Friday night. There's evidence that someone tries. The porch has been painted recently. It's neat and clean on the outside, which is more than can be said for some of the other trailers I see.

She must have been waiting right inside, because as soon as I park, she's out the door, hurrying toward me.

It's early, so it should be silent, but I hear muffled yells. Searching for the source of the noise, I see a guy standing on a stoop two houses down in a worn T-shirt, his large belly hanging over the top of athletic shorts that have probably never seen any real activity.

I press the button to lower the window, catching the end of what he's saying. "A BMW." The guy snorts. "You always think you're better than the rest of us here. But you aren't. Just a slut like your mother."

The words curl white-hot through me. *What the fuck? Who is this guy?*

For her part, Hannah ignores him, keeping her head up as she hurries toward me. The only signs of discomfort are the scowl on her flushed face and her pace. She's in some kind of short, flowing dress with tights and a pair of green Converse. The outfit shows off her legs, miles long and gorgeous. Her peacoat's buttoned up to her chin, her hair falling in waves around her face, and her huge glasses on. A giant scarf is wrapped around her neck. She's carrying a guitar case that I hope fits into the space behind us. The whole thing gives off a sexy-librarian, eclectic-musician vibe that I never thought I would find hot, but I completely do.

"Off to your fancy college. They can see through you, too, little girl."

Is this guy wasted? I roll the window the rest of the way down. "Hey, buddy," I call, waving. I offer him a smile, the one I give opposing teams when I'm about to skate all over them. The guy pauses in his rant, so I continue. "Morning. Bit early to be such an asshole, don't you think?"

Obviously, Mr. Congeniality hadn't expected anyone to test him this morning because his eyes flare briefly before he starts back up. "Shut it, pretty boy. This is none of your business."

The passenger door opens, and Hannah fumbles to find the lever to put the seat down so she can get her guitar in the back. I can feel her tension, and it pisses me off. No one should feel like this leaving their house. Especially not Hannah.

I shift the car into park then open my door.

Under her breath, Hannah says, "Cord. Please. It's okay." But the whispery voice she uses hints at her embarrassment, and that makes everything worse.

From what I can tell about Hannah Marshall, she's a force of nature. Super-talented musician, spicy enough to stand up to me, and yet too kind to pass a bunch of drunk-asshole hockey players on the side of the road late at night. No way this fucking guy gets to disrespect her.

Pushing the button to pop the trunk, I slide out of the car, unfurling to my full height, holding eye contact with the big-mouthed guy. I'm tall and at peak physical condition, and I like watching this guy recognize that he's completely outmanned. I'm not one to throw my weight around. In fact, I'm one of the most level-headed players on my team. But I've never backed down when I think something is wrong.

Like the way this man's speaking to Hannah.

"When you talk to my friend like that, you make this my business." I keep my voice mild and stare him down. I know his type. He feels big when he's picking on someone smaller than him, but guys like him can rarely back it up with action. "She deserves an apology. At the least, she deserves for you to go away."

Predictably, he looks away first. "Fuck you," he says, throwing a trash bag over the porch railing and into the trash can there. Giving me the finger, he waddles inside and closes the door without another word.

"Good comeback," I mutter, going around the car to Hannah's side. "You okay?" I ask quietly, taking the guitar from her. She nods, and I search her face, but she won't look at me. I need to know she's fine andthat she realizes that guy's a pile of shit, like I do. "Hannah."

When she meets my gaze, her brown eyes are big behind her glasses, but her mouth is tight. "You shouldn't have done that."

"Oh, I should have. Come on. You'll be late." I help her into her seat and close the door behind her. After depositing the guitar in my trunk, I swing back into the driver's seat. As we pull out, I glare at the guy's door as if daring him to even look our way. I see nothing.

"It'll only be worse next time."

That makes me grind my teeth. "Does he bother you often?"

"Not when Ken's home. That's his son. Usually when he's here, Mr. Murphy keeps to himself."

I keep it slow over all the potholes. "You should call the cops." No one deserves to be harassed every time they leave their house, especially a young woman.

"He's not violent. Just mean." She sighs, pushing her glasses up on her nose. "At least he is to me. He doesn't like my mother."

I glance at her, but she is staring out the front window. "How does that have anything to do with you?"

Her shoulder lifts in a shrug. "Some people don't separate their kids from their parents."

That's true enough. I'm completely different from my father, yet the comparisons never end. He'd played center, but our styles are different. I'm level, a calming agent on the rink, while my dad was a hothead, able to rile up his guys with his physical play. Even our interview style is different. No matter how much I try to set myself apart from him, I can't shake their associations, and it grates at me. I work hard. I only want to be judged on my own merit.

"It's not right," I say mulishly as we pull out of the neighborhood.

"No, it's not. And it's not fair. But that's life." I watch her fingers tighten on her purse in her lap.

"You should call the cops next time." I don't know why I'm pushing this, but the way she's acting bothers me. She should do something about this.

"And what, Cord?" She furrows her brow, anger flaring in her eyes. "I call the cops. They come out and talk to Mr. Murphy. Then what? They issue him a warning, maybe. But then they'll leave, and I'll still live two doors down from him. And Ken? Doubt he'll be too happy I brought them trouble. Do you think that man looks like he'll stop because the cops warned him?" She snorts. "I know you live in some other world, but in my world, that's not how it works."

My jaw tightens. "I don't like how he talked to you. Don't pretend it didn't upset you too."

“Of course it upset me. Especially because every time he calls me a slut, it reminds me that he really wants to tell my mother that she’s a slut.” She exhales. “She slept with him once when she was too high to know better, and then she never gave him the time of day again. I’m around more than she is, though, so I’m an easier target.”

I don’t know how to respond. I cast a glance at her, but she’s staring resolutely out the front window at the February gray, her jaw tight.

We drive for long minutes in silence. I can find something to say in most situations, but words are missing now. But if she expects an apology, she’s in for a long wait. “I’m not sorry I got involved, Hannah. It’s not right.”

She cocks her head, the hint of a grin on her face. “Not Marshall?”

She’s right. I’d called her Marshall Friday night because she’d been so stiff, severe. It felt appropriate to use her last name. But that girl isn’t like this one. “Don’t get sentimental on me now.” I watch the hint of a smile on her face bloom into a real one.

“Never,” she responds, still grinning.

We don’t say anything else the rest of the way to campus, but it isn’t an uncomfortable silence. As I pull up to the music building, she says, “Thanks.”

“No problem. I told you I was going to drive you. Your detailing should be done this afternoon. I’ll text you.” I shift into park then hit the hazards. She stops me as I reach for the door handle to get out and get her guitar. The feel of her fingers on my arm is so surprising, it stills me. No polish and nails cut short, but they’re graceful fingers, callused at the tips.

I meet her gaze. The guarded look is gone from her wide, coffee-colored eyes.

Without the suspiciousness, she looks more like the singer at the bar last night. Open, even raw. Whatever it is, it changes her features. Even at her haughtiest, Hannah Marshall's pretty in a fresh kind of way, with long straw-colored hair and natural skin. But when she looks like this…she's breathtaking.

"No," she says, her full lips tilting again into the real grin she gave me earlier, the one that had nearly stolen my breath. "Thank you for sticking up for me."

The way she says it, it sounds like it's a rare occurrence, and I wonder exactly what this girl has to deal with in her life. I've seen her around and know she works at the library, but I assumed she's like all the Chesterboro kids, raised wealthy or at least well-enough off. She certainly has the confidence of the rest of them. But Hannah looks like someone used to relying on herself.

I have the sudden raging desire to be someone she can lean on.

To avoid all that, I pop the trunk, slide out, grab her guitar out of the back, then slam the trunk closed. She joins me, hiking the same leather bag she'd carried on Friday onto her shoulder. "Have a good jam session."

She wrinkles her brow and nose as if trying to figure something out. "It's a composition class."

"Writing?"

"No." She laughs, and the sound hits me in the groin. "Music composition."

"So writing music. Like I said." She laughs again, and the sound makes me so happy, I immediately want to hear it again.

"Right." She shrugs her guitar onto her back. I hadn't realized the case had straps like a backpack. "Thanks again for the ride."

"No problem." I step back and clear my throat.

She grins. My gaze drops to her mouth, lingers. I stifle the sudden urge to step closer, to get into her space, to cover her lips with mine. She's lovely, sure, but I've met lots of pretty girls. There's something about her, though, a thread of steel that makes me want to learn everything she's trying to hide behind her walls.

Except she said she wasn't interested, and getting any closer to her isn't an option for me. I've got playoffs coming, and it's my last chance to impress scouts. My life doesn't need any more complications. That means it doesn't need Hannah Marshall.

Thank God she turned my "fake dating" offer down on Friday night. This girl is already a distraction. I'm not sure what I was thinking.

She backs up to walk away, and it feels wrong in a way I don't want to think too much about. Unable to help myself, I call, "See you around, Marshall."

She stops to roll her eyes at me, laughing. I offer her a salute. Shaking her head, she sets off again toward the fine arts building.

I chuckle, and the smile doesn't leave my face. I get back into my car and head for the gym. I have two hours before my first class, enough time to get a workout in. Maybe that'll help me stop thinking about Hannah Marshall's full lips.

Hannah

WHEN I STEP INTO my eleven o'clock a few hours later, I still haven't been able to get Cord Spellman out of my head. Knowing he's going to be here isn't helping.

Fine, he's hot. It's impossible not to notice. His big body is the sort that Greek sculptors idolized, gorgeous and chiseled. I'm smart enough to know I'm attracted to him, along with the rest of the female population at Chesterboro University and probably some of the male population.

Except it isn't only his body, though that is first-rate. It's his goofy half smile distracting me today, and though I hate to admit it, he made me laugh in the car and via text all weekend. He's sharp and witty. And he stepped up for me with Mr. Murphy.

Even now, my stomach sickens, thinking about the things Mr. Murphy said. Not the words—I've heard those plenty of times before. No, it's the fact that Cord heard them. The other neighbors ignore him, and I do, too, most of the time. But listening to him say that stuff in front of Cord was a new level of embarrassment.

For him to hear all that and then defend me reached into my chest, softening me in a way that was irresponsible. It's not only that he's good-looking and desirable but that he's practically worshiped on campus already, more experienced than I am, and infinitely popular.

He's not in my league, at least not for real.

His fake-relationship proposal flutters through my mind again, and I shake my head. I'm not interested in having my heart steamrolled. I've got grad school to look forward to. Every step I've made over these past years has been to get out of Chesterboro, to become an elite musician, to be respectable, not just someone's choice for a fake girlfriend.

I grimace, dropping my bag next to the piano in the auditorium, shrugging out of the straps on my guitar case, then setting it against the wall. I open the keyboard cover and run my fingers over the keys. The piano is beautiful, a baby grand. Someday, I'm going to own something like this.

I stretch my neck and sit down to warm up. As the notes ring out, I sigh. It's perfectly tuned. Nothing makes me happier than a well-cared-for instrument.

This is the first class I've assisted in. Usually, I'm too busy working, but Dr. Pierce's Intro to Music Theory class is a paying gig. Pierce is my adviser, and he's taken me under his wing. When he asked me to help, I couldn't say no.

"Sounds beautiful, Hannah, as always." I glance up to find Dr. Pierce at the end of the piano. I smile. With gray hair and kind eyes behind his bifocals, he's one of my favorite people at Chesterboro.

"Good morning, professor. Let me know if there's anything outside the syllabus that you need today."

"I appreciate that." He smiles, patting the piano, giving me a wink. "One of these days, I'll actually stump you."

I cup my hand over my mouth and play whisper. "You can try, sir."

He chuckles.

People always talk about my ability to pick up music that I hear, but it's just something I do. Some people can recite word-for-word conversations or draw faces after seeing them once, but for me, it's music. I usually only need to hear something once before it's easy for me to remember and play.

The room is getting crowded, and I stretch my neck and flex my fingers, checking the audience out. This is a 100-level class, so I expect mostly freshmen and maybe a few upperclassmen that are still fulfilling their general education requirements.

Upperclassmen such as Cord, who sidles through the back double doors, his backpack on and shoulders hunched, earbuds in. Usually, he sits in the back, probably because he has to miss so many classes for hockey. Today, though, he heads down the aisle toward me.

My stomach flutters. I don't think I'll ever get used to the way my body feels around him.

I'm not the only one, though. A few sorority girls in front wave at him, trying to get his attention. Maybe he doesn't see or hear them, because he walks right by and doesn't stop until he's standing next to the piano.

What is he doing?

He pulls one of his earbuds out, letting it hang in front of him. The corners of his mouth turn up, and then I've got the full weight of his gray eyes on me. "Hey."

"Hey," I respond, glancing around. "Why are you up here?"

He looks confused. "I came up to say hi?"

I'm amazed he even realized I'm the assistant in this class. "Hi?"

He looks at me like he's questioning my sanity when Pierce breaks in. "Good morning, Mr. Spellman. I'm looking forward to watching you and our Bulldogs in the playoffs this year."

"Thank you, professor." Cord smiles at him, still casting me confused glances.

"You like hockey, Dr. Pierce?" Everyone's surprising me today.

"Absolutely," he says. "You don't?"

I shrug. I don't think it'd be polite to say I don't care one way or the other.

"I loved watching Mr. Spellman's father in his heyday. I'm really looking forward to cheering you through your career as well," Pierce says to Cord.

"Thank you, sir. We think we have a really good chance at bringing home the championship this year." It's smooth, gracious, exactly what Cord's known for. "I just stopped up to say hello to Hannah."

"Do you two know each other?" Pierce asks, obviously taken off guard. Of course he is. We spend a lot of time together, and he's my mentor. He knows my few friends. They're in the music department, like me. I don't have time for a wide social circle.

"We just met," Cord hurries to say, smoothing over the awkwardness with ease, "Friday night. We were out, and she was kind enough to give me and a couple of the other guys on the team a ride home." He shrugs, the picture of boyish chagrin. "We'd had a bit too much."

"Really?" Pierce studies me. "That doesn't sound like you, Hannah."

It isn't. "I wasn't drinking, sir. Only there."

"She was in the right place at the right time Friday, for sure." Cord rubs the back of his neck.

"It wasn't a big deal." I wave off his gratitude, wishing the entire conversation was over.

"Well, I'm glad to see you getting out there and socializing, Hannah." Dr. Pierce pats my shoulder, obviously pleased with me. "It's time to start class. If you'll take your seat, Mr. Spellman?"

Cord nods, patting the piano. "Later, Hannah." He bounds up the stairs to the back where no one has taken his seat. No one would dare.

As the class begins, I remain acutely conscious of him watching me. I play the pieces when Pierce asks, even the ones that aren't on the syllabus.

I hadn't expected Cord to seek me out, unprovoked. I don't know why. I just figured when my car was cleaned, we'd go back to acting like we didn't know each other. I mean, he probably knows half the sorority girls he walked past to say hello to me. *Why me?*

By the end of the hour, I'm stressed out and hyperaware of the handsome hockey player in the back with the intelligent gray eyes who doesn't act how I expect him to.

Finally, the class ends. Dr. Pierce thanks me, and I'm already up as he's still assigning the reading for the next class. I throw my guitar onto my back, gather my coat and bag, and hurry up the auditorium stairs, trying to see if I can catch Cord on the way out. At least I try to hurry. Everyone's filing out of the aisles, and there's a traffic jam.

When I finally make my way to the top of the stairs, he's gone. *Damn.*

I shuffle into the line to get out, and when I clear the door, I find him leaning against the wall outside the auditorium, backpack on, looking like a male model.

I stop short only to get jabbed by the person behind me. “Excuse me,” they say, and I shift forward, feeling stupid and tongue-tied.

Finally, I offer, “Cord.”

He smiles like something I said is funny. “Marshall.”

Why does he call me that? I mean, it’s my last name, but no one calls me that. “Hey.”

“Hey.” He outright laughs.

I doubt I could be more awkward. I snag his sleeve, and he lets me drag him away from the rest of the exiting students. No way I could have moved him on my own. When we’re out of earshot, I say, “What are you doing?”

His brow crinkles, and he makes even confusion look hot. “Waiting for you?”

I inhale, desperate to get control. “I mean, why are you waiting for me?” I keep my voice low.

“Because I wanted to talk to you?” he whispers back.

“Okay…”

“Your car should be finished this afternoon. I just thought you should know. We can drop it at your place if you want.” He lifts his brows askance.

I blink at him. It strikes me that Cord Spellman is a really nice guy. In fact, he might just be the kind of guy I’d want to be friends with, if we had ever moved in the same circles or if he ever noticed a music nerd in the first place or if I didn’t work thirty or so hours a week on top of going to school.

It’s my last semester. I wonder offhand how many other friendships I might have had if I hadn’t needed to spend so much time handling the basics. Maybe Dr. Pierce is right. Maybe getting out, socializing, would be a good thing for me.

"Do you still want to be my fake boyfriend?" I blurt out then look around to see if anyone heard.

His eyes flare, and I wonder if I've miscalculated. "Absolutely."

"You do?" I hate how unsure I sound.

"It was my idea, Marshall."

"Right." Of course. "And if I agree, it would all be fake?"

"Exactly. Totally platonic. I can give you the rides you need while we get your car fixed up. I said I'd get that done, and I will. And we'll hang out at a party or two, maybe show up a few places together. To sell it."

Going to a party with him as friends, even though no one else would know that, actually sounds like fun. When I get to graduate school, I'll need to work there too. No way I'd be able to afford it without taking some side jobs. This might be my last chance to do the kind of stuff that the rest of the kids at CU do without thinking about it, on the arm of the hottest guy on campus. That doesn't sound so bad.

"And nothing happens between us," I clarify. Not because I don't want it to. All I've been thinking about the past twenty-four hours is his body. But between work and school, I don't have time to get distracted, at least not the kind of distracted that would end up with us sweaty in bed. Sex would make this messy.

"No. You said you aren't interested. And neither am I." He nods decisively. "You don't even like hockey guys."

"Exactly. I don't. And I'm not. Interested, I mean." Because there can't be anything between us. Even if it wasn't for work and school, we're from completely different worlds. Nothing could work out long-term between us. Sex would make this complicated and anything real would be disastrous. A struggling musician headed to music school and a hockey player destined for the NHL…ridiculous. Pretending anything different would only hurt me.

I study his face. "This isn't a joke."

"No way. Furthest thing from it. It's our little secret."

"And all you want me to do is pretend to be with you so Rachel Murray leaves you alone."

He nods. "Rachel and the other girls."

"There are others?"

He shrugs, adorably helpless. "A few…"

"Right." *Of course there are others. Well, here goes…* "Fine."

"Really?" He seems surprised. "Great."

"But the second this goes sideways, I'm calling it off." I don't expect it to, but it's good to get that out in the open. I don't know Rachel personally, but she strikes me as a pretty standard, garden-variety mean girl. As the girl from the trailer park, I handled that sort of bitchiness in high school.

"No problem. Absolutely. What could go wrong, though?"

Right. What could go wrong?

"Come on," he says. "Let me walk you to your next class."

Cord

AS I PULL INTO a parking spot at the rink after lunch and my phone's Do Not Disturb turns off, it vibrates with texts.

I snag it from the top of my gym bag. Four new notifications.

The first one is from Hannah: *I'll meet you at the rink at 4PM. Thanks for offering me the ride home.*

I want to shoot back that she doesn't have to thank me—I'm her boyfriend. I mean, her fake boyfriend. But I plan to play the role. That means rides if she needs them. And a whole lot of time spent with me.

An unwanted thrill of anticipation washes over me. Our conversation after Intro to Music Theory had only left me more excited to see her after practice. She has a smart mouth and is always quick with a comeback, and I can't resist that.

Except I shouldn't be looking forward to seeing her this much at all. My smile fades. I need to bench all this shit hard. I've got playoffs coming. I don't have the time to split my focus.

Maybe this is a bad idea. I could call it all off. But I genuinely like Hannah, and if we can do this, it'll help us both.

I just need to be sure that I keep anything I'm feeling for her completely in the friend zone.

The other notifications are all voicemails. The first is from my dad. I don't listen to that one. He probably wants to know about arrangements for the first weekend of playoffs. He'll be traveling from Tennessee to Pittsburgh, where they're holding the Frozen Four this year. He would want me to stay with him, even though he knows I need to stay with the team.

Sometimes his interest in my hockey—my life—is stifling.

The next message is from Rachel, and I ignore that, too, though with a lot less guilt. It's probably another rambling mix of frustration and desperate pleading with a whole lot of apologizing in between. I usually get one every week or so.

Looking back on our relationship, I regret letting it go on so long. When I first started college, I had a few quick relationships but mostly just random hookups. By the end of freshman year, something was missing. I was sick of one-nightstands and surface conversations with girls who cared more about dating a hockey player than getting to know me.

Then, last year, Rachel started at CU. Her dad and mine played together at Chesterboro, and I've known her most of my life. According to my dad, Rachel's exactly the kind of girl who could manage being married to a professional hockey player. She's from the life, knows about the travel and the ruthless schedules. She grew up with money, and she can handle herself in social situations. She's also beautiful.

Apparently, my father thinks it's okay that she's also the kind of girl to have affairs when she's lonely. Then at least she won't leave me with an expensive divorce that ends up all over the tabloids like my mother did to him, or so he insinuated last summer after Rachel and I broke up when pictures surfaced of her leaving the apartment of a winger with a newly signed contract at five o'clock in the morning.

I was the stupid one. I thought we were in love.

My dad had been right about one thing—Rachel will be happy in the lifewith the money and the prestige. She just needs to be happy with someone else.

Still, every chance Dad gets, he reiterates how Rachel would be a good fit. She's beautiful, smart, poised. Worldly.

I always hold my tongue, even though I want to tell him to mind his damn business. I get the feeling our breakup reminds him of the end of his own marriage to my mom. My mother came from a happy, middle-class family, and she expected a nine-to-five husband. She struggled with his travel schedule, and they were unhappy for years before they separated. When allegations of infidelity surfaced, she left him. I know my father thinks it would have been easier for them if she'd been able to deal with the long months of separation.

After Rachel, I decided that I'd avoid personal entanglements entirely. No more talk about perfect wives or even perfect girlfriends. I've seen the life, and I can see how relationships suffer. Why put myself through that? It would be easier to just find a warm body when I need one and keep my main focus on hockey.

Shaking my head, I focus on the last message. Harry Swanson, my agent. I tap the icon to listen."Cord. News from New Jersey. Call me."

I dial him back. He answers as he always does, as if we were in the middle of the conversation already. "Hey, kid, ready for playoffs?"

"Just on my way to practice."

“Great.” He barely breathes as he switches subjects. “New Jersey contacted me. They’d like to set up a meeting.” New Jersey drafted me the summer before college, and we agreed that I would play at Chesterboro to develop. But they still haven’t offered a contract.

I pause next to my car, my hand on my hip. “They have an offer?”

“Maybe. But it’s different. They have been watching your tapes from the fall. They’re interested in you for defense.”

“Defense?”I’m a center, like my dad. But when Linc, one of our top defenseman, struggled with concussions in the fall, Coach asked me to step in for a little while, until one of the other guys was ready. I had, of course. I’m the captain. I do what needs to be done. What I hadn’t expected was to love the position so much. Part of what makes me such a good center is that I hustle on the backcheck and I respect how much of the center’s job is defensive. In the two months I covered for Linc, I was a chaos agent on the blue line, creating opportunities.

It’s been a couple of months since I played defense, returning to center when someone else stepped up for Linc. It surprises me how much I miss it.

“They need your kind of dynamic play on defense. You’re fast, you see the whole rink, and you’ve got a cannon from the neutral zone.”

“I expected to play offense.”

“Straight shooting, kid? They don’t need you at offense. If they sign you for that, you’ll spend some time—maybe a long time—in the minors. At defense, you’d move up faster, maybe even be out of the minors by the holidays.”

That makes me pause and stare up at the gray winter sky. A lot can happen in a year, maybe two. Injuries, trades…all sorts of pitfalls. If I can get to the big show faster, that's an obvious bonus. But still… I've always wanted to be a center.

"You like defense, right?" Harry's voice interrupts my thoughts.

"I do." In fact, I never even admitted to myself how much I enjoyed it because it hadn't been part of the plan. But the position fit like a second skin. I hadn't expected it to feel so comfortable. "But I've always been on offense…"

"I think it's worth a conversation."

"Okay, when did they want to have the call?" I ask.

"Not a call." He inhales. "They want to meet you in person."

"Harry…"

He hurries on. "I'll fly in. We'll go together. Just let me know when you can do it, and I'll set it all up." Harry sighs. "Listen, kid. I know you always expected to be a center. But you like defense. It's worth exploring the opportunity."

I bury a hand in my hair, staring up at the rink where I've played for the past few years. "I don't know, Harry. I only played defense for a month or so. Before that, it was, I don't know, in peewees?"

"I understand that. But they see your potential." He pauses. "I know this is a lot to take it, but you need to have the conversation."

It sounds risky. I could suck at it and end up a mediocre defensive player stuck in the minors. "What happens if I don't want to play defense?"

"If they offer at offense, you'll spend time in the minors. If they don't offer, you become an unrestricted free agent in August and hope that someone else offers for you."

That all sounds risky too. I sigh. "You're right. It's worth a conversation." Talking doesn't bind me to anything. "I'll shoot you my availability when I get home."

He hangs up without another word.

I've been waiting for New Jersey to offer a contract for years, but this isn't what I expected. My first instinct is to help out. If they need defensemen, then I can do that. But I can't tell whether I want that or if I just want the contract, no matter the conditions.

I honestly don't know.

Hannah

WHEN MY TWO O'CLOCK is over, I sling my guitar onto my back and wrap my bag cross-body, preparing for the walk across campus to the hockey rink. I button my coat all the way up and tuck my hat on. I know a lot of the students here complain about the cold and gray. It's overcast in Chesterboro from October until April, with snow and rain taking turns, depending on which would make everyone more miserable at any given time.

But I always love the season changes, the leaves in the fall, the snow, and even when it gets sweaty hot in the summer. Today, there isn't any rain or snow, just what's leftover. The sidewalk is white with dried salt, and chunks of the stuff crunch under my boots. The snow in the grass between the street and the walkway that had been pure white a few days ago is dirty and iced over.

I catch myself hurrying and slow down. I've been looking forward to seeing Cord all day like I'm his real girlfriend, not his fake one. That's stupid. If I don't watch it, stuff like that's going to get me in trouble.

Worse, if I get to the rink and there's still a bunch more practice to go, I'll be sitting there awkwardly. I have my guitar, and I have work to do, but I'd like to avoid being there for long. So I veer down a side street, detouring away from the rink.

As I fade into Chesterboro, I take a deep breath. In the streets, I can remember the times when I was little, before my dad died and my mom dissolved into a puddle of alcohol and drugs. As I make the turn onto Dennings, the corner bakery where my dad used to pick up pastries on Sundays comes into view.

I haven't been inside in years.

The same bell hangs above the door, and it jingles when I push inside. A sour-faced woman comes out of the back. I don't recognize her. "Can I help you?"

I spare her my nostalgia and order two apple cider donuts and a coffee. I only had a protein bar for lunch, so I'm hungry. But I didn't usually eat at school, waiting to eat something cheap at the truck stop or make my own food at home. This is a splurge. Still, I can't resist donuts. Anyone who can is stronger than I am.

I take the bag of still-warm, sugary donuts and the to-go cup of coffee from the grouchy cashier. Sipping it, I sigh. It's strong and smooth, way better than the stuff I drink at home. I grin, saluting her with my coffee cup on my way out. She gives me a head nod then returns to the back.

I almost finish my coffee by the time I reach the rink, so I chug the last sips and throw out the cup before I push through the door, maneuvering my bulky guitar case behind me. There's a lobby with a bunch of benches and cushy chairs. I find one in the far corner, trying to stay inconspicuous.

Glancing at my phone, I realize that despite my attempts to waste time, I still have almost a half an hour until four, when

Cord said he would be done.

Well, might as well get some work done, then.

I take off my guitar case, set it on the ground, and unsnap the latches. When I open it, I smile. During this morning's composition class, I had an epiphany about the piece I'm working on, and I'm excited to get it sorted out.

The class examines different periods in musical history and studies their prevailing properties, and then we write a piece highlighting those properties. Right now, we're working on the Baroque movement, and I'm pretty sure I have something that will work.

Testing the tuning, I start in, humming along as I work. I fumble in my purse for my composition notebook, flipping the pages until I get to the right one.

Time fades as I pick apart what I have, changing parts that aren't as strong, adding where I can. Finally, when I read through it, it's the cohesive piece I envisioned. I quickly scan it again, memorizing the patterns.

Closing my eyes, I strum it from the beginning, tapping my foot.

"What the hell is this, some sort of concert venue?" My eyes pop open. An older man stands in front of me with his hands on his hips. Behind him, there are half a dozen hockey players in varying stages of undress.

"Um…" It might be all the acres of sweaty boy skin or the man's grumpiness, but I struggle to find words.

"This wall is as thin as paper." He nods to the stall behind me. "And though your music is lovely, listening to it had my guys unfocused in there."

"Yo, whose bunny is that?" One of the guys behind the coach asks. "She yours, Mitch?"

"Nah." Declan Mitchell, another of the playboys on the team, holds onto the ends of the towel around his very naked neck and chest. "Though I'd be happy to get to know her better if no one else claims her."

"Shut it, all of you," the coach barks. Some of the guys behind him smother grins, while others elbow Declan or give him a shot on the arm. "Can I ask you why you're here, Miss —"

"Marshall. I'm Hannah Marshall." I swallow, putting the guitar down in its case. "One of the hockey boys puked in my car Friday night, so they're cleaning it and getting me a ride home." I lock the guitar into its case, stand, and swing it onto my back.

He studies me. "Who threw up in your car, young lady?"

Behind the coach, Mikey waves his arms frantically, panic on his handsome face. He looks so mortified, I can't throw him under the bus. From the disapproval on the coach's face, I sense the repercussions would be heavy. So I keep my face neutral. "I'm not at liberty to say."

Coach's brows kick up further. "Not at liberty, huh?" The side of his lips tip up, as if he's holding back a grin. "Interesting. Well, then who's giving you a ride home today, Miss Marshall?"

"She's with me, Coach," Cord volunteers from behind him.

The humor fades from the coach's face, and he glares at Cord. "You throw up in her car, Cap?"

"It wasn't him, sir." I jump in quickly. "He offered to help."

The coach grunts. "Well, Miss Marshall, if you're here again, I'd appreciate it if you keep your music down in the foyer. Sound travels in this place."

"Sure. I'll remember that if I'm ever here again." I can't imagine that happening, so I don't have a problem with his terms.

"*When* she's here again," Cord offers, crossing his arms over his chest. He lifts his eyebrows, and I remember that we're supposed to be together.

"Right." I agree. "When."

Coach grunts, turning back toward the locker room. He pauses next to Cord and mutters something to him. I don't catch what he says, but Cord grins. "I do, too, Coach."

After he's gone, Cord joins me, slinging an arm around my shoulders. His smell envelops me. At least he's wearing clothes, but still, the contact sends electricity straight to my stomach. Over his shoulder, Mikey covers his heart and mouths "thank you" as he and another guy I don't know leave together.

"What did your coach say to you?" I ask Cord as everyone else disperses.

Cord hikes his hockey bag up on his shoulder, still smiling, and holds his arm out for my guitar. I hand it over without argument. I'm coming to learn that Cord takes chivalry very seriously. Shifting the instrument on his back as if it doesn't weigh anything, he drops his arm onto my shoulder again. "He said he liked you. So I told him I did too."

He likes me? "We're fake dating."

He shrugs. "That doesn't mean I can't like you, too, Marshall." He grins. "Come on. Let's get you home."

I swallow hard as we start out the door together. This fake relationship could become more than I banked on.

Cord

IN THE PARKING LOT, I unlock the car with a beep. Hannah stays quiet. I cast a glance her way. Her brows are furrowed, and her lips are tight. Something's brewing.

I've had enough experience with women to brace myself. I run the past five or ten minutes over in my head, trying to pinpoint what upset her so I can smooth it over.

Coach Chandler is intimidating sometimes, and I've seen guys bigger than me shrivel under the glare he gave her. She'd caught him at a pissy time. Her guitar had echoed through the meeting room, distracting everyone. When he'd gone storming out at the end, I'd expected to hear screaming. Instead, I found her standing there, calmly smoothing Coach's feathers.

She climbs in the passenger seat while I stow her guitar in the trunk before sliding behind the steering wheel. Next to me, she scowls out the window, clutching a white paper bag. I break the quiet. "What's up?"

"Why's it a bunny?"

"What?" That's not what I was expecting.

"Puck bunny." She scrunches up her nose. "Why bunny?"

"I mean…"

"I know about Playboy Bunnies, obviously. But why always bunnies? Is it because rabbits aren't discerning about who they sleep with? Or that they're transitory in general? Or maybe because they aren't supposed to be very smart."

None of that sounds good. "Yes?"

She blows out a disgusted snort. "Nasty. Who calls women that?" The color's high on her cheeks.

"Hannah…"

"It's demeaning."

I shrug, shaking my head. "They like it." She huffs, so I hurry on. "No, really. I think it makes them feel like they're part of a group or something. And I think most of them enjoy sleeping around with the guys as much as the guys like sleeping around with them. If no one gets hurt, what's the harm?" That had become my new philosophy since the summer. It's only when one lets their emotions get involved that things get messy.

She snorts as if she doesn't believe me. "I'm not some… groupie who is hanging around you guys."

"I know." No doubt about that. Hannah's nothing like any other girl I've met.

She keeps ranting even though I agreed with her. "Look at me. I mean, what about me says 'groupie'?"

We stop at a stoplight, so I take my time, looking her over. I have to admit that I like what I see. Sometime during the day, she'd pulled her hair into a braid and tucked a floppy beanie over it. Her wide brown eyes are huge behind her glasses, but again, it's her lips that catch my attention. They really are perfect, full, and lush. I want to sip at them.

Forcing myself to look back at the road, my floundering brain struggles to refocus on what she said. "Our fans"—I stress the word because "bunny" and "groupie" seem to have negative connotations to her, and her tone makes me feel the need to defend them—"come in all shapes and sizes. You, too, can be included, Marshall."

She rolls her eyes, and I can't help but grin. Man, I love riling this girl up.

Finally, she blows out a long breath. "How embarrassing. Why didn't you come out and tell me you guys could hear me?"

I consider it. We'd been sitting in the meeting room, going over film from the team we're facing this weekend. I heard the guitar and immediately knew it was Hannah. Around me, I watched the other guys tune in on it. Worse, Coach noticed. I'm surprised he didn't say something sooner.

I debate making some excuse, but I finally shrug. "I liked listening." I bet that was why Coach didn't put a stop to it either. Next to me, her mouth snaps shut, but she doesn't look quite as upset. I press my advantage. "What were you playing?"

She pauses, probably deciding if she's still pissed, then sighs. "It was something I wrote for my composition class. We're working on the Baroque period in musical history. I needed to write something that had elements of the time period." She says it offhand, as if everyone just writes something that good for a class all the time.

"Do you write a lot of your own music?"

She cocks her head like she's trying to figure me out. Or maybe she's trying to decide how much to say. Either way, I hold my breath, waiting for her response. "I do. I write all kinds of stuff."

“Yeah?” I keep my curiosity mild, because it scares me how much I want to know more. “What kind of music do you write?”

Her grin is playful. If she were any other girl, I might think she was flirting. But this is Hannah, and I’m sure she’s not. “I write love songs. What other kinds of songs are there?”

Is she serious? With her, I assume yes. I didn’t expect her to be the romance-y, love song sort. Then again, how much do I really know about her? But every second I spend with her makes me want to know more, which is problematic, considering that this is supposed to be a fake relationship with a targeted end date.

“Right.” I grit my teeth, motioning to the bag in her lap. “What’s that?” My voice is so gritty, it doesn’t even sound like me.

She clears her throat, lifting the bag and not making eye contact. *Is she nervous? Uncomfortable?* I would give anything to know what’s going through her head.

“I got us donuts.” She shrugs one shoulder. “They’re from a bakery my dad…I mean, we used to go to.”

“You got me a donut.”

“I figured you might be hungry after practice.” She holds the bag out to me, still not meeting my eyes. “Here. You can have them both if you want.”

I have no idea why this touches me so much that my throat tightens, but it does. Probably because in the course of all of my girlfriends, I can’t remember any of them doing something like that—even Rachel, and I dated her for almost a year. She never brought me something simply because it might make me happy.

If I wanted to kiss Hannah before, now I want to crawl inside her. “Hannah.” I wait, wanting—no, needing—her to look at me. When she finally does, it uncoils something inside me. I clear my throat. “Thanks.”

“You’re welcome.” A buzzing sounds from her purse, and she reaches inside to get her phone. Reading the face of it, she frowns. “Damn it.”

“Something wrong?”

She shoves her phone back into her purse. “My boss at the truck stop. Canceling my shift tonight and for the rest of the week.” Her mouth tightens. Lots of kids would be stoked to find themselves free. Apparently not Hannah.

“This is bad?” I suggest.

“Yeah.” She sighs. “I need the cash. There aren’t any elite graduate programs within driving distance, so I’ve got to get ready to move in a few months. That takes money. I’ll have to call some places or see if Josh will let me sing again this week. Any chance you know when my car will be ready?” She worries her lip, her brow furrowed.

“After class, I had a mechanic look at it, like I told you. It’s in bad shape.” I stop there, but the way the guy explained it, the muffler and exhaust system were really messed up, dangerously and expensively so. I told him to fix the entire thing, not just the muffler. He also said the alternator should be replaced and her tires were bald. I gave him the green light for all of it. I don’t like the idea of Hannah driving around in something unsafe. I’m not sure why I don’t want to tell her, though. Probably because she would feel bad or insist that she pay me back or something, and I don’t want her to. “They need a couple parts, and since it’s an older car, it’s going to be a few days before they can get them." I shrug apologetically. "He said he was trying to finish by the weekend."

"That sounds expensive." Fresh worry troubles her features. "I don't have a lot of money for that."

"I said I was getting it fixed." I was right—she'd been planning to try to pay.

"You don't have…"

"Stop." I hold up my hand. "I told you I'd fix it. Besides, I can take you to sing. Wherever you need to go." Anticipation at spending the time with her zings through me. I tamp it down.

"But…"

"What's the point of having a fake boyfriend if you can't make him drive you around?" I ask, trying to lighten the mood. Whether I'm doing it for her or for me, I'm not sure.

"Yeah, but no one will be there. What's the point of being a fake boyfriend if there's no one around to see it?"

I hadn't thought of that. Why hadn't I thought of that? "Either way, it's just a ride."

"Let me think about it. And send some texts."

"Sounds good." She reaches for the door handle, and I stop her. "Hey. Why didn't you tell me you were working tonight?" I hadn't made plans to take her.

"I figured my car would be ready." She shrugs. "Besides, I wasn't going to make you take me. It's the munchies shift. Nine until three."

"In the morning?" I can't keep the horror out of my voice.

She laughs. The sound warms me. "Yeah. In the morning."

"There are a few things I like to do that late, but none of them are work."

"I've heard that about you." She rolls her eyes as if everyone talks about my sexual prowess. Maybe they do. I'm not a monk. But something about hearing her talk about it doesn't feel right. "Anyway, I was going to catch a ride with the other girl on the shift with me." She waves it off like it isn't a big deal or like she's trying to be casual. "No need to be faking our relationship at the truck stop. No one's going to see you there either."

I stretch my fingers. All this talk about faking it is messing with my head. Because the way I want to touch her isn't fake at all. But I don't because I have no right to touch her, no matter what my body says. I promised her something straightforward and friendly that would help with Rachel.

Which makes me wonder…"Why are you doing this?"

"What?"

I tick off one finger. "It sounds like you didn't want me to mess with your car."

"That's not true. I really appreciate that. It's just expensive."

"And I told you not to worry about it." I tap another finger. "So you're acting weird about your car…"

"It's not weird." She glares at me. "It's rude not to worry when people spend their money on me."

When I dated Rachel, she used to want to go on trips to New York and fly places over breaks. Skiing, the beach… I paid for most of it. Either one of us could have—rather, our parents could have. I never thought much about it. The guy always paid because that was how my dad said a gentleman should act.

Hannah obviously wasn't raised like that.

I go on as though she hadn't replied. "So, why did you agree to fake girlfriend me?" I don't know why I'm complaining. My gain, after all. But I need things to be clear. It won't be fair if she expects something different than I do.

I pull into the drive for her development, if you could call Dreamland Homes that. The potholes, the rundown trailers… the place really is a mess.

Hannah doesn't respond as I park in front of her house, staring out the front window. Finally, she says, "I've been really busy. No time for parties or bars or whatever. At least not bars I'm not singing at." She smiles, but it's the kind of expression that is full of more sadness than joy. "You said that we'd go places together. I'm assuming that means parties and bars. I graduate in a few months. I thought it might be fun, you know, to see what that was like."

I study her. "You've never been to a party?"

"Not a real party in a long time. A couple times freshman year." She shrugs. "I've gotten together with people to practice, have pizza, stuff like that." She exhales. "Though, admittedly, I haven't even had much time for that lately."

That's not a real party. I can't imagine what it must have been like for her to spend the past few years stressing about money. I have responsibilities, and hockey weighs heavy on me, but I still have time to cut loose sometimes.

"We can definitely change that." I watch real happiness light her eyes. This girl's smiles always hit me like a punch in the chest, stealing my breath.

"Good." She reaches across the seat and squeezes my hand. The brief contact is nothing, just a friendly gesture. But the feel of her fingers on mine is comforting and sends heat racing through me.

I force my voice level. "But you promised you'd let me drive you around. So next time you need to work, let me know, okay?"

She tucks a strand of hair behind her ear. "It wasn't a big deal, Cord. Didn't seem like a reason to drag you out. Like I said…no one would see us. Fake should be fake."

She makes it sound like I only care about appearances and how she benefits me. That doesn't sit well with me. *But isn't that the point of this whole arrangement? This isn't supposed to be serious. What the hell am I doing?*

"Fake relationship doesn't mean we can't be friends." It's a good explanation, and it eases some of my discomfort. I squeeze her cold fingers for only a second before I take my hand back, patting the wheel and trying for an easy grin. "And I'm almost looking forward to going back to the Pig's Tail. Scene of the crime."

"Mikey actually barfed in my car in an alley downtown."

"Right. Well, the Pig is nicer."

"No, it isn't." She laughs.

I can't argue with that. But she's smiling again, and whatever that heavy feeling was is gone. "You're right. It's not. I'll take you anyway. Or anywhere else. Just let me know."

"All right. But keep me posted on my car, okay?"

"Sure." When she gets her car back, these conversations will probably end. Sure, I've only known her a few days, but I'm already not looking forward to our time together being over. She slides out of the passenger side, and I pop the trunk then follow her around the back to get her guitar. "What time do you need to be at school tomorrow?"

She hikes her guitar onto her back. "Not until after lunch."

"I'll pick you up at noon. We can hit the dining hall together."

"I don't have a dining plan, so I usually eat at home."

“My treat, then. Besides, we could use some exposure.” Friends with good optics. That’s what we are. “See you at noon.”

“Right.” She backs away, tossing me a wave and bouncing up the stairs to her place. I try not to stare at her legs until she slips inside and closes the door behind her.

Hannah

THOUGH I HAD THE entire night to prepare and I've been there countless times before, walking into the dining hall with Cord is an out-of-body experience.

I spent three years being invisible at this school unless I was sitting behind a piano or playing a violin. Even then, music blocked me out. But when Cord wraps his arm around my shoulder, everyone can see me. I dressed this morning in a slouchy sweater and my favorite jeans, a vintage pair from the nineties I'd picked up at a thrift store, and the Doc Martens I'd saved up to buy in high school. The outfit is the equivalent of emotional body armor, comforting and familiar. I am glad that I spent extra time on my hair, though. It falls around my shoulders in what I hope are stylish waves.

A handful of people call out greetings to Cord, and there are fist bumps and high fives. This must be what it's like to be a celebrity, onstage all the time. Cord doesn't seem to notice. He's as easygoing as usual. I'm not sure I could ever get used to that kind of attention.

There's a line for food. Of course, Cord knows the person in front of us and introduces me to a guy who helped him with chemistry last year. I smile and do my best to make small talk, but it's never really been my thing. When we get to the front of the line, Cord picks up a tray and bows. In a horrible French accent, he says, "Dinner is served."

I can't help but grin at him. Everything he does is just a little over the top, but when he acts silly, it puts me at ease. In fact, it's surprisingly easy to feel comfortable with Cord.

"I'm good. I ate at home." Even as I say it, my stomach clenches in hunger. I'm not lying—I had eaten at home. Peanut butter and jelly at home is cheaper than anything they serve here. But I only had toast and black coffee for breakfast to follow the ramen I had last night for dinner. There isn't much food in the house right now, not until there's more money in my bank account. Sometimes I need to make do.

Cord scowls, and his gaze follows the length of me from the tips of my boots to meet my eyes again. "Humor me." He puts his tray on the rails in front of the sandwich bar and orders a hoagie.

I glare at him. "I said I was fine."

"You are." He points at the sandwiches.

"I don't need to eat my vegetables, Cord." I keep my voice low because I don't really want to make a scene. It's peak college-exposure zone. The last thing I need is people to see us arguing before they even realize we're a couple.

Fake couple. Whatever.

Cord leans in. Suddenly, I'm surrounded by him, and his scent fills my head. He cups my shoulders in his hands. When he whispers in my ear, I can't stop the shiver that runs through me. He studies my face, and if I didn't know any better, I might think it's real concern I see there. "I heard your stomach growl, and I saw how you just looked at my pie. I don't usually see passionate glances like that outside the bedroom." The words ricochet along my spine, sending tingles into my stomach and my girl parts. *Damn. This guy even makes food talk sexy.*

His fingers press into my shoulders, and the press—almost a soft massage—feels so good that I want to groan. "So if that's the truth, and you're really not hungry, cool. I'm happy. But if you are, you don't have to pretend for me. I see you."

Then he's gone, stepping back next to his food with his usual easy grin.

"Come on, Marshall. Get something. For me." He winks. "It'll look weird, me eating all this"—he motions to the tray, which is piled high with his sandwich, some fries, a bowl of fruit, and the aforementioned piece of pie—"while you sit there and watch."

I've got two choices. I can lie. I can bristle, tell him he doesn't know what he's talking about, that this is all fake, and he should mind his business. That I can take care of myself. Because his words struck a lot closer to home than I'm comfortable with.

I might have done that, too, if I were smart. I need to keep some kind of distance between us.

Yesterday, he offered friendship when he dropped me off, as if that could actually happen. I'm graduating in a few months, and he'll be off to play professional hockey somewhere. What universe includes us interacting at all after graduation? Maybe he needs to think of this as a friendship, but I can see our expiration date looming.

Still, I can't lie to him, not with that softness in his eyes. Because he's right. I am hungry.

"I'd like a donut." It's the first thing that comes to my mind, and it's true. I always want a donut.

"Donut, huh?" Cord blinks, probably as surprised by my response as I am. He rubs his chin, and I notice he wears a layer of stubble well. Who am I kidding? He wears everything well.

His hand slides down my arm to my elbow, and he gently guides me to the dessert station. Next to him, I'm small and feminine. "Let's see what we have. Looks like glazed, powdered, and…"

"Cream-filled. Obviously."

He grins. "Obviously." He motions to the server. "We'll take two."

"I can only eat one."

"Hey there, one-way street. The other's for me."

I laugh, tapping his tray. "Of course."

He flattens his hand against his finely chiseled abs. "Got to keep this girlish figure, Marshall."

Shaking my head, I follow him to the checkout. He motions to the drinks. "Coffee? Water?"

"Coffee." He waits while I pour some into a to-go cup, closing the lid.

"You don't put anything in it?" He reaches around me to snag three bottles of water and a carton of milk. Being this close to him is liable to give me a contact high.

I shrug. "Not usually." I stopped buying cream and sugar because they're expensive, and then I just started liking it better black.

I follow him with my cup to the checkout. He takes the cup from me, which makes me feel kind of bad because he's already carrying my messenger bag, his backpack, and all the food. But he doesn't seem fazed by the weight of it all. He motions for me to go ahead of him, so I start forward, my hands free, while he's laden with our stuff like a pack mule.

Or like I'm a queen and he's my loyal subject. Have to admit, I don't mind that feeling one bit.

No sooner have we sat down than Mikey Dischenski slides in on the bench next to me. "Hannah, right?" He nudges me with his shoulder. "I'm Mikey."

"I know. You threw up in my car," I remind him in a conspiratorial whisper and give him a wink. Now that Cord's sorted my car out, the whole thing is a lot funnier than it had been the other night.

I swear he blushes. Ducking his head sheepishly, he shrugs. "I'm really sorry about that."

I can't resist a guy who blushes. I bump him back. "It was your birthday. You get a pass."

"Not like that. Like I said, I'm really sorry. But I'm going to make it up to you. You're not even going to recognize your car, it's so pretty. And after it's all fixed up…" He gives a chef's kiss.

I grin. "Thanks."

He leans in and says more softly, "And thanks for not ratting me out to Coach. That was cool of you."

"Don't mention it."

In front of us, Cord sifts through the smorgasbord of food on his tray. "Hey Dizz…wanna back off my girl while we eat? You're cock-blocking me."

Mikey lifts his hands, leaning away. "Oh, this is a date." He whistles under his breath. "Whoa, the dining hall. Didn't know you were so fancy." But I notice he scoots back a few inches, giving me some space. Cord nods at him in approval as he slides my coffee and donut across the table.

Mikey scowls at my food. “Dude. That's no date. That’s a snack. Where’s the girl’s food?”

What is with these guys, worrying about my caloric intake? “The girl ate already, thank you very much. I’m not that hungry.” I sigh in happiness. *Seriously, is there anything better than cream-filled donuts?*

Mikey eyebrows lift. “If you say so.” He pats the table and stands. “But I’m going to need more than that. Off to the buffet.”

He swings his leg over the bench and heads toward the food at a trot. He’s immediately replaced by Linc Reynolds and Declan Mitchell. Linc slides in next to me, taking Mikey’s spot, and Declan sits next to Cord.

Cord grumbles under his breath, “Why did I think we would be able to talk here?” But as he ducks his head, I catch his grin. It’s like he’s enjoying the guys chatting with me.

I don’t understand why he enjoys his teammates talking to me, and they mostly ignore him. Linc bumps my shoulder, same as Mikey had. “Hey, how’s it going?”

Across the table, Declan tilts his head in the imperial nod of introduction. “Hey. I’m Declan Mitchell. I don’t think we’ve met.”

I finish chewing then pat my lips, afraid I might be covered in powdered sugar. “I believe you offered to claim me if no one else did at the rink the other day.”

Linc snickers next to me, and Cord’s eyebrows shoot up.

Declan even cracks a smile before studying me closer. “So you and Cap? Interesting.” He leans back, crossing his arms over his chest. “My offer still stands. If you want to hang out with the best hockey player on the team, you let me know.”

Cord snorts. “She already is.”

Their eyes hold for a long minute. I'm not that familiar with guy interactions, but this feels like some weird male standoff. I'm about to break the awkward silence when Declan claps Cord on the shoulder and tosses me a wink.

Cord meets my gaze, and then nods toward my food. "Your donut's getting cold."

He doesn't need to remind me twice. As I polish off the surprisingly delicious donut, considering it's from a college cafeteria, the guys carry on their conversation. I'm glad Cord recommended food because I hadn't thought through how sitting with them might be. The food gives me something to do while I listen.

The conversation turns to hockey. Not surprising, I guess. They're away this weekend then play one more home game before playoffs begin in a few weeks. Heated debate breaks out about different aspects of their team, different players, and what they think their strengths and weaknesses are against them.

As I listen, I try to rationalize the difference between the airheaded jocks I'd thought they were with the well-informed athletes in front of me. The three of them are serious, intense, and similar in temperament to the focused musicians I'm used to hanging out with. As much as I hate to admit it, it's hard not to respect their passion and to completely disregard the airhead prejudice.

"Are you coming to the last home game, Hannah?" Linc finally asks.

"I don't…"

"Of course she is," Cord fills in. His eyes widen as if he's silently reminding me that I'm his "girlfriend." "It's next Thursday."

"Right. Of course." I smile. "I'll be there." Since my shifts were all cut, I don't have any other obligations.

Linc grins then turns to Cord. "Shea uses my ticket in our section if she's in town. If you're not using yours, you can give it to Hannah." He shrugs. "Maybe you guys could sit together."

"That'd be great." I'm not lying, either. I like Shea. She's the kind of girl everyone likes.

"So, you're in the music department?" Declan asks.

"Yes."

He pops one of Cord's fries in his mouth. "You're good."

I blink. These guys aren't anything like I expected. "Thanks."

Cord nudges his head toward the door then gathers all the trash onto his tray and stands, so I follow him. We say our goodbyes and make our way to the conveyor belt to deposit our dishes. The others follow us, and they clap Cord on the back, waving at me as they go, and I even get a high five from Mikey. As the hockey players tumble out of the cafeteria like a bunch of puppies, shoving and horsing around, I grin. "They're good guys, aren't they?"

"They're a huge pain in my ass." Cord winks at me as he throws out the trash and puts the dirty dishes on the belt. "But yeah. For the most part." He's playing it down, but it's clear that he adores them.

I can see why.

Someone slides up behind Cord, wrapping their arms around him. "Hey, lover."

Rachel. I'm partly shocked and a lot disgusted. *Who even talks like that?*

Cord stiffens, extracting himself from her grasp. "Rachel."

I have to admit that she looks amazing. In a short skirt with over-the-knee boots, she's showing off long and curvy legs. Her long brown hair is straight down her back, and her makeup's perfect. She's gorgeous and expensive.

I straighten, tilting my chin up.

Cord's lack of enthusiasm doesn't faze Rachel. "I've been trying to get a hold of you." She grins, squeezing his hand. "Haven't you gotten my messages?"

"I have." Cord tugs his fingers from her grasp and tucks his hands into his pockets.

"Oh. Well." Her grin slips a fraction. "I just…I heard you were going to be talking with New Jersey, and I wanted to wish you luck."

Cord's face darkens. "Wait. Who told you that?"

"I don't know." She waves dismissively. "Maybe my dad, or I might have read it somewhere…"

"It's none of your business. We aren't together," he grits out.

"Not if I had my way." She places her hands on his chest. I'm standing right next to them, but she's completely ignoring me. If I wasn't only his fake girlfriend, that would really piss me off.

I'm not sure what happened between them. He told me they broke up over the summer, but the rest had been vague. One thing's for sure, though. I hate that she's swiped the relaxed grin that I've become used to from his face.

Chuckling, he drops his arm onto my shoulder. I'm engulfed in the smell of him. It isn't cologne. It's soap and mint and full-scale male deliciousness. I flatten against his side. It's impossible not to notice just how hard and muscled he is, and I'm not prepared. I suck in a breath. Every inch of him is chiseled and cut. There are acres of abs there, and I step even closer. I’m supposed to be his girl. Just because I’m not, really, and my body isn’t supposed to be acting like this doesn’t mean I can’t enjoy it anyway.

Time to put on my fake girlfriend pants.

“Rachel, have you met Hannah?”

“I don't think we have.” I stick out the hand that isn't wrapped around Cord’s waist, even as I try to ignore the acres of muscle pressed against me. I plaster my best confident smile on my face, sure it looks fake because it is. “Hi. I’m Cord’s girlfriend.”

The words sound foreign to my ears, and Rachel doesn’t believe them either. It takes her one glance to disregard me. She smiles up at Cord. “Why don't we get together tonight? We have some things to talk about.”

“I don’t have anything to say. Besides, Hannah and I have plans.”

Rachel doesn’t even spare me a glance. “I'm sure she won’t keep you busy all night.”

He stares her down. “Let me be clear. I don’t want to talk to you.” He steps away, gripping my hand. “You ready?” he asks.

I nod, and we leave her there.

Cord

I LEAD HANNAH THROUGH the crowd of people heading to their one o'clock classes. Once we're outside on the quad, she drops my hand. It shouldn't bother me. Sure, we're fine holding hands for the purposes of our act, but there isn't a need out here, away from Rachel. But I rub my palms, my fingers missing hers. Catching myself, I zip my fleece up to my chin.

"Have to say it, Cord… she's terrifying." She shivers dramatically.

I can only sigh. We set off toward the music building, side by side. "What I really want to know is how she found out I was supposed to talk with New Jersey. I just agreed to the conversation last night with my agent, and it isn't public knowledge."

"New Jersey?"

That's right—she doesn't really like hockey. It's so weird that she agreed to fake boyfriend me and she isn't even a fan of the sport. "Yeah. They're the ones who drafted me a few years ago. But I'm a center. Now, they want to talk about signing me to a contract as a defenseman." I tuck my hands in my pockets and round my shoulders against the cold.

When I don't go on, she prods me. "And this is a big deal."

I blow out a slow breath. “No. Yes. I don't know.”

She laughs. “That cleared it up.”

I grit my teeth. “I’ve always wanted to be a center. But this opportunity is interesting. Risky, maybe.”

“Why risky?”

“It might not pay off. I played defense for a couple months, when Linc first got hurt.”

She tilts her head.

“Concussions.”

“Ah.”

“What if they sign me, and I absolutely blow at defense in the professionals?”

“What if you’re great?” she asks.

I don’t have an answer to that, so I only shrug. It’s not like me to lack confidence. I don’t like the feeling.

“Why is it a problem that Rachel knows?” she asks, dragging me from my thoughts.

“Honestly, I was hoping to get through the conversation with New Jersey without talking about it with my dad.” Not because I’m afraid to tell him. I just want to make the decisions on my own. My dad was a center and had a long career. His perspective is bound to be different than mine, and this is my life.

“How would your dad know?

“Her dad and my dad are good friends. And I wouldn’t put it past her to go directly to my dad to ask about me.” My dad always treated Rachel like the daughter he never had.

“They talk like that? She’s your ex-girlfriend.” She wrinkles her nose. “In my book, calling your ex-boyfriend’s father is… odd. I mean, I’ve been out of the dating scene for a while, but even I know that.”

I glance at her from the side. Suddenly, I'm thinking about her old boyfriends, about anyone who's kissed her, who's held her. Just the idea of other guys kissing Hannah… I stretch my suddenly tight neck muscles. Probably from the cold weather. "Sometimes, I think he likes her better than me."

"I see." She glances at me, and when our eyes meet, it's like she gets it. Like she might understand, even though I barely said anything. Suddenly, she pulls me to the side of the walkway, letting others get past us. Standing this close, I can see the flecks of gold in her brown eyes. I clear my throat. In the intensity of her gaze, I feel like she's seeing all the things I try to hide.

Then she's on her tiptoes, wrapping her arms around me in a quick hug. Between the strange vulnerability and the sudden feel of her in my arms, I'm in a tailspin.

When she pulls back, she squeezes my hand. "Listen, you should do what makes you happy. Our parents don't live our lives, and they can't determine how they go. You should follow your heart."

*God, this girl…*I smile at her, my chest swelling. I tug on the piece of hair that had fallen over her left shoulder. "Did Gandhi say that?"

"If he was smart, he did." She offers me a smart-ass grin. The subtle tilt of her lips draws my attention to her insanely full and kissable mouth.

"That's Zen of you, Marshall." My voice is huskier than usual. Because right now, I realize that this is the perfect chance to test out this fake relationship with a kiss. Because people in relationships kiss. Even though ours is fake, we need to make it look real.

I drop my hands onto her shoulders and allow my fingers to curve around them, to learn the lines of her. Everything about her is slight, but still, she radiates that strength that really just turns me on. Her pupils are dilated as her gaze meets mine, and her breathing hitches. That along with her lips…*fuck. What are they going to taste like?* The anticipation has me tightening up.

"Please don't kiss me."

The words are soft, but I hear them. I pause, pulling back, staring into the depths of her coffee-colored eyes. "Okay."

"It's fake." She swallows, licking her lips. "I don't want fake kisses."

"It would be a real kiss." My thumb traces the curve of her jaw. There's nothing fake about how much I want to taste her.

"You won't mean it. So please don't do it." Her voice is low, earnest. Maybe some girls would play games with something like this, but there's nothing manipulative in her face. I should know—I spent enough time with Rachel to know what controlling looks like.

She's right, though. Not about it being fake, but that I shouldn't kiss her. I haven't wanted to kiss someone since… well, since Rachel. I don't know what that means, but unless I know what the hell I'm doing, I definitely shouldn't be dragging her into my mess. How much I want her is throwing me off.

She's perfect for this "relationship" because she's not interested in me. Why am I complicating this by wanting her? Maybe this really is a bad idea. It defeats the purpose if I'm distracted from hockey by the girl who's supposed to help me focus on it.

But it doesn't sound like she wants me to cross that line either. Maybe that's a good thing. It will hold us both in check.

She blinks up at me, her eyes huge behind her glasses. I tuck a stray strand of hair behind her earthen lean closer, slowly, giving her every opportunity to step back or away. She doesn't, even when my lips are only an inch from her ear and I can breathe the lavender, citrus scent of her.

"I promise," I whisper. "I won't kiss you unless you ask me to." I retreat, retrieving my hands from her and tucking them into the pockets of my coat. I drop my gaze, using the moment to head to the walkway to get my shit together. A deep breath, and I'm pretty sure I've got everything under control when I turn back.

"I won't do that," she says. It sounds like a vow, and I wonder whether she's convincing me or herself.

I nod because I don't know if I'm relieved or disappointed or what. We set off again toward her building.

"We don't need to…" She swallows. "To do that for this to work."

I shrug because I can't refute that. "It would definitely sell it."

"It'll be easier if we don't." She glances up then licks her lips again. "After this is over."

"Easier."

"Yeah. Easier."

"To stay friends, you mean?" That was what we agreed to. Friends. Nothing more.

"Right," she says with a decisive nod. "To stay friends."

"If we don't make out in public all the time."

She glares at me. "Right."

"Right," I repeat, laughing. I throw my arm around her shoulders again and bump her hip. "Come on. Let's get you to class, baby."

She pushes her glasses up her nose. But as we continue, she shakes her head, even though I can see the ghost of a grin. "And I told you not to call me baby."

"Sorry, beautiful." I laugh, squeezing her closer. This time, she curls in like a real girlfriend might, like it's the most natural thing in the world, and I try to remember this is all make-believe.

When we reach the steps of her building, I check to make sure they've been salted before I let her head up alone.

She goes up a couple before pausing and skipping back down. "Oh, I forgot to tell you," she says, leaning in close again. Her hair looks so soft that I have to force my hands into my pockets to resist the urge to touch it. "I got a gig. Thursday night. At a bar about thirty miles away called Yesterday's Party. Can you take me?"

"Sure." I have practice earlier—twice every day until playoffs—but I'll snag a nap. "What time?"

"Can you pick me up around nine?"

"Absolutely. Mind if I bring Linc?"

She snags her lip with her teeth. "I guess not."

"You sure?" She doesn't sound it.

"Yeah. I just haven't made my singing a thing here. At Chesterboro, I mean. But I guess it isn't a big deal."

"Okay. Sounds good, then. Thursday at nine."

"Thanks." She grins again, waving, and starts up the steps again, her Converse crunching on the salt, her guitar strapped on her back.

I stare at her gorgeous legs in those crazy-colored tights. I never thought I'd be a tights-and-Converse kind of guy, but on her, I definitely am. "Hey, babe?"

She stops so fast someone almost runs into her. She twists back, scowling. “Yes?” she asks through gritted teeth.

I burst out laughing and wink at her. “Have a good day, Marshall.”

“Will do, Spellman.” She cracks a grin, shakes her head, then scurries up the rest of the stairs.

I chuckle to myself on my way to class on the other side of campus.

One thing’s for sure: I like Hannah Marshall more than might be safe for either of us.

Hannah

JENNA DEWITT STANDS AT the top of the stairs, watching me approach. When I reach her, she glances below us. "Is that Cord Spellman?"

Damn it. I should have known she had a reason to wait outside instead of going in to avoid the cold. I hike my guitar up. "Yeah."

Her eyebrows disappear under her sweeping bangs. "The hockey player Cord Spellman?"

"Yeah."*Is there another Cord Spellman I don't know about?* The world can't handle two of him. Or maybe that's just me.

"You hate jocks."

We shuffle inside with the flow of traffic. "Hate is a strong word."

"I think that was close to what you said. Especially about the hockey team." She puts her hand on her chest, doing a striking impersonation of me. "Jenna, they're so arrogant and full of themselves."

That sounds exactly like something I would say, so I divert as we start up the staircase toward the upper levels. "Cord's an okay guy."

That's unfair. A couple of days ago, sure, I might have said that. Now he's the guy I can't stop thinking about kissing, the guy who's making my breath come out ragged just thinking about his mouth on mine.

When Jenna looks at me, clearly confused, I blow out a shaky exhale as if climbing the stairs is winding me.

As we continue the trek upstairs to class, my mind returns to the sidewalk. To Cord's hands on me, to staring into his eyes and that delicious anticipation. He was going to kiss me.

I wanted him to. No surprise there. But he wanted to kiss me? Was he serious? Or was it only part of the act?

At least I'd had the foresight to stop him. We hadn't discussed the physical part of our faking it, but I should have seen it coming. Couples kissed. We're in college. What college couples don't kiss?

I can't, though. Maybe if I wasn't so attracted to him. But I can't pull it off now, not without making a complete fool out of myself.

It's better if I don't trust the kiss was real. It'll be better when this is over if I don't kiss him now. I doubt kissing Cord is something I'd forget easily.

"I think we're actually kind of seeing each other," I offer, trying to sound casual.

I must have failed. "What? How did you go from 'ew, jocks are gross' to 'we're actually kinda sorta seeing each other'?" We hit the landing on the second floor where our class is held. It's an advanced class, with only six of us in it, so the stairwell is empty.

When I agreed to…whatever this is with Cord, I didn't think about explaining how it happened so fast. Jenna knows me. She knows I didn't know Cord.

"I gave him, Mikey Dischenski, and Linc Reynolds a ride home last Friday night." That much is true enough.

"They were at the truck stop?" It makes sense that she would assume that. "And how did you end up shuttling the ice hockey team?"

"No, they weren't at the truck stop." No one from school is ever caught dead there. "They were walking. Mikey got sick in an Uber, and they got thrown out. They were on the road from the highway, trying to pick up another ride."

"Shit. That sucks." She giggles, though. Now I can see how that's amusing, especially having spent time with the hockey boys. They're royalty. Thinking of them walking because they couldn't get a ride is actually pretty funny. I grin along with her.

"It was Mikey's twenty-first." That's all the explanation needed. "I stopped to give them a lift. I guess Cord and I happened after that. Over the weekend and stuff." That sounds like we hooked up and makes me feel gross. I've always worked to be respectable.

But apparently, it's enough explanation for Jenna. It's Cord, after all. A lot of girls would fall right into bed with him, though that doesn't exactly comfort me.

"Wow. And that was why he was walking you to class today?"

"He drove me to school yesterday and today," I add.

She side-eyes me. "He took one look at you in the moonlight, saving him from a long, cold walk, and realized that he never wanted to leave your side from then on." She bats her eyelashes, all the drama-department energy, and I laugh.

Because that's ridiculous. Stuff like that doesn't happen. And if it did, it definitely wouldn't happen to girls like me.

"More like, Mikey threw up in the back of my car, too, so he's going to get it detailed for me and offered to drive me around for a while."

She pauses to consider before nodding. "Definitely makes more sense than love at first moonlight."

Though the words make my stomach pang, I laugh along with her as we shuffle into class. Sure, he came to my rescue with Mr. Murphy, and maybe he'd wanted to kiss me. But that's a whole lot different than love at first sight.

Love at first sight…that's hilarious. We've only known each other for four or five days. We're just a means to an end, help with an ex-girlfriend problem and a fixed-up car and some fun for me. The girls he's really connected to—girls like Rachel Murray—are glamorous and confident. They wear beautiful clothes, have beautiful hair and bodies.

They have money and prestige. They aren't like me.

Even he said it. The only reason I'm a good fit for this arrangement is that I didn't want him.

And I don't. Maybe I want to kiss him and run my hands over him and do any number of other things purely in the imagination of a girl who hasn't had time to have a relationship in, well, ever, really. But that's all purely physical. He's going off to make millions playing hockey, and I'm going to grad school in the fall. I don't have time to date, even if he is honestly interested. Which he isn't.

Kisses are physical. The attraction I feel for him is straight-up physical. All of that is as real and temporary as our fake relationship.

I set my guitar case at my spot then open it to tune the instrument and consider him.

Even though we aren't ever going to be together like that, it's hard not to genuinely like him. He's not only the hottest guy I've ever seen. He's the kind of guy who teases me and comes to my defense. A good guy.

Still… Me, friends with the captain of the hockey team feels weird. Shaking my head, I twist the tuning keys. It's as implausible as love at first moonlight. I only plan to enjoy his company, for now or whatever time we spend together. When the playoffs are over, we will be too.

As I settle in and class begins, my mind keeps straying to him, in the moonlight and then in the morning, holding my guitar out to me with a grin. I think about him calling me "baby" and laughing when it ruffles my feathers.

Despite all my friend-zone and temporary-relationship peptalking, it's difficult to stop thinking about him.

Hannah

I'M SUPPOSED TO GO onstage at Yesterday's Party at ten o'clock, so I asked Cord to pick me up at nine. As I slide into the passenger seat, he looks at me funny.

"What?" I run a hand over my hair. I don't have my wig, so I styled my hair this time. He offered to replace the wig, but I decided it wasn't worth it. The thing's hot. I thought in the beginning it might make me look glamorous. I always wanted darker hair. But I hadn't considered that it would make me so sweaty all the time.

Tonight, it had taken a while to do my hair because I hadn't used a curling iron in forever, but I thought it turned out okay. I'd managed to coax it into what I hoped were beachy waves. I don't know how I'm going to explain the different color, because my wig was a caramel color and my real hair is blond, but I hope even my "fans" aren't discerning enough to care. I put the visor down and check my makeup in the lighted mirror. "There's something in my teeth?"

Cord clears his throat. "No. Just…you look… great."

The way he says it makes my heartbeat pick up. Under the weight of his gaze, I close the cover on the mirror, not wanting the light to show the flush on my cheeks. "Thank you." I spent longer than usual on my makeup tonight. Not because Cord is going to be there but because I won't be wearing the wig. Its curls covered more of my face. At least that was what I told myself when I was getting dressed.

"You have everything?" he asks, shifting into reverse.

I pat my bag. "I have my tablet with my music. That's really all I need."

"Okay. We just have to double back to pick up Linc." He backs up to turn around and head out of Dreamland. "He had to finish powdering his nose or whatever." He snorts.

"All I need is a ride. You guys don't have to stay." After all, Linc and Cord won't really fit in at Yesterday's Party. Sure, it's not exactly the safest place, but I can take care of myself. I've been doing it for years.

"It's over half an hour away, Hannah. Where are we going to go if you're only singing for an hour or so? Besides, I want to hear you sing. And I'm not going to leave you alone at some dive bar." His hands tighten on the steering wheel as we pull up in front of his apartment. "I looked it up. The place isn't safe for a girl alone. Maybe you had to go alone before, but you have me now. What kind of a boyfriend do you think I am?"He looks honestly insulted.

"My fake boyfriend." *Seriously, what is happening here?*

"Exactly," he says as if he missed my point completely.

I blow out an exasperated breath as Linc jogs down the stairs from their apartment building. Cord jumps out, pushing his seat forward so Linc can climb in the back. For a few moments, it's all elbows and legs as he rearranges himself, trying to put a giant, nearly six-and-a-half-foot body into a capsule-sized space. But once he's settled, he smiles at me. "Hey, Hannah. I'm excited to watch you sing again."

He's so kind and appears so genuine, I don't feel as bad for dragging him out. Still, I say, "You guys absolutely don't need to watch me. But thank you for coming. Sorry you had to give your night up. Cord is under some misguided chivalrous notion that I need bodyguards."

Linc's face sobers, his eyebrows dropping. "Of course you need us. Cord says the place is sketchy." He smiles again, all dimples. "And it's our pleasure to go. You were awesome on Friday night. Like, really good."

I try to ignore the wash of pleasure that gives me, but I can't help my smile. "Thanks."

"No problem," he says, grinning back and touching his brow.

Even though I don't want to admit it, it's kind of nice to have them along. They're right—the Party isn't the safest place for a girl by herself. And it's cool to have people worried about me.

Linc leans forward. "So, what are you going to be singing?"

I shrugged. "Who knows? I usually see how things are going. Watch the audience. Then I sing whatever I think they want to hear."

He cocks his head. "How exactly do you know that?"

"I don't know. I just do."

"That's pretty obvious." Cord grins at me, squeezing my hand. The brief contact sends a shimmer of awareness through me. More disconcerting is how natural it all feels. He's really good at pretending.

The rest of the drive is them giving me suggestions of songs that they think I would slay, as Linc puts it. Some of them are songs that are already on my playlist, but they actually have a couple of good ideas. I pull out my tablet, making notes as they chat.

The ride is definitely better with company.

When we exit the highway, cars line the drive to the bar. Cord slows to a stop before we even get to the parking lot. “Are all these cars for the bar?”

I shrug. I've never seen it this packed. Cord circles back and finds a spot on the shoulder that doesn’t have too many potholes. As we head to the bar, Cord and Linc fall into step on either side of me, their hands in their pockets, their shoulders rounded, definitely like bodyguards. I’d drawn attention showing up here before, but flanked by two tall, good-looking guys, people turn to stare before we even reach the entrance. The line to get in snakes around the side of the building.

“What’s going on?” Linc asks.

A girl shivering next to her boyfriend answers. “Hannah is singing. Someone posted on the forums.” She pauses, her gaze falling on me. “Wait a minute…”

We keep walking, though, before she fully recognizes me, heading around back to the employee entrance. As he grabs the door to usher me in, Linc chuckles and winks at me. “Did you hear? Hannah’s singing.”

I can’t smother my smile. “I might have heard something about that.”

They are here for me. This is surreal. It’s completely packed. I’ve wanted to build a following. More people means more money, and this looks like it’s going to bring me a lot of cash.

There’s a block holding the back door open, probably so the employees can come out to smoke without getting locked out, so we slip in. I pause to take off my coat and hang it on one of the pegs on the wall.

“Do you want me to hold that for you?” Cord asks.

I shake my head. “That's okay. We’ll probably need to leave this way, anyway.” If the line is any indication, there’s no way I’ll be able to walk out the front door when this is over.

Even thinking about that is crazy.

He nods as if he understands. I’m still not sure I do. This is all a shock. I noticed the crowds getting heavier the last couple of times, I think, but this… this is next level.

I’m excited, and anticipation courses through me. This is the kind of exposure I need. My take of the earnings tonight will look great in my bank account.

A bar back is lifting a box of liquor next to us. I signal to him. “Hey, do you know if Ronnie Brandon is here?”

He shuffles the box to get a better grip. “Who?”

“Brandon,” I yell over the music. “He books events, got this job for me. About this high.” I motion. “Thinning hair. Mustache?”

He points, recognition on his face. “Oh yeah. Looks like a pimp on a TV show?”

I sigh. *Fair assessment.* “Yeah, that’s him.”

The bar back lifts a shoulder. “Haven’t seen him tonight. But ask Danny out front.” He jostles his box and leaves us there without another word.

I run my hand over my hair, trying to hide my irritation. This is the third event that he’s missed. What’s the point of a manager who doesn’t manage things?

“Everything okay?” Cord asks.

This isn’t his problem, so I put on my best smile. “Absolutely. Why don’t you guys watch from the bar? Ask for Danny. He’s the bar manager, and he’ll set you up.”

“If you’re sure.” He drops his hands on my shoulders as Linc heads to the front.

I smile at him. “I got this.”

He nods then follows Linc out to the bar, leaving me to prepare to sing for a huge crowd…including him.

I shake out my hands and stretch my neck, taking some deep breaths. This audience is bigger than any that I’ve ever been in front of before.

All my nerves disappear when I step onstage. The crowd greets me with whoops and claps, and the sounds are beautiful to my ears. I take the microphone and begin as I always do. “It's nice to be back,” I call. Except this time, the crowd goes wild, and I can't help but laugh along with them. I hook my tablet up to the sound system with an HDMI cable. I’m surprised to see a keyboard. They’ve never had a keyboard here before, and I’ve never played at one of my singing gigs.

Shaking my head, I flip through the songs on my tablet, looking for something upbeat. There are a lot of good vibes in the room tonight. Usually, I start with something slow to get warmed up, but that doesn't seem to fit. I cue up “Don’t Stop Believin’” by Journey. At the first strains of that distinctive piano solo, the crowd loses their mind.

What follows is a whirlwind. There’s so much energy. My whole body buzzes with the joy in the room. It’s raw and powerful.

After a few upbeat numbers, things start to feel frenetic, so I decide to switch it up. Skipping through my songs, nothing feels right. I glance out at the audience, but I can barely see them without my glasses. I can feel their expectations, though, their expectation. They want something from me. *Why haven’t I just fully fallen into this?*

I set the tablet down on the stool next to me. Heading to the edge of the stage, I retrieve my bag and riffle through it. There are murmurs behind me from people waiting to see what I'm doing.

I pull my glasses case out and slide my glasses onto my face. Then I step back up to the microphone.

"I'm going to try something new, you guys," I say, glancing at the keyboard. "Bear with me, okay?" I slide the microphone stand over, positioning it so I can still use it behind the keys.

I sit and take a moment to acquaint myself with this machine. It's nothing much, but it should do. I turn it on and warm up with a few scales. The crowd immediately starts applauding.

I laugh. "If you guys think that's something, wait."

It feels so good to be behind the keyboard. I always feel the most comfortable playing, but playing and singing is electric.

I know exactly the song I want to play.

I start to sing "Shake It Off" by Florence and the Machine, accompanying myself with the keyboard. During the first lyrics, the crowd in front of me stops moving, all of them watching. Some have their arms wrapped around themselves, and others are swaying.

But then the beat picks up. The crowd starts to dance, and it's so cathartic to sing this song about leaving baggage behind that tears roll down my face when I'm done.

It takes me a moment to recover, but the people don't seem to mind. At least the thunderous applause says they don't.

I play a few more songs. "Believe" by Mumford and Sonsthen "Driver's License" by Olivia Rodrigo. My fingers hover over the keys. I could play one of my songs. But I don't.

Instead, I say into the mic, "Thank you for being with me tonight" and start "Faithfully" by Journey.

When it's done, I stand, sweating and exhausted, and the crowd in front of me is so loud they shake the whole place. Adrenaline races through my veins, and I ride that high. *This is what my life is missing.*

Exhilarated, I stumble down the stairs off stage, almost running over my manager, Ronnie Brandon, an older man who hasn't quite figured out how to dress. Tonight, he wears an ill-fitting suit and has too much gel in his hair, every bit of him so slick it borders on slimy. The guy with him, however, looks normal in jeans, a button-up, with glasses. He's probably in his thirties.

Brandon opens his arms, pulling me into a hug I can't avoid in the small area behind the stage. "There's my girl!" he yells.

I shrug out of his grasp. "You're here." It's the politest thing I can say. He's missed my last few shows, but he keeps finding me gigs when I need them, so I'm wary to insult him.

"Of course," he says as if it's ridiculous to suggest he wouldn't be there.

I can barely contain my eye roll. "Right."

"Great job out there," he enthuses. "I didn't catch the beginning, but you really finished things off well. I didn't know you could play the piano."

"And the guitar." I've actually told him that a few times.

"Right." He waves that off like it's not important information, and I grind my back teeth together. "This is Milo Parker. He's an event coordinator and manager in New York. He apparently came to see you." Brandon's smile is too smooth.

I hold out my hand. "Nice to meet you."

He smiles, and his eyes are kind. “That was a very intense performance. I represent a handful of acts, and I was wondering if you would be interested in opening for one of them.” He rattles off a list of names, some I’ve never heard of and a few that I have.

“She would love to,” Brandon pipes in. I hold my face impassive, but it irritates me that he doesn’t let me answer for myself.

“Wonderful.” He hands us each a card from his pocket. “Give me a call this week. We can set something up.” He smiles at me. “I think you are going to be an amazing talent, Hannah.”

“Thank you.” I take his outstretched hand again. Over his shoulder, I see Cord and Linc picking their way through the cramped area backstage.

“She’s pretty great, isn’t she?” Brandon chimes in. My smile slips. He slings his arm around me, and I try not to cringe out of his grasp. “No doubt about it. I can really spot the talent. With a few changes to her clothes and maybe makeup… something a little sexier”—he pulls me closer as if we’re conspirators—”I really think we can push you over the edge.”

I stiffen, not sure I heard him correctly. “You want to change my clothes and makeup?”

“Yeah,” he says. “You know, slut it up a bit more. That’s what really brings in the crowds.”

Around me, the cacophony of the bar fades away. I can’t hear the dance music they piped in after I finished, only the heavy beat of my pulse.

Slut it up. Slut it up. The words echo in my head, bouncing around like bumper cars. This is exactly what I’ve worked to avoid my whole life, at least since my dad killed himself.

There'd been all the talk. After he died, the rumors circulated. He stole money and laundered it through the lumber company he worked for. There were creditors. I was only twelve, so I didn't understand it all, but I saw how people we knew suddenly pretended they didn't see us at the grocery store or at church. Then came my mom's drinking. Maybe she drank before. Maybe she didn't. I didn't remember, but I recognized when it got bad, along with the rest of the town. And the men she slept with…

The first time a boy in high school asked if I was a whore like my mother, I decided that my life would be different. Yet, here I am.

My eyes meet Cord's, and his expression is unreadable. He glances between me and Brandon. "Everything okay here?"

Maybe he hadn't heard what Brandon said. It's loud in here. It's possible Brandon's voice didn't carry this one time.

"I'm Hannah's manager, Ronnie Brandon. And this is Milo Parker." Brandon nudges his head toward Mr. Parker, further mortifying me. "You must be her…"

"I'm her boyfriend." Cord stares at Brandon's hand without taking it. "Are you ready, Marshall?" he asks, dismissing Brandon as if he isn't here.

He must have heard. *Great.* I nod, squaring my shoulders. "I look forward to hearing more from you, Mr. Parker," I say with as much dignity as I can manage. "Thank you for coming." Then I pull my coat off the peg. Cord nods to the other men and ushers me out the door.

Cord

IT'S SILENT ON THE way to the car. Linc and I flank Hannah, but she doesn't say anything. Her coat is buttoned up to her chin, and she doesn't look like a woman who just sang her heart out and brought an entire bar to their feet. She's closed off. As I click my key to unlock the car, Linc strides forward, opening the passenger side and crawling into the back.

"That was your manager?" I ask as we follow him. I didn't like the look of the guy. I especially didn't like the stuff that came out of his mouth. I'm not sure if Linc heard him, but I did. And by the tight set of his mouth and the stiffness in his shoulders, I bet he did too.

What an asshole. Some guys—lots of them—are dicks to women, but this guy is her manager. He's supposed to be looking out for her well-being. To talk like that in front of her, in front of a handful of others…that's fucked up.

I'm riding a heavy dose of protective instinct, too, and I'm not really interested in examining that right now.

We both climb into our seats. "Yeah. That's my manager."

When she doesn't continue, I start the car, and the radio breaks into the tension. As we pull out, no one says anything else until we hit the highway.

"Does he talk to you like that all the time?" I can't help it. I'm sure she'd rather I let this go, but that's not who I am.

When she doesn't immediately respond, Linc pipes in. "What he's trying to ask is if your manager is always a dickhead."

Hannah stiffens in the seat next to me, and I grit my teeth. "Thanks, Linc. I got it."

I glare at him in the rearview mirror, and he settles back in his seat, crossing his arms over his chest. Undoubtedly, Linc would have thrown hands at the guy first and asked questions later. Hell, that had been my first instinct too. But it's her manager, and they're supposed to have a professional relationship. The guy didn't act like a professional, but I want to respect her wishes. I followed her lead back there, but I'd like to know what the hell is going on now.

After a long moment, I prod her. "Does he?"

"What?"

I exhale. "Talk to you like that a lot."

"You mean tell me that I need to dress like a slut?" She stares out the window. "No. That was the first time. And he's definitely never said anything like that in front of other people, especially another manager who wants to book me to open for bands in New York."

"New York?"

"Yeah. The other guy he was with was Milo Parker." Hannah drops her hands to her lap. "He's another event organizer. I don't know much about it all, honestly. But he told me who he represented." She rattles off a few names that are familiar.

"Wait. The Dazed Zealots? That band is one of my new favorites," Linc pipes up from the back.

Mine too. I'd downloaded a couple of their songs earlier in the week to work out to. "Do you think he's legit?" I ask.

"Don't know. I need to look into it." She grimaces. "Or have Ronnie do it."

My nose scrunches as if I smell something bad. "I don't like that guy."

"No one likes that guy," she responds. "But he gets me gigs, so I put up with him."

"There has to be a better way. Other managers. He shouldn't talk to you like that." Inspiration strikes. "I can call my agent. Harry is with a major talent agency, and I know they represent some musicians. Or I can call my dad. My grandfather was a politician, and our family has contacts. I'm sure he knows someone else who would be a better fit for you."

She glances at me, but I can't read her expression in the dim light in the car. Then she goes back to staring out the window. It's dark out, so there's nothing interesting to see, which means she doesn't want to talk more about it.

But I can't figure out why. It isn't as if we hadn't given her an opening. Maybe it isn't that she doesn't want to talk about it. She just doesn't want to talk about it with me.

That stings. We haven't known each other long, but I thought we were making progress. Becoming friends, maybe, or something. I'd spent the last two days exchanging goofy texts with her. We talked about New Jersey, about defense. I've even told her some things about Rachel.

We lapse into silence. Linc tries chatting about the Dazed Zealots and Hannah's set. He might as well be carrying on a conversation with himself, though, because neither Hannah nor I add much. Before long, he quiets.

I'm probably making too much out of this. After all, as she keeps reminding me, this is a fake relationship. If she doesn't want to talk about something, that's her prerogative. It's my reaction that unsettles me.

I pull into the trailer park to drop her off. It hits home again just how run-down her neighborhood is. I try to keep from bottoming out on the potholes in the drive. When her place comes into the headlights, there's an older, rusted-out Oldsmobile parked out front and lights on inside.

"Were you expecting company?" I ask.

Next to me, she stiffens. "No."

I stop then, still a ways from the house. "Should we call the cops?"

"No." She sighs. "I know who it is. I just wasn't expecting her." She gathers her bag, reaching for the handle. "It's my mother."

"Wait. Let me pull up, then." Someone with a good relationship with their mother doesn't act like that. If my mom showed up out of the blue, I'd be ecstatic to see her. When I park, she says goodnight to Linc, and she's out so quickly that I barely have enough time to get my door open before she's scurrying toward her porch. I trot to catch up. "Hannah. Wait." I snag her hand. "What's going on?"

She gazes up at her place, not meeting my eyes. I don't think I've ever had to drag information out of a girl.

"Is everything okay?" I ask. "You've been acting strange since we left the bar." I rub my thumb against the inside of her wrist. *What is it about this girl that makes me want to touch her so badly?*

"You don't know me well enough to know what's strange and what isn't." She gently pulls her hand from mine. She drags the crossbody strap of her messenger bag over her head and finally meets my gaze. "You should go."

"What does that even mean?" It sure as hell sounds like a brush-off.

She laughs, but it's hollow. "You're a nice guy, Cord. I didn't expect that. But this"—she waves her hand between us—"is a temporary arrangement." She points at the house. "What's going on in there? That's my life. Ronnie Brandon? He's my mess. And all of this will still be here when you're gone."

Her words sting, and that pisses me off more than I ever would have expected. I read this entire situation wrong. Or I'd forgotten exactly why we started this.

Fake. Not real. Temporary. I get it. Loud and clear.

I bury my hands in my hair and tug, thankful to feel that burn. "You know what, Hannah? Fine. I'll get going." If she doesn't want me here, I'm not going to force it. Still, I can't help asking, my eyes on her place, "Is it safe?"

"She's my mother." Hannah shrugs.

That isn't a real answer, but it's definitely my cue to exit. "Right." I offer her a salute. "Goodnight, Hannah. You really did a great job tonight."

Maybe I shouldn't have said that. Hell, I don't know what I should say at this point. What I want to do is crack that shell around her and prove that she can trust me. But I don't have words that can do that, so I back away before I say anything else to embarrass myself.

I keep my eyes on her, though, until she's inside. If I've learned anything since I've met her, it's that it's almost painful to look away from her. As the door closes behind her, I trot back to my car.

Linc must have done some contortionist work to get into the front seat. I slide behind the steering wheel and shift into reverse, offering the house one more glance before backing away.

"You really like this girl." Linc sounds surprised. "I mean, she's nice and definitely hot in a sort of eclectic way, but…"

"I called her my girlfriend, didn't I?" I grumble. In front of everyone else, I can keep up the act. But this is Linc. *And what is the act anymore? That she's my fake girlfriend? Or that I want her to be more than that?* Sure, I want to be her friend. But a guy doesn't want to touch or kiss his friends. Friends didn't get under your skin. I want to pierce that hard shell she keeps wrapped around herself, to find out what she looks like when she's soft and vulnerable. And all that stuff is messing with my head. After everything that happened with Rachel, I'm just not sure I'm ready for something else. Anything else.

"I thought you were just trying to get laid." Linc shrugs. "But it's more than that, isn't it?"

As I pull onto the main road, I run my hand over my hair before slapping it hard against the steering wheel.

I shouldn't talk to him about this. I told Hannah that I wouldn't tell anyone. But it's Linc, my best friend. He would understand. "I don't know what it is anymore." I exhale. "I screwed this up."

"What?"

"It's fake. The whole thing."

"You don't like her?" Linc's brows furrow. "I don't understand."

"I do like her. I mean the relationship. That she's my girlfriend. It's fake."

He cocks his head. "Start at the beginning."

In as few words as I can, I explain the details to him. I tell him about how it started, about things with Rachel, the pressure about playoffs and New Jersey, and how Hannah is supposed to keep me from getting distracted.

"Let me get this straight. You took a fake girlfriend so you could avoid your ex-girlfriend because you didn't want any girlfriends at all?"

"Fuck you, man."

Linc laughs. "Seriously, I don't know anyone who can make things more complicated."

"It was supposed to be easy. Fun. I need to focus on hockey. I promised to get her back on the road and fix up her car. She doesn't even like hockey—or hockey players, for that matter. It was supposed to be totally platonic."

"Then what happened?"

"Nothing. Nothing happened. She is still the same. She's not a hockey fan, and I don't think she wants anything to do with me. Except…I like her. I have from the beginning. She's fun to talk to."

"And this is bad because…"

"Because I want her." There it is. The truth.

"And she doesn't want you?"

"I don't know what she wants. She's always so hard to read."

"That bothers you."

"Yes. It does." Explaining this makes it seem even more ridiculous. At a time when I should be focusing on my career and killing it in playoffs, I can't stop thinking about a girl who's supposed to keep me from being distracted.

Linc gives a thoughtful grunt. "Well, I like her," he finally says. "She is a little prickly, though. Maybe she's just scared." Linc has three sisters. He's usually solid for advice about girl emotions.

"Of what?" I don't like the idea, but I roll those words around in my head. If he's right, what's she afraid of? *Me?* My whole body cringes at that. More, it doesn't seem legit. She's not afraid of me, but something is scaring her, and I don't know how I can get past that if she won't let me in.

Linc shrugs. "Just take it slow, I guess. If she's anxious, you"—he waves, indicating all of me—"might be too much for her."

"What does that mean?"

He blows out a laughing snort. "Please. You're a real beauty, Cord. Everyone loves you. You always want to help everyone, fix everything. Everyone around you leans on you. Your first instinct is to be open to everyone. It's why you're a great captain. But it might not be the best play with her."

I want to argue, but I close my mouth. He's right, but he makes wanting to help people sound like a bad thing. Still, maybe he's on to something. We drive the rest of the way home in silence.

Hannah

THE DOOR TO THE trailer's unlocked. As I step inside, I glance back, watching Cord's taillights fade down the driveway.

"Fancy car." My mother stands at the window next to the door, a glass of amber liquid in one hand. She must have brought whatever alcohol is in it with her, because I don't keep any in the house. She lets the curtain fall. "Friend from school?"

"Yeah." I shrug out of my coat, hanging it on the hook next to the door.

"He's hot. Saw he had a nice ass in his headlights." She shrugs, taking a sip.

I haven't seen my mom in over a month—since she showed up on Christmas—and all she can do is comment on Cord's ass. No hellos, no hugs. Not that I expect any. We don't have that kind of relationship, at least not anymore.

I think we did before my father died, when I was a young girl. I remember her singing in the kitchen while she made breakfast on Sunday mornings. She used to fall asleep reading romance novels in the living room. She hugged me too tightly at bedtime.

But that was before Dad killed himself and everyone in Chesterboro started to tiptoe around us and whisper behind our backs. I heard the whispers. They wanted to know why he'd done it. There were the rumors of financial ruin, an affair, even drugs. If I'd heard it all, I'm sure my mom heard more.

She started drinking. Before long, I found the painkillers in prescription bottles with the labels peeled off. When I was a freshman in high school, she stopped coming home most nights. One night, when she did come home, some guy came with her. His clothes were ratty, and he smelled like a distillery. His appearance had nothing on his personality, though. When I came home from school, he looked me over like I was a buffet and he'd just paid for all he could eat.

His hand "accidentally" touched my breast. My mom caught him, and she kicked him out. He cussed her out, calling her names Mr. Murphy had never even dreamed up, and slammed out the door.

After that, I got a job. Not long after that, she signed the title of this disaster of a trailer over to me. There's no mortgage, just all the utilities and the rent for the lot. My mom barely shows up at all anymore.

"Guys like that are only looking for one thing, Hannah Marie." She offers a sad smile. "You don't have enough of it to keep them interested."

"Thanks, Mom. Welcome home." I narrow my eyes at her. "When is the last time you ate anything?" She's as thin as a rail, and her once-shiny blond hair, similar to mine, hangs dully on her shoulders. Her skin's ruddy, and deep circles darken under her eyes. We used to look similar, but now she's strung out. Who knows what she's on today. She's definitely drunk, though, and I don't need the half-empty bottle of whiskey on the table to tell me that.

I open the fridge, scanning my meager groceries. Eggs and toast it is, I guess. That's bland enough. I start the one burner that still works on the stove and get to it while my mother continues ranting.

"A BMW, huh? A rich boy from school, then." She stumbles, sloshing some of her drink onto the carpet.

"He does go to Chesterboro." I scramble the eggs right in the pan. Mom isn't a foodie. She won't notice if it isn't mixed properly. She's so wasted, she probably won't even be able to taste it.

"You need to be careful with men like that. Rich men. They think they're better than everyone else."

Hearing her put Cord down like that bothers me. "You don't even know him, Mom."

"Do you know him?" she asks. When I don't immediately respond, she continues, railing against wealthy men, powerful men. I tune her out as I continue mixing her food.

Do I know him? A week ago, I thought I knew him, just like everyone else on campus. Hockey god, rich and entitled, too charming for his own good. But that was before… he stuck up for me with Mr. Murphy. Before he waited every time I went into the house before he left and told me about his father and about how difficult it had been to live up to his expectations.

He's more than the dumb jock I'd assumed he was, and I like him a lot. Too much.

After he overheard Brandon, my skin felt too tight, and Cord had been worrying about me, wanting to hear my thoughts and giving me a chance to share with him, to bounce my ideas off of him. Like he actually cared.

More, as I'd looked into his eyes, I'd wanted to talk it over with him. It had freaked me out.

"Hannah." My mother's tone said I'd been ignoring her for longer than what was polite. "Are you even listening?"

"No, Mom. I'm not." My mom had made herself scarce from my life years ago. She doesn't get the right to endless commentary now. I glance at the food I made for her. She's barely eaten anything. "Are you done?"

She shrugs. "I'm not hungry."

I know better than to argue with her, so I pick the plate up and eat her leftovers before putting the plate in the sink. I can't afford to waste food. As I wash the dishes, I ask, "Why are you really here, Mom?" I'm not naive enough to think that she's stopped for a friendly visit.

She inhales, and I brace myself. "I need some cash, sweetie."

Her voice has taken on the wheedling tone I've come to hate. I close my eyes, bracing my hands on the sink to steady myself. "I don't have any money, Mom."

"I don't need much. Just a little to get me through the weekend. Barry's friend is paying him back some money he owes him on Monday."

"Barry, huh?" Newest boyfriend, I assume. Probably who owns the car out front. "He know you're here?"

"I told him that my daughter would be able to help us out."

Of course she did. I smile, not because it's funny but because it's so predictable. "Mom…"

"Please, Hannah. We're in a bind."

She's always in a bind. Suddenly, I'm more exhausted than I've ever been in my life. I turn back to her, crossing my arms over my chest. "I'm behind on the land lease, and my money is low too. They cut my shifts at the truck stop, and I am between jobs." I definitely don't tell her about the singing. If she knew about that, I'm sure she'd find some way to use the knowledge against me. I work hard, and I'm not willing to derail my savings for grad school. I've given her money before, thinking it would help her or change her. It never does, and it's never enough.

That I need to protect myself from my own mother makes emptiness open in my stomach and a hollow, aching sadness fill my chest.

"There must be something," she pleads. "You always have a backup plan. What about your new rich boyfriend?"

I jolt as if she hit me. "Cord isn't my boyfriend. And why don't you have a backup plan, Mom?" The question lacks heat. "You don't have to live like this." I hurry on, even as she's shaking her head. "If you wanted, I could talk to the school for you. I bet that they'd give you your job back, working there. I could even talk to my adviser on your behalf." Even as I say the words, I'm sure that it's the sort of Hail Mary pass that's more wish than actual possibility.

At the table, my mom deflates. She used to be a pretty woman, with my fair and clear skin, but everything about her is brittle. The side of her mouth tilts up. "Maybe, sweetie. That sounds good."

The words fill me with hope, even though I curse it. I've heard it all before, but I can't help it. I want that life for her—for me—so much. Every time she comes by, I tell myself that I won't let it hurt me when she leaves. But it does, every time.

"Why don't you get some sleep tonight, Mom. I'll make the spare bed up for you."

"I should get back." She glances toward the door, and a flash of fear crosses her features. I close my eyes briefly, hating the man she's afraid of, somewhere out there, and hating her for choosing him and that life over me.

"You can't drive tonight," I say softly. "Just sleep for a few hours. We'll talk about this more in the morning."

She nods vaguely and sips from her glass.

I retrieve the spare sheet set from the closet in my room. I'd moved into the master bedroom a few years ago, when it became clear that she wasn't here often enough to leave it empty. Now, the second bedroom only holds the spare bed and a few things in Tupperware from our old life. Nothing of monetary value. All of that had been sold years ago. But there are pictures and things I keep for nostalgia.

As I put the sheets on the bed and lay a blanket over it, I wonder if this could be the time that my mom stays, tries to get herself together. Even as I flirt with the idea, I disregard it. In the morning, I'll try again to talk her into it. She'll be more sober then. Maybe she'll hear me.

When I return to the kitchen, she's practically falling asleep at the table.

I coax her up and into the bathroom before tucking her into bed. She pats my cheek as she curls up, but her face is sad. "I love you, sweetheart."

I swallow hard. "I love you, too, Mom."

As I brush my teeth and wash my face, I try not to be happy that the house isn't empty. I lay my head on my pillow and remind myself not to hope too much, because history proves that she'll be gone in a day or so.

When I wake, I'm wrong. She hadn't even waited a day or so. She's gone without a trace, and so is the wad of cash in my purse, my share of the cover charges from the Party last night.

I take a shower, standing there for longer than necessary when I'm done.

That money was supposed to pay for groceries and the electric bill, which is already overdue. Most of the venues pay me by Venmo or PayPal for tax purposes. But I needed the cash this time, so Danny had agreed. I hadn't expected my mother to be here. Now, I have no idea how I'm going to make my ends meet this week.

When nothing comes to me, I shut off the water and climb out, shivering in the morning chill.

I planned to get caught up. Not even ahead, only caught up. Now I'm back at the beginning again.

Part of me recognizes that I should be angry at my mother, maybe even try to track her down, because what kind of person steals from her own child? But when I try to get worked up about it, all I feel is emptiness and a healthy dose of shame.

I check the clock after I put on some warm clothes. It's still early, only eight in the morning. I glance at my phone. No messages from Cord. I stare at the empty notification screen. *Should I call him? Text?* He said he'd drive me to school until my car was ready, but I didn't know if he would after the way we left things last night.

Sighing, I throw my phone in my bag. I missed my eight o'clock but still have some time before my eleven o'clock class. It's a two-mile walk into town, but I can do it and see if I can put in some applications. If I have any luck at all, I'll be able to find a new job in the next few days. I'll need to call the landlord, but if I have a new job, maybe I can buy some time.

As for groceries, I'll just have to stretch things out for a few days.

Sifting through my bag, I see Mr. Parker's card from last night. Pulling it out, I run my fingers over the embossing. I have no idea if singing is a long-term solution in my life, but it sure might be able to fix some of my problems right now.

An excited thrill races through me.

I'm going to New York to sing. I'll call Brandon later today. I tilt my chin up, sick of pretending I don't want the things I want. I'm going to do it without slutting it up, too, as Brandon said. I'm going to stay myself, no matter what.

I tuck a hat on my head, settling in for a long walk into town. But when I open the door, my car is parked out front. Mikey had been right—I barely recognize Cherry at all. She's clean, first of all. That's something that hasn't happened in a long time. And the rust spots on the front are gone.

I look around, but there's no one there. I skip down the porch steps and try the door, and it's open. A card sits on the front seat. I rip it open, reading:

Hannah: Mikey got your car last night. I thought you would want it. Keys are under the front tire. C.

I know why he hadn't knocked on the door, and I can't blame him. I make it hard to get to know me, and he's really been nothing but great.

He's been great, and I've blown it.

Bending down to retrieve my keys, I curse under my breath. I slide behind the wheel then start it up, smiling as she purrs like a new car. Getting it back has given me new life.

First, I'll see if I can find a real job. Then I'll call Ronnie. It's time I stop pretending. I don't sing only for money—I love it. And just because I love singing doesn't mean I have to stop loving playing the piano or the guitar or anything else. Music is my soul, and however I want to embrace that will need to be fine. So if I want to sing, then I will. I'm not going to let the chance to open for a real band in New York pass me by.

After I do all that, I'm going to find a way to make things right with Cord. I just don't know how.

Cord

BEFORE OUR LAST HOME game the next Thursday night, team warm-ups are off. Not for everyone—only me. The rest of the guys are loose and fired up. The playoffs start in a couple weeks, and though it won't change our standings, it's important to go into the tournament with good energy.

I can't seem to get it together, though.

I miss two easy passes, I'm a second late off the line, and I whiff on a gimme goal in front of the net. I can even see our goalie, Nate's, questioning eyes through all of his equipment.

I'm supposed to visit with New Jersey on Monday. It isn't the time for me to lose my mojo.

As I step off the ice, I curse quietly because I don't want anyone to hear. But I'm sure they get the idea.

I need to get my head in this game. This isn't the time to lose my shit. Except…I haven't heard from Hannah in a week, and that—she—is all I can think about. When we dropped her car off on Friday morning, something kept me from going to the door. Maybe it was because I didn't have anything to say. She had been doing what we agreed to, keeping things platonic. So I snagged some paper from my backpack and left her a note, tucking the keys under the car tire. I told myself I was giving her space, that I was sticking to the agreement, and that we'd sort it out after I got back from my weekend away games.

Except we haven't. I saw her in Pierce's class on Wednesday, but she stayed to talk with him after. I wondered if she was trying to avoid me.

All of this has left me thinking about her, wondering what the hell I should do, and obviously being distracted at exactly the time I shouldn't be.

Head down, I make my way off the ice. That's why I don't see her leaning against the wall in the hallway outside the locker room.

I stop. "Hannah. What are you doing here?" I have my helmet and stick in one hand, so I use my other hand to swipe the hair and sweat out of my eyes as I walk up on her. In my skates, I really tower over her, instead of the six or so inches I usually have on her.

She looks up at me, rocking back and forth from heel to toe, and swallows hard. "Cord. Hi."

It's so good to see her that I can't help but smile. Whatever has been wrong and off inside my chest loosens with her in front of me. "That's me."I can't pretend anymore. I've screwed up my fake relationship. I don't know what we are, but I want something real with her.

She glances away, wringing her hands. "Yes. Well, I wanted to wish you luck on your game."

"You came." She said before that she'd never been to one of our games. I'm going to take her presence as a huge win.

We stand there with her looking more uncomfortable than I've ever seen her and me wondering what's going on. I search for something to say that will settle her down. "Thanks for coming." Not much in the way of comfort, but I'm not sure what I'm working with here.

"Girlfriend, remember?" she says as if it hasn't been a week since we spoke. But then she shakes her head. "That's not it, though. I came because I wanted to see you."

My stomach dips. "Thank you."

"And because I need to talk to you." She inhales. "I'm sorry," she blurts out, "for the other night." She pushes her glasses up her nose and meets me with wide, honest eyes. "I was shutting you out. And it wasn't you. It was me. Which is a stupid thing to say, but it's true. And it wasn't fair. So I just wanted to apologize."

She's talking too fast, and we're in the hallway, outside a room full of stinky hockey equipment. I'm smelly, and the lighting isn't great, but to me, everything about her being there is perfect. "I'm really glad you came."

She smiles, exhaling, and I wish I wasn't so gross right now because I want to drag her into my arms… except she hasn't wanted me to kiss her. And I definitely don't smell good enough to be standing near anyone.

"I'm glad I came too."

I look her over. I haven't seen her in over a week, and the sight of her is a breath of fresh air. I can't quite figure out what it is about her. She isn't classically pretty, but her brown eyes are huge, her lips are full, and something about the combination of her makes me want to see her more, make her smile, figure out what makes her tick.

I want her to be mine. She isn't like the other girls I date, but that shouldn't have blinded me to what was in front of me…a savvy, smart, talented woman with the ability to see through me and the most kissable mouth I've ever seen.

"Hold on for a second, okay?" I don't wait for her to respond as I open the door to the locker room and make my way to my stuff. After dropping my stick and helmet, I sift through my bag until I find what I'm looking for.

Declan Mitchell tries to stop me on my way back to Hannah, but I hold up a finger for him to give me a second as I shuffle past him on my skates.

In the hall, I hold my away jersey out to Hannah. "Here. If you wanted to wear it," I offer. Wearing their guys' jerseys is a thing among the girlfriends on the team. As I stand there, the jersey between us, it feels like a big deal. I shrug, trying to play it down. "It gets cold near the rink."

She slowly takes the shirt from me. "Oh, I'm not close. I'm up near the top."

"No, you aren't." I shake my head. "You can sit in our seats." There's a section of seats that the team keeps open for family and important guests, and Hannah is important.

"You don't have to do that," she says, but I notice that she hugs the jersey to her. It isn't much, but that small action makes me more sure.

"I know. Come on. I think Shea's there this game too." I motion for her to follow me and walk with her back toward the ice. When I get there, I motion to the letters on the stairs. "Follow this to rows *D* through *F*. All of those seats are ours. I can't go up." I point at my skates. "My blades."

She nods but glances up at the stands like I'm sending her into the gladiator pit as she clutches my jersey to her chest. That's when it hits me—Hannah can be a little shy. Even though I've watched her stand on a stage and lead hundreds of people in covers of Journey and Garth Brooks, one-on-one situations like this overwhelm her.

Bending down, I quickly untie my skates. Then, when I'm in my socks, I take my jersey from her and help her slip it over her head. It's gigantic, and she swims in it, but I don't think anything has made me so happy in a long time. "I think the other girls knot them or something." I have no idea, really. I grab her hand. "Come on. I'll introduce you."

A relieved grin splits her face, and she nods, following me up the stairs. Shea's sitting toward the end, thank God. That'll make this easier. "Hey, Shea. You remember Hannah, right?" I like Shea Carmichael a lot. She's around a lot because Linc grew up with her, played club hockey with her twin, Colt. Even though her twin's signed to Philadelphia now, Colt and Linc stayed close. "She's going to be sitting with you guys."

Shea offers an open smile. "Hey, Hannah. It's good to see you." She motions to the two girls next to her. "This is Violet Tannehill and Tanya Steyer." The other girls take in Hannah wearing my jersey.

Violet, a tall sorority girl who's dating the goalie, Nate, waves her over with a huge grin. "Come on, Hannah. You can sit with us."

Hannah nods, straightening her shoulders. When she looks up at me, she offers a determined smile. "Good luck tonight. I'm rooting for you."

That smile squeezes my heart. This girl… This is what she asked for out of our deal, to be introduced around, to have some fun. Yet, she's obviously not completely comfortable in social situations. Still, she's willing to try to put herself out there.

I run my thumb over her fingers, even though I want to do so much more. She's here, and it's the best thing to happen to me this week. "I'll see you after the game?" I say it like a question, because I have no idea what her intentions are. I have no idea where we stand, and it's got me off-balance.

She nods, though. "Yeah. I'll wait for you by the locker room?"

"Perfect." I drop my hand, winking at the other girls. "Take good care of her for me, ladies."

Tanya's eyebrows shoot up. I wonder if she'll be nice to Hannah. She's good friends with Rachel. But Shea's here, and Violet, for all her party-girl ways, always struck me as a nice person. Besides, Hannah managed Coach and Rachel. She's tougher than she looks, probably tougher than she thinks. She'll be fine.

The other team is finishing up their warm-up, so I need to get back into the locker room. I bound down the stairs in my socks, grab my skates, and head in with what is probably a stupid smile on my face.

Declan must have been watching for me, because he makes a beeline for my locker. "Cap," he said.

I strip off my warm-up jersey, drying off. "What's up?"

He leans in. "Is everything okay?"

Declan and I didn't start off on the greatest terms. The guy comes off like an arrogant asshole half the time and a growling shit the other half. But since we've been on each other's line for a couple years, we've become friends. I trust him.

Which is why I say, "It is now. Hannah's here."

That doesn't seem to make him as happy as it makes me. "Christ…"

"I know what you're going to say, Mitch. I've heard it before. Hell, I've said it before. It's stupid to get distracted by anything on the way up to playoffs—"

“Why am I even talking to you, then?” he grits out, cutting me off.

“Because I can’t help it,” I hiss back. We stare each other down. I can tell he has no idea what I’m talking about. I exhale, rubbing my hand over my head. “It’s too late. I’m distracted by her already. But when she’s here, it’s better. I can’t explain it.”

He drops his hand onto my shoulder and gives me a look containing what looks like pity. “Listen, whatever, man. But if you’re off your game, don’t think I won’t kick your ass from here into next week.”

I grin at him. I can’t help it. Nothing can piss me off right now. “As you should. Though I’d like to see you try.”

He snorts, his lips tilting into a smirk. But then he sobers. “I’m serious, Cord. I need you.”

This is Mitch’s last year of eligibility to be drafted. He needs to impress the teams during this playoff, and he’s one of my wingers. It’s our job to work together. He needs me.

I clap him back on the shoulder. “I got you.”

He nods, retreating to his own locker to finish getting ready.

As I lace my skates again, I wonder if I am being stupid, going any further with Hannah. I originally thought this would keep me on the right track. But now, it could be Hannah who poses the biggest threat to my focus. If I was smart, I’d cool off. I definitely wouldn’t have given her my jersey.

Seems that when it comes to her, I don’t care about the risks.

Still, all of that fades away as I meet my team in the hallway on the way to the rink. I’m not the rowdiest in the bunch, so I let Mikey and Declan lead the chants. With a “one, two, three, Bulldogs” yell, we make our way back out on the ice, the sound of our music on the intercom and the roar of the crowd in our ears.

As I skate around the circle, loosening up, my eyes find Hannah in the stands. Shea must be explaining things to her, because she looks intent, watching us. I stretch my neck from side to side. Having her here makes me feel invincible.

It's showtime.

Hannah

I'VE NEVER BEEN TO a hockey game before. I wasn't much of a sports girl. I tried softball and soccer when I was little, but I never got far, and hockey definitely hasn't been on my radar. Add that to the way some of the hockey and football guys seem to think they're the best things ever, and… well, it just isn't my thing.

Maybe that was why I hadn't realized how fast-paced and exciting the game would be.

I'm glad I have Shea and Violet with me. Tanya moves to sit with a couple of other girls as soon as the game starts, but Shea and Violet explain the rules and some of the strategy. Before long, I'm holding my breath along with the rest of the crowd as the skaters zoom around the ice.

And Cord… I heard he was good and that he went in the first round of the draft. But none of that prepares me for how impressive he is.

He scores twice and has an assist, Shea tells me, which I figure out means that he passed the puck to someone else who then scored. Apparently, that got him points on his stats or something, but I start to fade when she explains that part to me.

After the second goal, I'm sure he's looking for me in the crowd. I wave and cheer as loudly as I can, not even caring that I probably look ridiculous. He spins his stick back and forth, and Violet giggles in my ear, telling me that's a stick wave. A part of me wants to think that's silly, but I don't. In fact, I'm only happy and proud of him.

Our Bulldogs win four to one, and the place goes crazy. There are announcements at the end about the beginning of the Frozen Four in two weeks and how they'll be held in Pittsburgh, but I don't know if anyone is really listening besides me.

Pittsburgh… I have no idea how I'm going to afford to go to that, assuming that Cord wants me there, which is a huge assumption. Our arrangement is only supposed to be until playoffs. *Does that mean the beginning of playoffs? Through all of playoffs? How long are they, exactly?* I have no clue, and thinking about the end bothers me more than I want to admit. I've already wasted a week, trying to get up the nerve to apologize to him.

"Come on," Violet says, practically beaming. Girls like her usually intimidate me because she's so pretty that she almost hurts my eyes. But she's so full of sunshine that it's hard not to like her. "We need to meet the guys at the locker room."

"Right now?" I thought they needed to go in and, I don't know… smack each other's butts or something.

"Yeah. Right now. Don't you want to see them?" She bounds ahead of me, skirting around a few slower spectators. Shea rolls her eyes, laughing, and grabs my hand. Together, the three of us hurry into the tunnel and toward the locker room to greet the victors.

Violet snags our arms, dragging us back to stand against the wall with a whole bunch of other fans. The amount of noise in the tunnel is deafening. When the guys shuffle through, everyone punches them on the arms or pats them on the head. It's so crowded, I almost miss when Cord comes through. But he reaches over and nudges my shoulder. I wave, feeling awkward but also carried away in the excitement. He grins back, offering me a tiny salute before following the rest of his teammates into the locker room.

The other fans start to disperse, but we hang out with some of the other girlfriends, waiting for the guys to come back out. Violet keeps up a steady conversation, and Shea and I mostly nod along.

When Nate comes out, freshly showered and beaming with happiness, he sweeps Violet into his arms, and they start making out right there. Then Tanya appears next to us…with Cord's ex, Rachel.

Rachel's sweet to Shea, but Shea doesn't look thrilled to see her. Then Rachel smiles at me, and I tense. She glances over me, taking in Cord's jersey. "It's Hannah, right?"

She knows who I am. I'm dating her ex. Well, fake dating. Either way, I nod and play along. "And it's Rachel, right?"

"You and Cord. That's interesting." She shrugs as if us being in a relationship is inconsequential to her. She pulls her coat closer around her. Her long dark hair, arranged in perfect waves today, falls over her shoulders.

I don't know how to respond to that, so I don't say anything, crossing my arms over my chest.

She leans closer. The noise in the hall probably drowns out her words for everyone else, but I hear them loudly and clearly. "Don't get comfy in his jersey. I wore it before, and I'll wear it again."Stepping back, she nods to Tanya, and the two of them walk away together.

I can only stare after her, my arms dropping to my sides. *What sort of high school nonsense is this?*

Even though Cord seems to have no interest in revisiting his relationship with Rachel, she is exactly the kind of girl I can picture him with. Perfect hair, perfect clothes. I glance down at my motorcycle boots and jeans. I do what I can with thrift-store fashion. I have a secondhand sewing machine, and I update the pieces I find. I like to think I've got a vintage style. But Rachel looks and smells expensive.

Like Cord.

I tilt my head up, glaring after her. It doesn't matter. This is only a temporary arrangement, anyway. Cord might not want to be with her, but eventually, he'll pair off with someone like her, someone with money and class, someone with connections. Someone who understands his life and sees how wonderful he is, like I do.

Except she'll be someone who fits with him.

But for now, I'm the one he's spending time with. It won't last, but I've decided to enjoy him, his company, his time, for as long as I can.

"I don't like her," Shea says, her face twisting like something stinks. "What did she whisper to you?"

"Nothing." Nothing that changed anything, anyway.

"Right," she laughs. "I bet. Just ignore her. She's jealous."

"Of me? Sure." I snort.

"No, really." Shea gives me a side squeeze. "Cord doesn't look at anyone like he looks at you. She must see it too."

I grin. "And how does he look at me?"

"Like you're ice cream and he wants to lick you." She winks at me, and I can't help it—I crack up.

A few other guys file out of the locker room, and Shea's face shadows, as it did off and on during the game. Shea's one of those girls who's always so put together. Classy clothes, hair in place. She keeps smiling, but I've been with her all night. I've noticed she's off. "Hey," I ask. "Are you okay?"

She nods, that grin in place, but I don't believe it. "Sure. I'm great."

"Yeah?"

"I'm great. Just… great." She sighs, and the stoic smile she's been wearing fades. "Actually, I'm not. I was supposed to see my boyfriend this weekend. At State. But he called me earlier today and said he planned to hang low for the weekend. Catch up on schoolwork and relax."

"Yeah?" That doesn't sound so bad. Everyone needs to recharge.

"Yeah, except…" She pulls out her phone and opens Instagram. "He was tagged a little while ago." She lifts the screen so I can see, and there's a very good-looking, shirtless guy sitting on a couch with a girl in a bikini top on his lap. If the flush on his cheeks and the glassy eyes are any indication, he's been drinking.

"Ah. I see." Though I don't. I'm not sure what kind of relationship they have. Maybe he sits with pretty girls without his clothes on all the time. But Shea's expression says he doesn't—or at least, he shouldn't.

Violet comes up for air. When she detaches herself from Nate, she wraps her arm around Shea's neck and asks Nate, "So, where's the party?"

"Back at Shepherd. You guys are coming, right?" he asks us. But he doesn't wait for a response before he sweeps Violet into his arms, twirling her around. "We won!" he shouts, taking off toward the parking lot at a run.

"See you guys there," Violet calls back to us, laughing.

"Where?" Cord steps out of the locker room. Linc's on his heels.

I glance up at him, my breath catching. His hair's still wet, the longish waves on top combed away from his face. In jeans and a Chesterboro Bulldogs hoodie, he's a heart stopper.

Since I don't answer very quickly, thanks to being struck mute by him, Shea jumps in. "They're going to be celebrating our last home victory at Shepherd. Let's go. Unless you guys are planning on going home?"

That's right. Cord and Linc live off campus.

Linc's brows shoot up. "Wait. You want to go?" he asks her.

"Absolutely." Shea nods, her mouth firm. "I definitely want to go to a party tonight."

"Really?" He folds his arms over his chest. "Because you hate parties."

"Well," Shea says, linking our arms. "Not today, I don't. Hannah and I would love to go. If you guys are going." She leans in, whispering in my ear. "Please. I can't go back to my room and sit there, thinking about Justin. Come with me."

I want to go anyway, so I nod. "Of course." Besides, there's no way I would leave her alone tonight. Not with all that. I've been left to my own overthinking too many times. "I want to go," I answer honestly.

Shea's face lights into a bright grin, and she starts us toward the door. With a shrug, the guys follow. Shea breaks off to ride with Linc, and I follow Cord to his car. As we slide in, he asks, “Is everything okay? With Shea?”

“She’s upset about her boyfriend, and she didn’t want to go home.”

“Really?” His face storms over. “What happened?”

Too late, I realize I might have overstepped. I don’t know if Shea wants Cord or Linc to know about her boyfriend. “It’s her story to tell. But she wanted company tonight.” I shrug. “Besides, it’s a party. And isn’t this the whole point of me being your fake girlfriend? So that I could go to parties and take the heat off you with random girls?”

Cord buries his hand in his hair. “Yeah, but…I mean, that’s not what…” He exhales. “Listen, Hannah…”

When someone starts a sentence with “listen,” it isn’t usually good. But he’d given me the jersey to wear, and I can still do my part. Tonight, I don’t want to hear that he’s rethinking our arrangement. If he does or doesn’t, I don’t want to know tonight. I like him, and I like how I feel when I’m around him. He makes me laugh, and he sets off butterflies in my stomach. I live for the moments when he touches me, even with the shortest and most fleeting brushes.

I’m not ready for this to be over, whatever it is. I’m going to squeeze out whatever moments I have left.

“We can talk later. Shea needs me.”

He stares at me and finally nods. “Okay. Cool. Let’s go, then.”

I hate how relieved I am. This is supposed to be a temporary thing, nothing serious. Rides, a car fix, some help with some girl trouble. *When did everything get so confusing?*

Cord

I LOSE HANNAH ALMOST as soon as we get to Shepherd. Shea whisks her toward the general vicinity of the keg. I get overrun by people congratulating us on our win and guys stopping to talk about our next game in Pittsburgh. The conversation centers on strategies to use our opponents' strengths and weaknesses, but I can barely hold the thread of it. Instead, I'm struggling not to worry about Hannah.

We spent the trip to Shepherd, all eight blocks of it, talking about the game. She asked me a million questions, and I answered them clinically. I didn't want to talk about hockey. I wanted to tell her that I didn't want to do our stupid fake arrangement anymore. Except that isn't it either. I want to make our fake arrangement real.

I've been an idiot. I should have known from the beginning that we couldn't only be friends.

Seeing her in my jersey filled me with a whole lot of protectiveness and a softness I never expected. Having her there tonight told me all I needed to know. When she's around, I'm whole and lighter. No fake relationship does that. She put that jersey on and looked up at me from behind her glasses, and I wanted to take her face in my hands and kiss her.

I couldn't, though. I can't. Because of this stupid agreement we've made, I'm in some weird limbo with her. Every time I think we're getting past it and that maybe she wants all of me, too, she brings it up again, sending me right back to the starting line with her.

Maybe I'll never get past that, but I really want to. I just have no idea how.

About an hour after we arrive, Shea and Hannah weave by me, heading toward the kitchen. As they flit past, I notice their flushed cheeks and glassy eyes. Worry twists my gut. Hannah doesn't drink much, as far as I can tell. Neither does Shea. I pull myself from the guys I'm with and follow them. I need to keep an eye on both of them, especially if Shea's upset. Heartache and hard partying never mix well.

The two of them settle on a couch in the common room with Violet and Nate. They seem to be getting along, and both Shea and Hannah look happy, if a little drunk. I'm glad to see Hannah having fun. Her life seems so serious.

Linc joins me, handing me a Solo cup of light beer. "Any time Shea's agreed to go to a party, I've had to nag her. Any idea what's changed her mind tonight?"

Taking a sip, I shake my head. "All Hannah said was that Shea had been upset about something with her boyfriend."

"Right. Peterson." Linc scowls and tightens his jaw, but he doesn't say anything else.

Across the room, I watch Hannah shake her head. I have no idea what's going on until someone produces a guitar and presses it into her hands. Shea beams at her.

Shit. Someone's trying to get her to play. I hand Linc my beer, weaving quickly through the crowd. I'm a top-line hockey player, and I can thread the needle. In a handful of seconds, I'm next to her. "Hey, what's up?"

Shea grins up at me, her cheeks pink, obviously buzzed. "We were just going to have Hannah play."

"Violet sang in beauty pageants when she was younger," Hannah offers, her own cheeks flushed. The two of them are a couple of lightweights. "She was going to sing something. I was going to play for her." She nods at me, silently telling me it's fine. I try to decide if she's being straight with me as she checks the tuning on the guitar. I can't find any indication that she wants to be rescued, so I step back. But not too far. If she's going to play, I'm sticking around for it. I settle on the arm of the couch. "What are you going to sing?"

"Do you know 'Leaving on a Jet Plane' by John Denver?" Violet asks.

Hannah winks at her. Even before her fingers dance over the strings, I'm sure she knows it. The song's a classic, and she knows everything.

When it's time, Violet starts, her voice clear and clean. Then Hannah joins in for the harmony.

I've watched Hannah play and sing before, but every time, it surprises me how she transforms. When she's playing, it's as if all her defenses drop. I've seen glimpses of this Hannah—the open, vulnerable Hannah, the one who smiles easily and isn't always guarded. The girl behind that mask. I can't her get out of my mind.

Around me, everyone else is under her spell too. We lean in, holding our breaths. Hannah's a talented musician, and she has a gripping voice, but it goes further than that. When she performs, she glows.

One song leads to more duets. People bring her drinks, give her shots. She sings with Violet, and then people start putting in their requests. Some sing with her. Others ask her to do solos. That's when the dancing starts.

I take it all in, watching her shine, happier than I've been in a very long time.

"Your girl is something, Cap." Declan joins me in a lull between songs. "I see now that I should have worked harder to coax her away."

It's a joke, but the wave of possessiveness that washes through me isn't. "Just try."

He holds up his hands. "Relax." He shakes his head. "You're all in with this girl, aren't you?"

Am I? After Rachel, all I wanted was to stay unattached, to keep my heart out of everything. Yet here I am, and this girl is all I can see.

I don't respond because someone asks Hannah if she writes her own stuff. She shrugs, and because that isn't a direct no, everyone assumes it's a yes. That's followed by cajoling and encouragement.

I'm moving toward her before I even realize it. Because if she needs me, then I'll be there. If she wants to go, if she wants to sing, I'm there for whatever she wants.

Our gazes meet and hold. The moment heats, and in the middle of this crowded room, we could be alone. Either she didn't have time to hide behind her armor or she doesn't want to, because she doesn't drop the eye contact when she starts to play.

The melody is haunting, but when she starts the lyrics, they vibrate through me. She sings about a boat in a storm, about how it's tossed and thrown but finds its way. The song is about loneliness, about finding safety.

When she finishes, there's a long moment of silence before Nate says, "Holy shit." Then the entire room seems to contract in on her. They crowd her, asking questions. But I'm not looking at them. I only have eyes for her.

She's pale.

A wave of protectiveness sweeps over me. I take her hand and plaster a smile on my face, making eye contact with as many of the people around us as I can, drawing the attention away from her. I position my body to partly shield her and hold up my other hand, "Whoa, you animals. Get your own dates. Mine needs a break."

It isn't much, but it breaks things up. Conversations begin around me, and a couple of guys slap my arm, joking about how I always need to be the center of attention. Beside me, Shea whispers to Hannah.

I glance down, assessing the situation. She's not only pale—she's green. Shea meets my gaze over Hannah's head, her face full of concern.

She's going to be sick.

Damn it. I'd seen people bring her drinks, but she'd been playing so much for the past hour or so that I didn't think it had been too much. Then again, she isn't much of a drinker, and she doesn't weigh very much. I have no idea what that means for her tolerance.

"Hannah," I say in her ear. "Are you okay?"

"I'm dizzy." She presses her palm against her forehead. Then she giggles.

That seals it. Hannah doesn't giggle. It's time to go.

To Shea, I say, "You okay if I take her home?"

Linc steps in. “I’ll get Shea back to her place.”

Shea scowls up at him. “I can answer for myself.” She folds her arms over her chest. “Linc can get me back to my place.”

Linc rolls his eyes, but I see the softness when he looks at her.

“Let me get you home, Marshall.”

“You only call me Marshall when you’re bossing me around.” She giggles again as I tow her along behind me through the room.

“Correction, Marshall,” I yell back to her over the crowd noise. “I only call you Marshall when you need bossing around.” I wink at her.

Her laugh follows us out of Shepherd.

When we hit the fresh air on the porch, Hannah sighs. “That feels much better. It was so hot in there.” She sways, and I steady her, holding her against me to keep her from falling, or so I tell myself. But I don’t let go, and that’s definitely not all about her.

I’m selfish. I want to hold her.

In the dim streetlight, she tilts her face up to mine, leaning in. She looks beautiful. Her skin’s pale and smooth, her big brown eyes huge behind her glasses. Her hair falls over her shoulder, and her fucking mouth…I want to drag her closer and bury myself in her lips.

There are about a million reasons why I can’t. That promise I made not to touch her…did it mean I couldn’t even bring it up? I have no idea what it meant because I hadn’t had the foresight to think that I’d want her so fucking desperately.

But even if I hadn’t made the promise, she’s been drinking. If she asked me now, it wouldn’t count. I don’t take advantage of girls.

I can't stop from running my hand along her back, though. She fits against me like she's made to be there. I swear, I could hold this girl forever, and I want to do so much more than that.

"Are you going to kiss me?" she asks in a conspiratorial whisper.

God, my body practically burns with it. But right now isn't the time. I only hope that there is a right time soon. Very soon. "No."

I need to get her home, get her rehydrated, and make sure she doesn't get sick. Gently, I pull away from her, making sure she doesn't lose her balance, and tuck her arm in mine so she can lean on me as we start toward the car.

"Thank you," she says, patting my hand.

"For holding you up?" I wave her off. "Rather than letting you fall on your face?"

"No," she laughs. Under the streetlights, the color's high on her cheeks. Much better than the paleness earlier. Her glasses have smudges on them, but even that can't dull the shine in her eyes. "For bringing me to a party."

I swallow and nod because I don't know what I can say right now that won't give away everything I'm feeling. But I'm not sure she wants to hear that. The other night, she didn't seem to want anything from me. For now, this is enough.

Finally, I manage, "Let me get you home."

Cord

"HOW ARE YOU FEELING?" I venture, scanning her for any signs that our ride home might be dangerous. I'd parked behind the building, so it isn't a long walk. I review the stuff I have in my car. *Do I have anything in case she gets sick?*

It's ironic, considering what Mikey put her car through the first time we officially met.

"I'm good." She grins, stumbling on nothing and gripping my arm tighter.

"Not feeling nauseous?" There aren't any immediate signs of distress.

She shrugs. "I don't drink."

I can't stop my chuckle. "Apparently, you did tonight." I unlock the car.

She grins. "I did." Her eyes light up. "And I sang. A lot." She swings her arm wide, as if she might take off dancing. I steady her, guiding her around to the passenger side.

"You did." I help her into her seat. As she looks up at me, I can't resist the joy on her face and run my thumb over her cheek. "You were great."

Our gazes hold too long, and she finally glances down. I retreat, pulling my hand back and closing the door. As I make my way around to the driver's side, I shut my eyes, bracing myself.

I get it together by the time I slide into my driver's seat. As we pull out of the parking lot, she says, "I'm supposed to go to New York on Monday to sing in some venue in the Meatpacking District. I'm opening for the Dazed Zealots."

"You are? Did this happen because of that manager last week?" That was fast.

"Yeah. Mr. Parker. He told Ronnie he has an opening to fill."

"That's great, Hannah." Her manager still gives me bad vibes, but it's her decision. If she's happy, then I'm happy for her.

She doesn't respond for long moments. "Singing's how I'm going to pay for grad school."

"Why is it so important to go to grad school right now?" I ask. "With all the interest you seem to be getting for your singing, it seems like you could follow that up, see where it goes. Grad school could be something you do later, you know?"

She shakes her head and winces. "I've wanted to go to graduate school forever. Since my dad taught me how to play piano. It was always his dream for me to play with the greats."

She hasn't talked much about her father. "*Was* his dream?"

"He died eight years ago." She glances at her hands. "Suicide."

"I'm sorry, Hannah."

"It's been the goal for as long as I can remember. Even though he isn't here, I feel like if I make it, he'll know."

I get the impression that this is more information than Hannah would give up if she hadn't been drinking. "Aren't you already into graduate school? Haven't you kind of already made it?"

"I'm in, sure. But paying for it is a completely different problem."

I don't know much about that. I don't come from a place where money has ever been an issue.

She sighs. "Besides, singing is so dangerous."

That isn't what I expected her to say. "How?"

"No stability. No guarantee that I'll make it, be able to make a living."

"Is there any guarantee of making a living with a music degree?" That doesn't seem like the most stable career choice either.

"Music's not my only major. I also have one in business."

Why am I not surprised that Hannah, with all her insane talent, is an overachiever? "Right. I'm only saying that there aren't guarantees for anyone."

"Easy for you to say. You're rich."

That stings. "Technically, my dad is rich. Him having money definitely made things easier. But I've been working my whole life to make it to the NHL. Nothing can buy me into that. And there aren't any guarantees even now. I could tear my Achilles tomorrow or break my hip. Any number of injuries would end that dream. That doesn't mean it isn't worth chasing."

"You don't get it." She exhales, obviously frustrated. "If you don't make it to the NHL, there's a billion other things you could do. You've got a home. Your family knows people, people who would be willing to help you out. I'm me. I don't have the connections that you have."

She slurs, and I have the distinct impression that she wouldn't say any of this if she hadn't been drinking. I try not to be offended. “You could do a bunch of other things, too, Hannah. You still can, even if this doesn’t work. You’re a double major from CU, and I assume your grades are good.” I can’t imagine it any other way. “But don’t you think it’s worth shooting for something that could be wonderful? What if you actually get it?”

She blinks at me. “What if I don’t?”

“Then you don’t.” I shrug. “You’re not only this dream. You’re lots of dreams. And I know you can do just about anything you want.” I’ve only known her for a short time, but I’m sure of this.

Her eyes, still glassy and not entirely focused, find me in the streetlights as we make our way to her place. “You don’t know me well enough to know that.”

“I think you don’t know what I know,” I tease.

She opens her mouth to respond as we pull into Dreamland, hitting a huge pothole. After jostling around in her seat, she groans and presses a hand to her stomach. “Yuck.”

Alarmed, I slow to a near crawl the rest of the way to her house. She closes her eyes. When we pull up at her porch, I exhale.

As soon as I turn the car off, I hurry around the front to help her out. She takes my hand without any complaint, and I grin. She must not be feeling right. She’s not usually so receptive to chivalry. As she leans on me, her face twists. Even pale and scowling, she’s the most beautiful thing I’ve ever seen.

“Alcohol is mean.” She wrinkles her nose.

I laugh. “I’ve heard that before.”

I help her up the stairs, waiting as she digs around in her purse for her keys. When she can’t find them, she sighs, handing me the bag. Shrugging, she blows a stray hair out of her face in comical frustration. "My purse ate my keys."

"I hate it when that happens." I sift through the contents of her bag, finding them at the bottom. I make quick work of the lock and hold it open for her. She presses a hand to her forehead, groaning. "How are you doing?"

She moans. "Why do people do this?"

"Most of us learn to pace ourselves."

She drops her bag in the general direction of the table next to the door and misses. The purse hits the ground, half of the contents spilling. She doesn't seem to notice or care. "I need a shower."

"Do you think that's a good idea?" Prone position in a bed sounds better for too many reasons.

"Shower," she repeats. "Yes." She shrugs out of her coat and flings it toward the coat rack, missing again. Then she reaches for the hem on her shirt, lifting it so I catch the entire expanse of her stomach and the slightest hint of tan lace before I stop her.

"Whoa." I leap forward, catching her sweater hem and yanking it back down even as my whole body tightens. Jesus Christ, she's going to kill me. She doesn't appear to notice, abandoning the shirt and kicking at her shoes. Then she reaches for her shirt again. "Hannah. I'd wait to take that off."

She places her hands on her hips. "I need a shower."

"That's cool, baby. But save the strip for the bathroom, okay?" My voice is deeper, even raspy. Probably because the sight of her creamy skin has my heart beating, and I'm hard.

"Huh." She cocks her head, pulling out the tie at the end of her braid. "Good idea." She unravels her hair until it falls in bendy waves around her face. Our gazes meet, and I smother the groan in my throat. She's a goddess. My hands move as if they have a life of their own, smoothing over the soft strands to cup her face.

Holding her, I can imagine it. Leaning down, covering her perfect mouth with mine and tasting her. It's there, on the tip of my tongue, like a sweet promise. Her eyes search mine, and I wonder if she wants that too.

But even if she does, could I trust that it was real? Would she? I refuse to take that chance. Not like this.

Instead, I run my thumb over her bottom lip. Her breath hitches, and the tiny inhalation has me gritting my teeth. I force myself to stop there, dropping my hands. "Come on. Let's get you showered."

Immediately, my brain offers images of her under the shower spray. My cursed imagination expands on the skin I've already seen. I never thought myself a particularly creative guy, but where Hannah's concerned, my mind's especially innovative.

I'm a disciplined, principled, elite athlete. I can hold my shit together enough to take care of this girl.

My girl.

She nods then heads down the hall and turns into the bathroom, closing the door behind her.

With her out of my sight, I can finally breathe again. I lean my forehead against the wall, sucking in air. I wait, listening. The water starts to run, and I push away from the wall, stretching out my neck.

Desperate to focus on anything but Hannah's warm, wet skin only a thin door away, I stroll out into the kitchen to get her some water.

I haven't been inside her place before. If the outside looks run-down, the inside's decrepit. The cabinets are worn and lopsided, thanks to failing hinges. Part of the floorboards are exposed, and the other parts are worn linoleum. It's all clean, but that can't take away how depressing it is.

Down the hall, the water stops. The bathroom door opens. Hannah comes out, covered in a towel with her hair dripping wet, and I swear my heart stops. She's so tall that the towel barely covers her ass, and I can make out the curve of her rear as she strolls out down the hall. She doesn't pay any attention to me as she wanders into her bedroom barefoot and closes the door.

Fuck. I need to get a hold of myself. I haven't been this out-of-control attracted to a girl since middle school.

Hands on my hips, I force myself to slow my breathing and focus on what Hannah needs. After a calming inhale, I call, "Are you okay?"

When she doesn't immediately answer, I stare down the short hallway. "Hannah?"

The door opens slowly, and she's swallowed up in sweatpants and a beat-up CU sweatshirt. She looks delicious. "I think so."

"Good," I say. "That's good." I clear my throat. "You should drink some water."

She follows me to the kitchen. I hand her the glass I found, and she drinks greedily. "Whoa," I caution. "Slow down."

"I don't feel good again. This is the worst." She presses her hand to her cheek. "I should lie down."

"Maybe not yet." I set the glass on the table. "Lying down sometimes makes it worse. Why don't we sit, though? Close to the bathroom, just in case."

"Good idea," she whispers as if we're keeping a secret.

I expect her to sit on the couch or at the kitchen table. Instead, she heads toward her bedroom. I follow, unable to do anything else.

She rearranges her pillows on her bed so she can sit up.

I take her in, all pink from her shower, crawling across her bed. She has one of those seat cushions, and she flops down on it. Then she pats the bed next to her. "Will you stay with me tonight?"

There's nothing I want more than to slide up next to her. The combination of bed and just-showered Hannah is almost too much for me. Which is why I falter. "I don't think…"

"Please."

Any resistance disintegrates. Bracing myself, I stretch out next to her, tucking my arm over my head. The coziness tugs at my heart. I'm stuck in some complicated space between wanting her so much that I'm throbbing and being so content in her presence that I never want to leave. I don't understand it, but I definitely am not strong enough to fight it right now. "I'll stay for a little while." I swallow the lump in my throat. "Did you want me to get you anything else to drink?"

She shakes her head. "No." Shaking her head must have worn her out, because she leans back, resting. "Cord?"

"Yeah?"

She turns to look at me, tucking her hands under her cheek. "Why didn't you kiss me outside, Shepherd?"

The question surprises me, and I stiffen. "Did you want me to kiss you?" Even though her answer can't matter—she's drunk, so what she thinks she wants right now isn't valid—I hold my breath, waiting for her response.

She considers, her teeth worrying her lower lip and her eyelids getting heavy. "It's okay if you didn't want to."

That's not an answer. "I didn't say that," I whisper.

"This is all fake," she says, finally losing the battle with her eyes and letting them close.

"Is it?"What I really want to know is if it's fake to her. She doesn't respond, and I take her hand. She squeezes my fingers. As I wait for her response, I study her beautiful face. I swear, I could stare at her forever.

Her breathing deepens, and her hold on my hand relaxes. In sleep, her whole body softens. When she's awake, Hannah exudes energy. She doesn't over talk like some people, but her attention's alert, always watching, always studying, as if daring anyone to underestimate her.

Now, though, she's peaceful. I lie there, watching over her, for longer than I probably need to if I'm only worried about her getting sick.

I doze off, waking to find that it's almost three in the morning. Next to me, Hannah has hardly moved. *Guess she isn't an active sleeper.* I smile, happy to have learned something new about her.

I have no idea if she would be happy to have me here in the morning. We still haven't talked about the other night or the way we left things. But she came tonight, to watch me. And the way she asked why I hadn't kissed her had to be a good sign, *didn't it?*

I'm terrified to hope and afraid not to. Either way, it's probably best if I leave and text to check on her in the morning. It's been several hours. She doesn't seem like she's going to be sick. There's no excuse to overstay my welcome.

Already missing her, I lift from the bed slowly and quietly creep out of the house, locking the door behind me.

Hannah

THE SUN HURTS MY feelings, pounding into my skull.

I roll to the side, squeezing my eyes closed and pressing my forearm against them. Why do people put themselves through this? Sure, the first couple of drinks made me feel great. Invincible, even. But it had all gone downhill from there. The rolling stomach, the dry mouth, and now this godforsaken headache. *Ugh, this sucks.*

My groggy mind pieces together last night's events. *Shea.* I'd never seen somebody so determined to have a good time. She’d been steadfast, drinking shots and laughing too loudly. Even as I worried about her, I followed along with her drinks. I stayed by her side, too, because even though she hadn’t said anything else about Justin, she’d needed me.

And then Violet wanted to sing. I can't remember how it came up in conversation that I could play the guitar. My music major? Or maybe not. Who knew? I said and did a lot of things that I wouldn't have done last night without the alcohol running through my veins.

The singing.

I groan, rolling onto my stomach. It had been so natural to play for people, to sing. It’s always magic. I’m not going to pretend it's only the alcohol that made it feel so wonderful. In fact, until I sang my own song, everything had been super.

Then, as I sang, I met Cord's eyes, and I was sure I saw heat there.

Oh, no…Cord.

I shoot up in bed, immediately regretting the quick movement, and fall back, moaning. I press my hand against my forehead.

"Why didn't you kiss me outside Shepherd?"

Oh my God. Did I actually ask that? Desperately, I search for what he said afterward. It's foggy. I'd been so tired and dizzy. But nothing makes me believe that he regretted *not* kissing me.

What had I been thinking? Except I know. I wanted to kiss him. All night.

The last time he'd almost kissed me, I'd told him not to. Last night, I practically begged him to.

He took care of me, though. I've no idea whether that was real or fake caring. I'm having a lot of difficulty distinguishing between the two these days. There's something there, but I don't know whether it's real or fake or some combination. I'm just not sure, almost like I'm not sure if I wanted to know why he didn't kiss me.

Why would I ask that question if I didn't really want to know the answer? Worse, will everything be awkward now? If it is, it'll be my fault. I should have left it alone.

Because he didn't kiss me, and he didn't say he wanted to. Nothing is going to shorten our arrangement faster than me making everything weird in our fake relationship with my stupid real feelings. What if I've ruined everything with my uncomfortable questions?

I'm never drinking again. If this is the sort of trouble I can get myself into, I shouldn't be allowed near the stuff. Maybe I could just lie in my bed for the rest of the day or the week. Maybe then all of this would go away. Glancing at my alarm clock, I groan again. It's already ten thirty in the morning.

Staying in bed isn't going to change what I said to him.

I force myself out of bed, stretching and taking stock of the rest of me. Except for the headache and horrible desert in my mouth, I'm okay. At least I didn't throw up last night. There'd definitely been some near misses. My hair's damp. That's right —I showered.

And ran down the hall in a towel. Then I asked him to stay the night with me. I close my eyes, praying for deliverance.

Well, nothing to do for it now. I hoist myself up and shuffle into the kitchen, looking for my purse. My bag's next to the door, and I sift around inside until I find my phone. Not much of a charge left but enough that I can see the three messages on the front. One from Shea and two from Cord. Running my hands over my crazy hair, I unlock it.

Shea's message's first, so I click on it. And maybe I don't want to face whatever Cord has to say just yet. Because I'm a coward.

Hope you're feeling well today. Thank you for staying with me last night. You're a good friend.

I smile. At least I did something last night that I can be proud of. Shea's sweet. If I made her feel any better, that's a good thing. I'll have to text her back and see how she's doing today.

But first…

Anxious, I click on Cord's messages.

Hope you're feeling okay today. Talking with New Jersey on Monday. Can drive you to your concert if you're interested. Lmk.

I stare at those words. No mention of the near-kiss-slash-near-miss in front of Shepherd or my stupid attempt to ask him about it. In fact, this message says nothing.

Except he wants to see me and drive to New York with me. That has to be a good sign.

I scan the second message. *By the way, you look good in a towel, Marshall.*

I should be mortified, but I'm not. Instead, I can't stop grinning. Maybe I didn't completely wreck everything between us.

From here on, I'm going to stick to the program. And no more talk of kissing.

Hannah

THE WEEKEND TAKES FOREVER. Cord and I exchange a few texts, and I'm pretty sure they're enough to smooth over any awkwardness I might have caused.

But then I'm in a car on the way to New York City for the first time, and I chat Cord's ear off. He's got his meeting with the Jaguars on Monday afternoon, and I'm opening for the Dazed Zealots that night. I ask how he feels about the meeting, and he's lukewarm, definitely not sold on the idea of defense. He asks me about singing, and I tell him I'm trying not to think about it. He laughs at me, but it's not mean.

Then we get into random subjects. His life back in Tennessee. My mom. He mentions my dad, but I steer the conversation away. I only tell him that he's where I learned to play the piano.

We touch on his major—finance, on his anxiety about getting a contract, about his dad, who sounds overbearing, and his mom, to a lesser degree. He calls her every weekend, and she gets to some of his home games.

Thanks to all the talking, we go through the Lincoln Tunnel before I even realize it. I'm glad I was distracted. The nerves don't hit me until we're up at street level again.

The bar where I'm opening for the Dazed Zealots is in the Meatpacking District. As we drive there, the impact of New York is overwhelming. There's no space anywhere, it seems. It's crammed with people and buildings, sounds and smells. I've never been to the city before, but Cord appears to know where he's going. Just another reminder of how different we are. He's probably been here a zillion times.

We follow the GPS directions to the right street. When I find the sign for the venue, Cord pulls over and hits the hazards. "You're sure this is it?"

The Dazed Zealots are pretty popular, but there's no sign advertising the concert tonight. "Maybe they don't want a line?"

"Maybe." He shifts into park, skeptical. "Want me to go in with you?"

I want to say yes. "That's okay. I've got this."

He looks like he wants to argue, but he doesn't. "I'll have my phone on me all day. Call if you need me."

I already dread him leaving. "I won't call." He glares at me, and I laugh. "You're going to be in meetings with the Jaguars. You don't need me bothering you."

His brow tightens, and I refrain from grinning. I've only known him for a couple of weeks, but he's predictable. Nothing riles him up like suggesting he won't help someone. I hate to admit it, but it's adorable. "Hannah…"

"Fine, fine," I wave my hand, like his protectiveness isn't wrecking me. "I'll call you if I need you. I swear."

He sniffs. The way he's all puffed up makes me squeeze his forearm, trying to calm him down.

As always, the zing of electricity pulses through me when I touch him. Disoriented, my smile slips a fraction, and I remove my hand from his arm. "It's going to be great."

"Hell yeah, it is." He nods as if it's insane to believe otherwise. His quiet confidence steadies me.

"And you'll be here to see it?" He's already promised, but I want to hear it. Need to hear it. Knowing he's coming, that he'll be watching me, calms everything inside me.

"Wouldn't miss it for anything."

I inhale, squaring my shoulders. "Great." I slide out of the car, pushing the seat forward to get my bag out of the back. I hadn't expected him to get out, but he appears at my side, his hands in his pockets. Staring down at me, I can't read his expression.

"Good luck with the Jaguars." Impulsively, I throw my arms around him in a hug. As my whole front flattens against him, it's hard to breathe. He stills for a second. I must have taken him off guard. But then his arms wrap around me, and he squeezes. I worry that the moment goes on too long, so I push away, reluctant to go.

Stepping back, I tuck a strand of hair behind my ear, feeling awkward.

"Thanks." He shrugs, glaring at the door as if it could be a portal to another dimension. "Are you sure you don't want me to come in with you?"

His concern strengthens my resolve. "I'm good." I clutch my bags tighter. "I've got this."

He pulls his phone out of his pocket and waves it at me. I chuckle, shooing him away. He offers me a salute and walks around the car, sliding into the driver's seat with the grace of a model or an elite hockey player. I shake my head, grinning.

I plan to wait for him to go before going in, but he doesn't leave, gesturing for me to go inside first.

Right. Who am I kidding? He's not leaving until I'm safely in the building.

With more confidence than I feel, I march to the entrance, swing open the door, and step inside.

But as the door closes behind me, plunging me into darkness, I halt. It takes a minute for my eyes to adjust to the low light, but when they do, I'm disoriented. The outside doesn't look like much, but the inside of the bar is a different world. Everything is red, black, and silver, clean lines, modern. Much more like the sort of place I would expect an up-and-coming band to be playing. Still, it's a surprise that no one is in the lobby.

"Hello? Is there anyone here?" When no one responds, there's nothing else to do but search for signs of life. I walk past a black gleaming bar, the wall of glass shelves behind it covered in a wide variety of liquor. Definitely different from the sort of things they serve at the Pig or Yesterday's Party. There's no bartender, though, so I lug my bag through the door beside the bar.

It opens onto a hallway. "Hello?" I repeat, starting to panic. Seriously, where is everyone?

"Hi there, pretty girl," someone says behind me.

"Thank God," I breathe out, gripping my bag as I turn. "I was wondering if I was in the right place…" The words die in my mouth as I face Sebastian Taylor, the lead guitarist for the Dazed Zealots.

I've seen his picture, and the guy's hot, no doubt about it. But this guy has something else going for him. Charisma, maybe. Something vibrant, like being in a room with a live wire.

"Hi," I respond, blinking.

He tucks his hands in the front of his skinny jeans, his lips in a grin that shows off a dimple.

It's so staged, it shakes me out of my star struck paralysis. "Hi," I repeat, stronger this time, blowing my hair out of my eyes. "I'm Hannah Marshall. I'm opening for you guys tonight."

The polished flirting slips off his face, replaced by a genuine smile. "Oh. Hi. Sorry, I thought you were a groupie."

"I get that a lot." I laugh, thinking back to meeting Cord's coach at the ice rink. "There wasn't anyone outside, so I just came in."

A wrinkle forms between Sebastian's eyebrows. "Yeah, I think that Brandon promised Milo he'd cover some of the security. If the few guards I saw is any indication of how he works, we won't be doing more gigs with any of his artists."

I can't deny that Ronnie's managerial skills suck, but as his client, it doesn't feel right to let anyone else badmouth him. "He's gotten me some exposure." It's a lame defense. That's his job, after all, but it's all I have.

Sebastian snorts. "You're new to this shit, huh?" He shakes his head. "I've heard your music. You deserve better."

I file that away for later, changing the subject. "What do I need to do?"

"Bash." Another guy steps out of a door. "We need to get ready for sound check." If Sebastian's the charisma, this guy's the danger. With dark hair and eyes, he's got that brooding thing down. He screams mystery, and he's nothing I feel safe with.

"Hannah, this is Jack, our bass player." I sweep forward to shake his hand. "Jack, Hannah is our opener."

He offers me a nod and a wink. "Hey." Then he ducks back inside.

Bash rolls his eyes at me, and I grin. I might be able to like this guitarist, especially now that he put the flirting away. We follow Jack in, and the other members of their band are there. Liberty Rose, their singer, gets right up and walks toward me, an easy smile on her face.

"You're Hannah." She folds me into a hug. "I'm Libby." She motions toward the other girl, who twirls a drumstick. "That's Maeve."

The drummer only salutes with her stick, saying nothing. Guess she's not a talker. Or a hugger.

"Milo sent us some of your videos. We're excited to have you here," Libby says. Her face is so open, it's impossible not to smile at her. "Maybe we could do a song together?"

"You guys want to sing with me?" I'm sure I meant that to sound cooler, but it comes out as star struck as I am.

Libby laughs, and it's a trilling sound, full of music. "Oh, honey. We need to work on your poker face."

Heat floods my face, but I laugh along with her. "Accurate."

There's discussion of the covers we could do together. Libby and Bash do most of the talking, but it's obvious that if Libby is the idealist in their group, Jack is their cynic. It works for them, though. We decide to do a riff on "Monday, Monday" by the Mamas and the Papas. I'm skeptical, but Maeve gets excited when she starts tapping out a beat that doesn't sound much like the song I'm familiar with. Then, Libby starts in with the background vocals, and it becomes clear.

I sing the main vocals, and we move through the song roughly, but I can see how it's going to be great. Libby's excited when we're done.

"Let's run a quick practice on it." They file out, younger and more vibrant than they seemed when I walked in. Now, they don't seem like rock stars. They're just college-aged kids, full of excitement. I follow them until we shrug through a door that reads Stage Access.

Three steps more and I'm out, under the lights. The venue unfolds in front of me. It's two stories but open. The second floor is a balcony, and the dance floor spreads in front of us. Above me, there's a dome. This place is going to have amazing acoustics.

Maeve steps behind her drum set, already tapping. Sebastian and Jack chat quietly, staring at their phones as Libby hums under her breath. I leave them to their thoughts, gazing out at the empty dance floor in front of me.

I'm going to sing here tonight, in this hip club in New York City, opening up for a band that's on the verge of greatness. I'm mostly doing covers, but I decided to add a couple of my own songs. I have no idea how they're going to go over, but I need to know.

Do I belong here?

Since I was a child, I've wanted to play music. My father would sit with me for hours as I practiced the piano at night, commenting about how someday, I'd perform on stage with the living greats. Helene Grimaud, Lise de la Salle. But I don't know if this is what he meant.

I love to sing. At least, I've loved singing at small bars. *Will this be the same? What if it isn't?*

I don't need to think about it now because what I need more than anything is money. I don't need to think about forever. My bank account doesn't care about my future plans.

Standing here, staring out into that empty room, I miss Cord and wonder how his meeting is going. I can't wait to see him later, find out how it went.

I should be focused on my set, but instead, I'm thinking about him. *Is he thinking about me too?*

"Hannah," Bash calls, dragging me back to the stage.

"Yeah. Sorry. I'm ready to give it a go." A stagehand—probably someone from their group—brings another microphone onstage. Libby and I take our places as the others start to play the melody. Instead of the bubblegum tune I remember, they give it a punk feel. As they all play, riffing off one another, I can see Libby's vision come together as she coaxes them.

By the times we start to sing, I'm smiling.

Cord had been right—this *is* going to be great.

Cord

"IT WAS A PLEASURE chatting with you, Mr. Spellman." Mr. Johnson, the general manager for the Jaguars, rises, holding out a hand. "I think that there are a lot of ways that we could have a mutually beneficial relationship."

That sounds risqué, but I get the idea. Smiling, I shake his hand. "Thanks for meeting with me."

"Absolutely." He points at me. "You've got a promising career ahead of you. I really think that you will make a long-term defensive impact at our organization."

I don't have any response, so I can only grin and nod along.

"Thank you, Paul, for making time in your busy schedule." My agent shakes Mr. Johnson's hand, subtly shifting us toward the door. "I'm sure I'll be talking to you in the future."

"Of course, Harry. It's always a pleasure." Johnson's assistant steps in, speaking softly into his ear, and we're dismissed. Harry tilts his head, and I follow him out.

In the hall, he's more animated. "That went well. Do you think it went well?"

"I do." I glance back at the conference room and then around me, at the rest of the Jaguars' facility. The whole place is impressive. I met with someone from the training department, and I spoke with the defense coach. It's easy to see how I could fit in. The coach's perspective, his style of play, and even his personality meshes well with my own philosophy. Granted, coaches come and go, but the locker room mentality stays longer. The whole place has a scrappy, feisty feel about it, and I like it. It reminds me of why I was so excited to be drafted by New Jersey in the first place.

"Good. Good to hear." I can see Harry's brain working. "Why don't we go sit, have dinner and a drink, chat about it?"

"Can't." I shrug, shaking my head in apology. "I've got a concert I've got to get to."

His brow shoots up. "A concert?"

"My girl is opening for the Dazed Zealots tonight." Pride fills me. *Because she's got this gig, or because I called her mine?*

Harry cocks his head. "Never heard of them."

"You like alternative music?"

He snorts. "Alternative to what?"

I grin. "They're good. You should come."

He slaps me on the shoulder. "Thanks, but if you won't eat with me, I'm going back to the hotel for room service."

"Sounds exciting." We step out of the elevator into the lobby. "Are you sure, though? My girl…" I clear my throat. "She's really good."

Harry's quiet as we walk out the front doors. "You haven't dated anyone since Rachel."

It doesn't surprise me that Harry is clued in on my love life. It's part of his job to know what's going on with me. "Yeah."

"Be careful, kid," he says. He nods his head toward the facility behind us. "I think that this defensive opportunity would be a good fit for you, but if you end up a free agent, you really need to make an impact in the playoffs."

"I get it." And I do, but he has to know I've already thought of all that. Hockey's my life. I'm not going to lose track of the goal this close to the finish line.

Harry searches my face. I don't know what he sees, but finally, he nods, slapping my shoulder again. "Good." He jerks a thumb toward the top-notch hockey facility behind us. "Think about what we talked about in there, okay? We'll chat this week."

"Sounds good."

"Now go watch your girl live her alternative life." I don't think that means what he thinks it does, but I don't correct him. He waves at the car he called for upstairs, and the compact pulls up next to us. As he slides in, I pull out my phone to check the time. It's after six, but Hannah's not supposed to go on until eight.

Still, I hurry to the parking garage, not wanting to be late.

Rush hour traffic around New York City is its own special hell. It takes me almost an hour to go what's probably only ten or twelve miles. Trying to find parking near the venue is equally time-consuming, and by the time I'm jogging up to the entrance, Hannah's scheduled to take the stage in fifteen minutes.

There's chaos at the door. No one has set up any ropes for a line, so everyone's just milling around. The Dazed Zealots have amazing buzz, so I'm not sure why no one thought that would be necessary. But the front is being manned by only one bouncer. Behind him, a girl with a clipboard is arguing with a guy in a suit.

"Excuse me," I call to the frazzled bouncer. "I'm on the VIP list."

"Yeah, pal. Everyone's special."

"No, seriously. Hannah is my girlfriend." The guy snorts, his beefy arms still wide, standing in front of the door. But I'm pretty tall, so I can look him in the eye. "Is her manager here? His name is Brandon." I can't remember his first name, but that should get me somewhere.

Mr. Beefy shrugs his head behind him. "Talk to Trudy."

I guess Trudy's the hostess. I step around Beefy, and a pat on his shoulder earns me a scowl. Trudy doesn't look happy, either, so I try on my best smile. "Are you Trudy?"

"I am. What can I do for you?" Her voice is thick with a Bronx accent.

"I'm Cord Spellman, Hannah Marshall's boyfriend." The more times I claim her as my girl, the more natural it feels. "I'm here to watch her."

She glances at the sheet in front of her. I follow her gaze, and sure enough, my name is there. She runs a red pen over the letters, waving me past. "Sorry for the confusion. Go ahead in."

I sweep through the front door, dodging pockets of people. I search out the bars in the place, thinking someone working there can help me find Hannah. A bouncer guards a door. Maybe that's the entrance to the stage. I beeline for him.

The music is loud, and then the lights on the stage go down. I yank my phone from my pocket. It's only five until eight, but I guess she's going on early. The crowd quiets, but there's still nervous conversation and a sense of anticipation in the room. I stand and watch, excited to see her. I'm lucky, though—I know what to expect. The majority of the audience doesn't yet.

"Good evening, everyone." Her voice soothes every ragged edge in me. I didn't think that the meetings I'd had earlier had stressed me out, but hearing her settles me.

"I'm Hannah. I'm here to warm you guys up for the Dazed Zealots." Her voice is energy, and her enthusiasm for the headliners courses through the room. I don't know whether she means it or if she's just selling the place, but I find myself clapping along.

The lights go up, and there she is.

"How about we get started?" She looks amazing. Her blond hair is arranged in waves around her face. She's wearing some sort of bohemian dress, and she's got tights and boots on. It shouldn't work, but it does for her. She picks up her tablet. She glances at the audience and then at her songs. The rest of the people here can't read her, but I can. She's testing the room, letting it flow through her, so she can sing for them. The knowledge makes me smug, and I cross my arms over my chest.

These people don't know what they're in for.

I didn't know what she planned to sing tonight, but I'm a little surprised to hear the first strains of Bob Marley's "Three Little Birds." Around me, patrons who had been talking stop, staring at one another. Some of them even laugh, as if confused or embarrassed. My grin widens.

Hannah starts in on the song, and I'm dragged in, as always. Around me, others start to get in on it too. There's clapping and swaying. Then they start to sing along. Maybe some in the audience had Googled her before the show to see if it was worth coming in early to see her. But I know what they don't—that part of Hannah's brilliance is her ability to read a room, to sense what they want or need and give it to them.

By the end of the song, the entire tone of the place has changed. When I walked in, the room buzzed. Too much energy, too much frustration. Now, smiles all around. That's what Hannah does.

Hell, I know firsthand. The more I'm around her, the more I want to be. She makes me happy. Happier than I've been in a long time. Maybe ever.

As the audience erupts into applause, she shields her eyes, scanning the room. *Is she looking for me?*

My chest tightens. I told her that I'd be here. I raise my arm, waving. But everyone is flailing around. It's a fucking concert. There's no way she can see me.

She must have given up because she reaches for her tablet. I can see the rise and fall of her shoulders as she takes a breath. "How are you all doing this evening?" she asks into the microphone. When she's greeted with only mild applause, she cocks her head. "What? I missed that."

The crowd responds louder this time.

"That's a little better." She laughs, and the sound fills me with joy. I need to get to her. She needs to know I'm here, that I made it. That I wouldn't let her down.

As I hurry toward the bouncer-protected door, the strains of a Billie Eilish song fill the air.

I stop in front of the bouncer. "I'm here with Hannah." I point toward the stage. "She's expecting me."

He snorts. "Pal, everyone's here with Hannah."

I glance back at the crowd. He's right—they're all right there with her, but I doubt that was what he meant. I try again. "No. I brought her. She's my girlfriend."

"Sure, buddy."

That annoys me. "Talk to Trudy. I'm on a list."

The hostess's name must have opened some magical door. Still skeptical, he pulls out his phone and speaks quietly into it. "What's your name?"

"Cord Spellman," I yell. It's weird having to explain who I am. Back in Chesterboro, everyone knows me.

After a few more quiet murmurs, he slides his phone back in his pocket and steps aside to let me pass without another word.

I slide through the door. Back here is a lot different than out front. There are a bunch of bar backs lugging dishes around and wait staff running. A couple of people on their phones don't look happy.

I weave around everyone, searching for someone that looks like they might be able to help me. "Which way is the stage?"

A guy with purple hair peeks his head out a door. "Hey. What are you—"

"I'm with Hannah."

He scowls, and I recognize him. The guitarist for the Zealots. I don't even care. He points down the hall, and I don't even slow.

The music gets louder as I get closer. I turn the corner, and there are stairs that I take in one leap. At the top, I pause.

From this close, I'm awestruck by her. *How did I ever think she wasn't the most arresting girl in the world?*

She sways along as she finishes the song. When she reaches for her tablet again, our eyes connect.

Her smile loosens everything in me. The meeting with the Jaguars, the low-level worry about my father's reaction when he finds out, and the increasing certainty that the choices I'm considering are going to disappoint him stop mattering when she smiles like that in front of me.

"Now that we are all here," she says, "let's get everyone moving."

What follows might be one of the best performances I've ever seen. She shines, and the whole place agrees. She sings a few original songs, and they're the best ones, I think.

When she's done, the crowd still roars as she hurries across the stage toward me. She doesn't stop, throwing herself into my arms.

The press of her against me is perfect. If seeing her is a comfort, feeling her is the most delicious ache.

She pulls back, laughing. "Did you see that?" She vibrates with joy, and it steals all the words from my mouth. "That was amazing."

I find my voice, but I need to clear my throat to use it. "You were amazing."

Her eyes find mine, and the smile is replaced by something heavier, weighted, and hot. The urge to kiss her, to consume her, is so strong that my fingers tighten into her shirt as I fight it.

A voice cuts into the energy between us. "Hannah, that was perfect."

The entire Dazed Zealots lineup is behind us. I recognize them from their album cover. Liberty, the lead singer, folds Hannah into a hug, laughing.

"Thank you," she says.

"You ready to sing with us?" Sebastian throws a casual arm over her shoulder, winking at her.

Hannah rocks back on her heels, grinning. "Absolutely."

"Right on," he says, his gaze full of approval. I want to step between them, disliking the guitarist immediately.

I snag her arm as she starts to go back on stage. "Wait, you're going to sing with them?"

"Yep!" She sighs happily. My irritation with Sebastian fades. Hannah's excited. That's good enough for me.

"Break a leg, Marshall." I lift her hand, pressing a kiss to the back of it. She glances away, flustered.

With an unsteady breath, she steps back on stage. A roar rises. She waves.

"I know you all aren't here to just listen to me. You're waiting for the Dazed Zealots!" There's another roar from the crowd, and she laughs. "Would you all like to see them?"

There's a fever-pitch scream.

"You do?"

The lights on stage go down.

"Later, pal." Sebastian pats me on the shoulder as they all run out. Then the lights go up, brighter than ever. The place goes crazy.

Hannah hugs Libby and Sebastian, and I notice that he holds on a little too long. The drums start, and Libby steps toward the microphone. They start a song from the sixties, but somehow, the way they're playing it is edgy. Hannah sings the main lyrics, and it's perfect for her voice. I never would have pictured her as a Mamas and Papas kind of girl, but one thing is more than apparent as I can't take my eyes off of her—whatever kind of girl she is, she's definitely the only girl I can see.

Hannah

LIBBY ASKS ME TO stay until the end, to take a final bow. Cord and I watch from side stage, close enough that I can touch him. I don't, though, because I don't think I can again without making a complete fool of myself.

After my set, I was riding such a high that all I wanted was to share it with him. He looked so gorgeous there, in the dress shirt and pants he wore to the meeting with the Jaguars, his dark hair rustled like he'd been running his fingers through it. Then, as he held me in his arms, my joy mixed with everything I've been struggling to hold inside since I met him, comfort and happiness and the purest desire that I've ever experienced.

Because there is nothing, not even my music, that I want with the same kind of raw emotion as Cord Spellman.

The Zealots put on a great show, but I can't concentrate on it because he's there, beside me. By the end, when Libby calls me back onstage, my body is so on edge and attuned to him that my knees are weak with needing him.

"We're the Dazed Zealots, and this is Hannah." I stand on that stage with the members of one of the hottest up-and-coming bands in the country and watch the crowd in front of us go crazy. But even as I'm overwhelmed by the noise, the energy, all I can feel is Cord just offstage.

I follow the Zealots off while the crowd continues to scream. They congratulate one another, and I accept their pats on the back and high fives. Bash pulls me into a hug and swings me around. When he puts me down, I rock back on my heels. "Thanks for having me, you guys. It was a great experience."

"You're so formal." Maeve winks at me. "That's so cute." I roll my eyes as Bash tucks Maeve under his arm and ruffles her pink hair.

Jack barely nods at me. "Good job, Goldie."

I get the feeling that's high praise from him. "Thanks."

Libby hugs me again. If Jack is reserved, she's so open it's almost scary to watch. It makes me want to protect her. "You're going to be huge, girl. We're going to see you soon."

I swallow, nodding, unable to respond around how much I want that to be true. *But if I do, where does that leave graduate school?*

And Cord?

My eyes meet his over Libby's red hair. Worry clouds his features.

I don't have a chance to ask him what's up, though, because Bash tugs one of my curls and presses something in my hand. "Let me know if you want to talk to Milo. You need a better manager."

I open my hand. A piece of paper with a phone number is in it. Then he's gone, following his band before I can respond, leaving Cord and me alone, if it's possible to be alone in a bar with hundreds of other people.

"Thank you for coming. For driving me. For everything." I don't have the words to say all the things I'm thinking and feeling. I can only step forward and squeeze his hand. But touching him is a bad idea. Because his skin is warm, and I want to step closer, to be closer, to feel more of him.

I can't meet his eyes, and I drop the contact. He clears his throat.

I'm dangerously close to saying something that will change everything. This is supposed to be fake. I was ideal because I promised I didn't want him. And I didn't, at least not really. He was just another attractive guy, or so I told myself.

No one warned me that it would be impossible to know him without falling half in love with him.

Please, God, let me only be half in love with him.

What I do know is that it's getting too difficult to pretend I don't want him now. Just standing next to him lights me on fire.

"I'm glad I could be here," he finally says. When I glance up, he's staring after the Zealots. "Why was Sebastian talking about your manager?"

Much easier conversation. I shrug. "Ronnie didn't show. And he didn't send enough bouncers."

His brow furrows. "Just be careful. You don't know these people, and you don't know their manager. I don't like Ronnie, but you should be careful before you change anything. You need to vet these guys and anyone they put you in contact with. You can't trust they'll have your best interests in mind."

Maybe it's because my emotions are so close to the surface, but this irritates me. "I know that. I've been taking care of myself for a long time."

He sighs. "That wasn't what I meant."

"What did you mean?" I ask, my hands on my hips. "Because it sounded like you were trying to manage me."

"Hannah, no." He steps closer, putting his hands on my shoulders. "That's not it. I'm not trying to tell you what to do. I'm only…" He exhales, shrugging a shoulder. "I just really don't want you to get hurt." When I don't respond, he glares down at me. "Why's it hard to believe I care about you?"

My mouth opens, but I can't find words. He's right—it's hard to believe he cares. I don't make it easy for people to get close to me. In my life, depending on people is a recipe to be let down. I couldn't handle being let down by him.

What I need right now is space. Or him. One of those options is safer than the other.

Spinning, I head toward the door. The bar is too loud, too small. I need fresh air. I just need to get away from him, away from the insane idea that we might be able to be more than what we are.

I keep going through the hallway in the back and then out the side door.

I lean on the wall next to the door. I inhale, sucking in air, desperate to regroup. I run my hand over my hair. I need to get my shit together or I'm going to embarrass myself.

I wrap my arms around myself and stare at the sky. In Chesterboro, I can see the stars above me at night. Here, the sky is bright gray, probably from light pollution. It makes me homesick. Back home, everything is clear and everything with Cord makes sense. All the boundaries, all the reasons why we aren't together. But here, everything is murky.

"Are you the singer? Hannah?" The voice cuts into my pity party, and someone grabs my arm. "How you doing, pretty girl?" I pull back, looking toward the door. There's supposed to be a bouncer here, but there's no one to interfere between this intoxicated, handsy guy and me.

"Let me go," I say, yanking to free my arm from his grasp. I pull harder on his hand, my voice higher than usual. "You're hurting me."

"I just want to talk. Don't you want to talk?"

I scream. His eyes widen, and he pulls me against him, panicked. "No. Shut up. You're being too loud. People will hear." When I don't listen and keep screaming, he covers my mouth. But that makes it hard for me to breathe, and I struggle harder, which makes him pull me closer and tighter against him.

I'm crying, trying to yell with no air, my heart beating loudly in my ears. Desperate, I remember the self-defense classes I took when I started at CU. One of the moves returns to me.

Leaning back, I step down hard on his foot. Then I turn in his arms. He's expecting me to keep struggling away, so the change sets his balance off. I loosen my arm enough to shove my elbow into his gut then drive my knee into his groin. He lets me go, doubling over, and I scurry away.

I suck in a gasp, falling to my knees, my hands on my chest. I can't hear anything but the loud racing of my heart. It's long seconds until I make out the skirmish next to me.

Glancing up, I find Cord holding my Casanova up against the wall by his jacket. "What the actual fuck do you think you are doing?" He shoves him, and the guy goes flying, landing in a heap next to the door. "Why were your hands on her?"

"I only wanted to say hello," he babbles. "She started yelling…"

"You don't get to say anything to her," Cord hisses through gritted teeth, standing over the man with his legs apart. "You definitely shouldn't be touching any part of her." He looks like he's going to reach for him again.

"Cord," I rasp out. "Stop."

It might not work. He's so angry, he might not listen. But he pauses, and I stumble to my feet.

I'm intensely aware that there are people on the street about twenty yards away. They have phones, with cameras. They will take videos that will end up on social media. I brush myself off, stepping between Cord and the drunk guy. Meeting Cord's eyes, I place my hand on his chest. Beneath my fingers, his heart races as fast as mine.

"It's okay. We need to get back inside." I use my most soothing voice, like I'm calming a frightened animal. Or in this case, a furious star hockey player. When he doesn't appear to hear me, I say his name again, louder. "Cord. There are people watching. We don't need this kind of attention."

He's about to sign a hockey contract. The last thing he needs is to end up in pictures anywhere, especially from a brawl in New York.

It takes long moments, but I watch as he gathers himself. He finally peels his eyes off the other man, focusing on me. He nods. "Right."

Taking my arm, he leads me up the side stairs and inside, casting angry glances back to where Casanova still leans against the building.

The door closes behind us, the sound so loud I jump, gasping. In front of me, Cord jams his hands into his hair. "What the…" He swallows whatever is going to come next. "Jesus, Hannah…" It's as if he can't form the words properly.

“They said all the entrances would have bouncers, even the side ones,” I explain, but even as I say the words, I think of all the other missteps this evening, especially when it came to security measures. “Brandon was supposed to make sure there were enough bouncers.”

“Obviously he let that particular responsibility slide,” Cord grinds out.

I glare at him. “I see that.”

He drops his hands onto my shoulders. “My God, what were you thinking?”

How is this my fault? “That I needed some air,” I snap. “That it’s a free country, and there’s nothing wrong with needing some air.” If I’d stayed in that room, I would have said something I regretted.

“All those people are screaming for you. You didn’t think this could be dangerous?” His eyes are wild. “Do you know what could have happened?”

“It didn’t, though. Nothing happened. Because I handled it. I can take care of myself.”

“What if you couldn’t, though?” He grips my arms.

His frustration finds a home inside me. My chaotic emotions focus, and now I’m mad. “But I did. I don’t need you to save me.”

Abruptly, he pulls me into his arms, and I’m pressed against his hard chest.

With the immediate threat gone and folded in his arms, my heart picks up for a different reason, one that has nothing to do with fear. God, he feels good. I drop my head against his shoulder.

I’m lying. I do need him. I need his mouth against mine, his hands in my hair. Except that once I get a taste of him, I’m going to want all of him. What started as a façade has become everything to me. Now, instead of faking my feelings for him, I'm hiding them.

I allow myself these moments, wrapped in his arms, to close my eyes and pretend.

I run my hands up his arms, over the dress shirt he's rolled up at the sleeves. I trace the lines of his arms, reveling in the strength of him. Not only the physical perfection, though that's pretty extraordinary.

No, he's proven time and again that he's got the force of will to stand next to someone, to be their strength when they need it. I've never seen him shy away from anything, and he always does what's needed. Whether it's leading his team or standing up for me—with Mr. Murphy, when I'm overwhelmed, just now in the alley—he's supremely decent and reliable.

For a girl who's never had anyone to lean on, this steady, gorgeous man is a temptation I can't resist.

I force that aside, though, because right now he's in my arms and I can feel him breathing, I can hear his heart racing, and I'm only allowing myself to have this for a moment. As he pulls me closer, his hold tightening, I slide my face against him and inhale, and his scent weakens my knees, sending heat flooding into my stomach.

I press my lips together and open my eyes. I need to get a grip and out of his. "Please…" My voice is desperate, so I swallow, pushing back and away from his heat, despite every instinct I possess. "Please, Cord. Let me go."

He immediately drops his arms, and I step back, out of his reach. "Hannah…"

I can't do this right now, not with my emotions everywhere. I fold my arms around myself. "I'll go get my things. We should go."

Though I try not to rush, I run down the hall and away from him.

Cord

AS I WAIT FOR Hannah outside the side door, I pace back and forth, allowing the cool spring air to calm me down. It works some, but it leaves me with everything else.

She was so happy after singing and excited about the Zealots offering to help with her manager. I only wanted to make sure she's careful. Then I basically told her I cared about her, and she took off.

If I doubted before whether she wanted something real with me, she couldn't have been any clearer than running away. Message received.

But she surprised me so much that I didn't follow right away. When I did, I saw red.

She'd already thrown him off her, and that was a good thing for the dickhead because he wouldn't have wanted me to do it for her. As it was, I barely kept myself from bashing his face in.

I'm not violent. I play one of the most physical sports in the world, and I'm known for being level-headed. But seeing his hands on her made me lose my head.

The door opens, and Hannah steps out, her messenger bag crossbody over her jacket. "I'm ready."

"I parked a few blocks away." I motion in the right direction, and she nods, falling in step next to me.

We wind through the streets, neither of us talking. By the time we reach the car, the silence is killing me. I pause with my hand on the doorknob. "You're upset."

"Not upset, exactly," she says.

I hurry on. "You were right. There's nothing wrong with needing some air. I shouldn't have said that."I shouldn't have put her in a position where she felt like she needed to run away. I'll remember that.

She pulls her coat closer and tilts her chin up. "I did have that under control. I got him off of me. But you're actually right. I should have looked for a bouncer. But it was before that, Cord. Earlier. Inside."

Why can't she just tell me what I messed up so I could fix it? My brain frantically scans the minutes before she ran out. Sebastian had given her his number, which honestly was kind of a douchey thing to do in front of her boyfriend. Fake boyfriend, but he doesn't know that. "You want a new manager." My brain spins. "I told you, my family has a lot of connections. My agent. I can get you in touch with a lot of people—"

She growls and cuts me off. "I don't need you to fix my problems for me," she says, her face flushed in the streetlight. "I need you…"

Her voice trails off, but the words light me up, throwing fuel to the flame that's been slowly burning inside of me for the past two and a half weeks that I've known her.

"What is it exactly that you need, Hannah?" I bury my hands in my hair to keep from reaching for her. This close, in the streetlight, she's ethereal. But I don't dare. She took off the last time I brought up my feelings for her. "I don't know what you want from me. You don't need me to help you. You don't like it when I pay for things. I would help you do anything, in any way I can. You have to see that."

Her eyes search mine, and the air between us is heavy. Finally, she steps forward, placing her hand on my chest. "You keep trying to help me with everything, and that's really sweet, but I don't need your help. I only need you."

The words are devastating. Sweeping forward, I wrap one arm around her waist, and I curve the other around her neck. This close, I can almost taste her gasp. My fingers thread into her hair, lacing through so I can tilt her face toward mine. My gaze finds her mouth, as always, those damn full lips a temptation. I rub my thumb along her jaw. Her skin is insanely soft, so I do it again, unable to stop myself.

I drop my forehead to hers. Our breathing tangles, and I close my eyes, barely holding on to my control. "Hannah, I know I told you I wouldn't kiss you until you asked, but I've never wanted anything so—"

Her mouth silences me. It's the softest press. It's all the invitation I need.

Cupping her face, I capture her Cupid's-bow mouth with my own. I want to take it slow, to have some finesse here, but fuck… she tastes so good, and her mouth feels so right, and the way she greedily grips me to her is the sweetest thing I've ever felt. My entire body roars with need. I angle her head, and her tongue meets mine.

Her hands pull at my shirt, dragging the shirttails out of my pants. Then her fingers press into the skin at my waist. Her hunger revs me up even more. I growl low, tugging gently on her hair to tilt her head back so I can drag my mouth from hers to slide my lips along her jaw and then down her throat. Her skin is as smooth as I expect and slightly salty.

She moans, her hands on my back, pulling me closer. She's tall, so slight and wispy that I never would have expected that we would fit this well against each other. But somehow, it works because the way she fills in the hard planes of my body is a completion I never would have expected. With her in my arms, I never want her anywhere else.

She might have started this kiss, but it's mine now. It's a possession and a claiming.

Conversation behind us distracts me. We aren't alone here. I lift my head, surfacing from the lust raging through me. Hannah's pressed between the car and me, her hair tousled and her lips pink and swollen. It takes everything in me not to capture her mouth again. I groan, running my hands over her hair to smooth it. "We can't do this here."

"Where can we do this, then?" she whispers, her hands on my shoulders.

Closing my eyes, I breathe deep. "Baby girl, now that I've kissed you, I plan to kiss you anywhere, anytime I can." I murmur back. I drop my head, capturing her lower lip between my teeth, and running my tongue along it.

"More," she sighs. Her eyes open, honey-colored in the soft streetlight. "I want more than kisses tonight."

I search her eyes, and she holds my gaze. The color is high on her cheeks from arousal or embarrassment, and it's gorgeous on her. This girl is the one who said she wasn't into me, that we were fake. But the desire I read on her face is real.

"I want you, Cord. I want to spend the night with you."

I already told her that we'd get a place to sleep tonight because I assumed it would be too late to drive home tonight.

Technically, I'm already supposed to spend the night with her.

I need more clarity than that. So I capture her face again in my hands. I'm not rough, only insistent. "I don't only want to spend the night with you, Hannah. I want you. To kiss you, to taste you, to be inside you. All night. In any and every way I can have you." I've spent so much time wondering exactly where I stand with her. For this, I need to be crystal clear. I need her to know exactly what I want.

"Yes," she says, sighing out. "I want that too."

Thank God. I drop a hard kiss on her mouth then open the door of the car and tuck her inside.

Hannah

CORD PULLS INTO THE parking garage under the Standard, High Line. It's the fanciest hotel I've ever seen. He hands his key to the valet and ushers me into an elevator. It's late, after midnight, but when the elevator doors open into the lobby, there are people everywhere.

Not only people but hip and glamorous people. Girls in small dresses and high heels, guys in slick pants and button-downs, shoes right out of the pages of high-end men's magazines. For my show, I wore tights and a boho dress, but it's my usual vintage edgy stuff, nothing anyone would call high fashion.

Cord is what these people wish they were. Some of the gorgeous girls walking by check him out even as he places his hand on the small of my back, guiding me toward the registration desk.

I tuck my coat tighter around myself and square my shoulders. Sure, these girls are beautiful, but it's me he'll be spending the night with.

I shudder, wondering if I'm making a huge mistake. There won't be any going back from sleeping with Cord. Then again, after kissing him, I don't think there's any going back from that either.

I wouldn't even want to. I've never wanted anything more than him, no matter what happens next.

"Do you want a drink?" He motions toward the bar.

I shake my head. We're here to sleep together. Back at the car, I got the feeling he was as eager to do that as I was. But now he wants to stop and have a drink. Or maybe this is just what people do. I have no idea, because I could count the sum of my sexual encounters on my thumbs.

"Hang out here, then. I'll get our room key." He motions to a chair and squeezes my arm as he heads to check in.

Without him next to me, this place is even scarier with all its glass and trendy decor. By the time he returns, I'm totally psyched out.

He takes me in, and his brows crinkle in confusion. But he only says, "Our room is on the eighth floor. Come on." Again, his hand finds my back, and its presence there comforts me.

When the elevator opens onto our floor, he checks the key card and leads us down one of the halls, stopping at a door. With a click, the door swings open.

The room is breathtaking. It's sleek, hip, the kind of trendy that lots of money manages. I walk farther inside and gasp. The bedroom has floor-to-ceiling windows. We are obviously in the corner of the hotel because two of the walls are windows, and the view looks out over the city.

I cover my mouth. "My God, it's amazing."

Cord helps me out of my jacket. "I thought you'd like it." He drops his mouth to my shoulder, and I can't help but tilt my head back and to the side, giving him better access. He trails his lips up my neck, to the curve beneath my ear. "You said you've never been to the city, right?"

I can only nod because he's stolen my ability to speak. Except he retreats, leaving me standing there.

"Some other time, we'll need to come back, and I'll show you around. My mom's from New Jersey. I've been to the city lots of times." He talks about the future easily, as though it's somehow guaranteed for us. I know better, but it's appealing to think about it.

It's chilly without my coat, so I wrap my arms around myself then turn to find him at the mini bar, unbuttoning the sleeves of his shirt and rolling them up. He reaches inside the fridge and pulls out a bottle of champagne. He unwraps the cork and untwists the wire around it then covers it with a towel and pops it open like a pro.

I don't think I've ever even seen someone open a bottle of champagne.

I accept the glass he hands me and sip it. Because I can't talk about what could happen down the road, I focus on the rest of what he said. This is the first time he's spoken of his mom. He talks about his dad all the time but not her. He didn't ask to see her while we were here, either. "Where in New Jersey?"

"Menlo Park." I wrack my brain for what I know about the town. Not much. "She and my father divorced when I was thirteen."

"I'm sorry."

He shrugs. "It was a long time ago. My parents are very different."

"How so?" I take another drink of the champagne and realize my sips have almost emptied the flute. The stuff is better than I expected. I hold it out to Cord for more.

He looks me over and pours me some more. “Well, my dad grew up wealthy. His father was a politician. My mother’s family is more middle-class.” He takes a drink, draining his own glass. “I think she wanted a more traditional life. A husband who didn’t travel, who wasn’t in the news.” He pauses. “The kind of guy who didn’t cheat.”

I blow out a breath. “That’s awful.”

“They probably held on too long. For me. She was unhappy, and he felt responsible for it. It was a recipe for disaster.” He sets down his glass. “I split my time between them now. Some holidays with her, some with my dad. Divide the summers. She’ll come for a game or two during the year, and we talk on the phone every Sunday.”

Compared to my own mother, she sounds wonderful. To avoid thinking too much about that, I set down my glass. “So,” I offer. “How does this work?”

He stills. “Work?”

“I mean, how do we do this?”

He sets his glass down, too. “This?”

Is he going to make me spell it out? “Have sex, Cord. Isn’t that what we’re doing here, in this super-fancy hotel?” The champagne has loosened my tongue.

He scowls at me. “First of all, I reserved the hotel yesterday. Remember?”

“I know. That’s not what I mean. I only mean, how do we start?” Everything in this room makes me anxious. It’s slick and smooth and screams money in a way that I recognize as foreign. Add Cord’s big, cut, gorgeous body, and it’s claustrophobic.

He steps closer, placing his hands on my shoulders. When his fingers press into the tight muscles there, I realize I'm tense. "There's no way to 'start.' There's only what's working for us." He presses his lips to my forehead, and I close my eyes. "We don't have to do anything if you don't want to, baby," he whispers. "If you want to stop right now, that's fine. We can just go to bed."

My gaze meets his. *Is that what I want? Absolutely not.* Staring into his gray eyes, there's nothing I want in the world more than this man.

He presses a kiss to my temple and returns to the champagne, pouring another glass. With his back to me, I inhale a steadying breath and gather my nerve. Then I pull my dress over my head. With a quick flick of my wrist, I unsnap my strapless bra and let it fall to the floor.

With his champagne flute on the way to his lips, he catches sight of me. I kick one of my heels off and then the other. Slowly, as he watches, I pull off my tights, shimmying them off my hips and down my legs. Bending over, I pull them off my heels, leaving myself standing there in only my panties. Briefly, I wish I had on something sexier than the practical, nude-colored bikini that I'm wearing or that I even owned something sexier. But the heat in Cord's eyes says he doesn't mind these at all.

He sets down his glass and sweeps forward, curling an arm around my waist and dragging me against him. His other hand finds my hair, and his mouth falls on mine.

I've been kissed before. Not often but a handful of times. Some of the kisses have even been pleasant. But when Cord kisses, it's like nothing I've ever experienced before. He consumes me. I can't think of anything except for his lips on mine, his body against me. He isn't rough, only insistent. He kisses like he does everything else, with the kind of surety that demands attention.

It definitely works for me.

His fingers splay across my back, pulling me closer. Even in clothes, the feel of him against my skin makes me gasp.

With a quick lift, I'm in his arms. I'm not a short girl, but he carries me like I weigh nothing, and it makes me feel small and feminine. In my day-to-day, I hate feeling weak or fragile, but in his arms, it amps me up.

He pushes the comforter off the bed and lays me on the sheets. When he leans back, goosebumps erupt on my skin, but I can't tell whether they're from the cold or from Cord's gaze. I'd untucked his shirt earlier, and now he only bothers to unbutton enough buttons so that he can pull it over his head.

There's no overhead light in the room, but in the glow from the lamp, I can easily see the chiseled planes of his chest. I didn't even know people could have that many abs.

Reaching, I trail my fingers over them. He inhales sharply, and I smile. My touch affects him too. Satisfaction courses through me, so I use both hands, running them over his wide shoulders, all the way down his chest, and pause at his waistband. His eyes close on a groan. "Fuck, baby, that feels so good."

I move to unbutton his pants, but he covers my hand. "I think we need to slow down there, or this won't last as long as I want it to." He shifts, dragging my hand over my head, and settles beside me on his side. "My turn."

He runs his thumb over my lips once, twice, and then slides his hand into my hair, dropping his mouth to mine.

This kiss isn't like the others. It's slow and gentle, taking its time. Heat explodes through me, and I move, trying to get closer to him. He breaks off the kiss, quieting me with a finger over my lips and a shush, and then he drags his lips along my neck. I tilt my head back to give him more access. Then, he settles his mouth on my left nipple.

I cry out. He doesn't stop, only continues the kiss he started on my lips on the sensitive tip of my breast. He's still holding my right arm over my head, but I bury my other hand in his hair, rubbing and holding him against me.

"God, you're perfect."

Never in my life have I believed anything about my body was perfect. I'm tall and thin, with barely any hips and even less breasts. But under his gaze, I feel beautiful.

He runs his hands down to where my panties hit my waist, and he pauses. "You doing okay up there?"

I can only nod because I suddenly feel like I'm breathing through concrete. He places a soft kiss on my hip then starts to slide my panties down.

"Wait." I clutch his shoulders, shimmying up so I'm propped up on my elbows. He stops immediately. "Cord… I mean. What…" I don't even know what I'm trying to say here.

He takes his hands off my underwear, shifting onto his elbows so he can see me, cocking his head. "What's up, baby girl?"

I study him. Tucked between my legs, he goes from being completely consumed with what he was doing to laser focused on me. Or maybe his focus has been on me this entire time, whether it's on kisses or conversation. I've only had sex a couple times, but both times, it felt like the guy was going through the motions. Boob squeeze here, butt grab there. Quick kisses, rush, rush. Like they were checking off things on their to-do list on the way to a finish line.

Cord's not rushing, and he's not only going through the motions. He's here with me. Any nerves I might have been feeling a moment ago disappear.

"Nothing." I smile at him. "Everything's good."

His brows pop up. "Only good? Well, that's not what I'm going for here." He nudges his head toward my belly. "Mind if I get back to what I was doing? Couple things I need to do."

I laugh. "Proceed."

Giving a satisfied sniff, he slides my underwear down a few inches, my slit still covered. He runs his tongue along the top edge of my panties, and I fall back with a sigh. He blows on the skin he just licked, and I shiver. There's a smile in his voice when he murmurs, "That sounds better."

The bed shifts as he hoists himself up. He slides my panties the rest of the way off then returns, settling between my spread thighs again. He tucks his arms under my thighs so that my knees hitch up, opening me even further. Heat hits my face. I know he's going to go down on me. I hold my breath with the anticipation and vulnerability of it all. Only one of the other guys I slept with did this, but that was in the dark. Those few licks had felt nice, but this…I'm more turned on now from just knowing Cord's eyes are on me, and he hasn't even touched me yet.

His breath is warm against the center of me, and I moan, but I can't close my eyes, watching him watch me. Then his gaze finds mine, and the heat there sends lightning through my veins. As our eyes hold, he licks me, tongue wide, from bottom to top, and I cry out.

His eyes close as he runs his tongue along his lips, humming. "So sweet," he says as he drops his head and covers me again.

Cord's mouth is magic. At first, he's slow and gentle, his fingers holding me open as he learns how I react. Then I lose track of what he's doing, and I only feel. What starts soft becomes more insistent, his fingers and his mouth moving over the most sensitive parts of me. Fire licks through me, and I know I'm making noise and that I'm moving, but I don't even care anymore whether it's the right way to act or not. Whatever he's doing feels so good that I never want it to end. I only want more and more, and then I'm so close to coming that I need it. I'm desperate with wanting it. The orgasm is so close and climbing me so fast that there's nothing in the world that could possibly stop it now.

When it crashes over me, I gasp and cry out with it, even as Cord continues to work me over, letting me ride it out completely, sucking every last shudder from me. After it's over, my head falls back against the bed, and I pant, breathless and spent.

He strokes my hips, a pleased smile on his face. "That sounded like it was at least a step or two above good."

I laugh, whatever awkwardness I might have been working up disappearing instantly. "Several, I'd say."

"Hell yeah." He slides up next to me, rubbing his thumb along my cheek and dropping a kiss on my lips. I can taste a hint of myself there, and I would have never thought I'd think that was hot, but on him, it is. "How are you feeling?"

I pretend to consider. "If I say good, are you going to get mad?"

He growls, and I laugh again, shifting onto my side. In front of me, he's Greek god gorgeous, and I can feel the heat rising in me again. I have no idea what happens next for us. At Chesterboro, things confuse me. What we are and aren't, how long we're whatever we are… But I have him right now. Maybe we'll have more than this night together. Maybe a week, two. I don't know, but I'm certain we don't have forever. Our deadline looms in the near future, so I plan to make the most out of what I have as long as I have it.

Including him, right now, in this bed with me.

"You're still wearing pants," I tell him.

He glances down. "My God, you're right." His eyes widen innocently. "What are you going to do about that, Marshall?"

I grin at him then reach for his fly.

Cord

THE TASTE OF HANNAH still buzzes through my head as she slides my zipper down. Holy fuck, I don't think I've ever been this turned on. But Hannah, with her hair spilling over her shoulders, her lips swollen from kisses, and her tiny nipples tight and bright pink with desire…I'm so close to going off that the small of my back is tight with it.

I hike myself up to help her get my pants off. I left them on earlier because my damn cock is so sensitive right now, and I didn't want anything to distract me from licking her. I groan, thinking about her scent, the luscious taste of her on my mouth.

I breathe deeply. *Come on, I've got more control than this…*

As my pants and boxers hit my ankles, I pause, reaching into the pocket and retrieving my wallet and the condom I have there, dropping it onto the bed beside me. Then I toss the rest of my clothes onto the floor. Hannah shoves my shoulder gently, coaxing me onto my back. I go. Hell, I'd happily follow this girl anywhere right now, as long as I can stay with her.

Throwing her leg over my thighs, she settles, rubbing the wet core of her against me. I can feel her slickness, and I cup her hips, my fingers pressing in. God, I want her so badly. I grind my teeth against it, equal parts wanting to be inside her and never wanting to stop feeling this way.

She drops her head. The soft waves of her hair brush against my hips, and with her eyes watching me, she slides her tongue from the base of my dick up to the top in one slow swipe.

"Oh, fuck," I murmur. "Baby…" After that, she opens her mouth and takes the length of me inside, completely shutting me up.

My hips buck up, but she stays put on top of me. At first, her movements are tentative, but she must be making sense of whatever nonsense I'm mumbling because she figures out exactly what to do in an achingly short amount of time. Then the damn orgasm I've been holding off is so close that I'm pleading, "Baby, please, I need you."

My voice is gravel. There's no finesse left in me, only this raging need to get inside her, to make her mine, to move and hear the same noises she made earlier when she came except this time, I want to hear them while I'm buried inside her, with her body's gentle convulsions warm on my cock.

I grip her hips, and maybe I'm rougher than I should be—I don't know—but she doesn't seem to mind. I try to turn her over, but she shakes her head, keeping me on my back. She flicks the condom up with her finger and hands it to me. A quick rip and a roll, and I'm ready.

The smile on her lips is part Mona Lisa, part siren, and it's so much the Hannah I've seen, the real one that she hides from everyone else. My chest squeezes, and the emotion there is so heavy, so perfect, that it feels like it's too big.

I love this girl.

As she shimmies up my legs and poises over my hips, the words are on the tip of my tongue. But then she lowers, taking me inside her inch by inch, and I doubt I could have mumbled anything remotely coherent.

I'm a tall, big guy, and the rest of me is in proportion. Hannah wiggles a bit to accommodate me, and my fingers tighten on her hips as I growl, staying as still as I can as I wait for her body to get used to me inside her.

When she's seated hard on top of me, she stops, and I drag my eyes open to stare at her. Her hair is a halo around her head in the light, and her pale skin glows. She takes my breath away. When I meet her eyes, though, there's uncertainty. "Are you okay?" I ask. Whatever is there on her face shorts my brain. Whatever is causing her concern is the only thing that matters right now.

"I just don't know what to do here," she whispers.

Relief courses over me. That's easy enough to fix. I laugh, but it's more a groan. "Whatever you're doing is perfect."

"No," she shakes her head. "I mean, I've never done it this way. Maybe we should…" She gestures toward the bed. "Maybe you should…"

Absolutely not. No way my girl is going to feel self-conscious about anything we do in bed together. Not now and not ever.

I reach up and smooth her hair from her face, cupping her cheek. "There's no right way to do this, only whatever way works for us, baby. What you're doing is working for me." I thrust my hips up, and her eyes widen. "Obviously."

"Okay." She licks her lips, but she still looks worried. So I grasp her, tugging her down against my chest. The adjustment in position makes her gasp, and I catch the inhalation in my mouth, kissing her hard.

"Hannah Marshall, I want you so bad," I murmur. "Whatever you do, I can't imagine a thing that would change that right now." I lick at her lips. "I want to watch you on top of me, I want you to be in control. I want you to take whatever you need from me. Now. Will you do that, baby?"

The uncertainty disappears, and she nods, heat in her eyes. She presses up, her hands on my chest, and I groan again. *Christ, she's going to kill me.*

Then she lifts her hips and slides back down on me, and I'm in heaven. When she does it again, I decide it could be hell. It doesn't even matter which it is anymore, as long as she's here. I'm determined to let her ride this out, literally. And I keep my eyes open because there's nothing that could keep me from watching every erotic second of it.

Her mouth falls open, and a flush warms her cheeks and her neck. Her breasts are a temptation I can't resist, and I run my hands over her rib cage so my thumbs can rasp against the tips of them. She jerks, her eyes flaring open on a gasp. She's so responsive, and it revs up my own raging lust.

"You like that?" I ask, doing it again. Her movement falters again as she inhales, and then she's arching into my hands. *Fuck, yeah.*

I continue to tease her nipples as she rides me, the movements of her hips becoming more insistent, more demanding, and I'm so ready to go. When she cries out and her body stiffens, I can't hold on anymore. With a fluid movement, I've got her on her back, and I'm driving into her convulsing body. She hikes her legs up my hips, opening further, and her heels dig into my ass, sending me over the edge.

I spill into her with a shout, her body still softly pulsing and her hard nipples rasping against my chest. Everything about it, her in my arms, my body inside her, fills me with a kind of rightness I've never felt. It's the sort of out-of-body experience that I've heard described, but I've always thought was just bullshit spouted by overly romantic jackasses.

Who's the jackass now?

Still panting, I gather her against me and roll off her so she can breathe again. She curls against me, and I pull the sheets over us, holding her as we nod off to sleep.

Cord

WE WAKE AGAIN IN the night, hands seeking each other. But the sun comes up much faster than I would have liked. Hannah already planned to skip her Tuesday eight o'clock, but she wanted to get to her eleven o'clock. So at nine, I stumble out of bed, drop a kiss on her sleepy mouth, and trudge into the bathroom for a shower.

As I soap up, a grin plays over my lips as I replay our middle-of-the-night escapades. We tried a couple of different positions that time, ending with doggie style. Hannah's ass was luscious, and I'd leaned over her, fingering her clit while she held onto the bed frame…My cock wakes up, and I quietly curse myself. If we had more time, I would climb back in bed with her. I've been inside her twice, but now because I know, I crave her even more.

A soft knock at the door interrupts me. "Yeah?" I call.

Hannah steps inside, still naked. "I was wondering if you might want some company."

"Absolutely." I slide the shower door open, letting her in. I duck her under the water and proceed to make a huge deal out of soaping her up. After the slide of the soap on her skin, we're frantic. No condom in the shower, so we rinse off and stumble out, hands and mouths searching as we hustle back into the bedroom.

We're barely on the bed when I'm ripping open the last condom I've got. She hurries me, fingers in my back, and when I push inside her, both of us call out.

What comes next is fast and carnal, wild. When it's over, it's as if the air sweeps out of the room.

I hold her, still panting, aware that something is different now. I help her up, kissing her, but her expression is almost sad. Pulling back, I ask, "What's up?"

She shrugs, reaching for her bag and pulling out her clothes. We silently dress, but as she grabs a comb and slowly pulls it through her hair, I capture her hand, forcing her to look at me. "Talk to me, please."

She sighs. "We're going home today."

"Yeah?" I'm not sure where this is going.

"When we get back, we'll be back."

"That's how it usually works, Marshall." I tug on a lock of her wet hair.

"No, I mean this is supposed to be fake. Except now, we've slept together. That's something." Her eyes are everywhere in the room except on me. I can feel her panic, and foreboding seeps through me. Whatever I say next is going to be important. This is some sort of define-our-fake-or-real-relationship shit, but I don't exactly know what she wants me to say, and if I say the wrong thing, I get the impression I'm going to scare her away.

Which is why I don't do something stupid like bust out the *L* word.

My brain searches for the way to soothe her, to fix this, whatever is going through her head. "We don't need to do this right now, Hannah," I offer. "We are what we are, right?"

She crinkles her nose up. "I guess…"

"I mean, I like spending time with you," I explain. "In bed and out of it. Do you?"*Oh God, please say yes…*

"Of course."

I'm almost weak with relief. "Then let's just see how it goes. We can hang out like we have been, and we can sleep together. If you want to." My throat tightens even as I consider the possibility that she might not, sometime in the near future, want to. For me, last night changed everything. The playoffs, New Jersey, the future…I have no idea what will happen with all that. But Hannah is the one clear and true thing I want to stay exactly the same.

She swallows, and I rub my hands along her arms, even as all I want to do is pull her in my arms. I don't, though, instead holding my breath, waiting for her and praying that she isn't ready to give us up yet either.

Finally, after the longest moments in my life, she nods. "Sounds good."

I drop a kiss on her mouth, breathing her in, all the terror of a moment ago leaking away. My eyes close, and I pull her against me, glad to have this reprieve. Because more time with her means more time to convince her that we could be something great, something real, if she can give us a chance.

Hannah

THE WEEK THAT FOLLOWS is incredible. Cord and I spend every spare second together. He's busy preparing for playoffs, but when he's not at the rink or working out, he's at my place or I'm at his. I can't tell whether he's nervous about playoffs or not, but I do know that the increasing phone calls from his father are setting him on edge.

The team leaves for Pittsburgh on Tuesday morning. Their first game will be Thursday night, and Cord insisted on buying me a plane ticket out of Scranton to get there. I do my best to convince myself that I'm not going to miss him, but when I show up for Dr. Pierce's class and Cord isn't there, it hits me like a gut punch.

This emptiness without him isn't good, and it doesn't bode well for the future. He hasn't even been gone for twenty-four hours.

As usual, I'm a few minutes early, and there's hardly anyone there. I drop my things by the piano and try to shake off how much I miss him.

Dr. Pierce interrupts my pity party. "Hannah. I'd like to speak with you for a moment."

I force a smile. "Good morning, professor. Sure. What can I do for you?"

He retrieves his phone from his pocket then slides it across the piano. There I am, onstage in New York. "Is this you?"

"Dr. Pierce…" I don't know what I'm going to say.

"Hannah, this is wonderful." He skims his finger to move forward in the recording until it reaches the part where I sing one of my original pieces. "Is this something you wrote?"

"Yes, sir." I hug my arm across my stomach.

"The lyrics as well?"

I nod. "Yes. They're mine too."

"Hannah, I knew you said you were singing, but this"—he points at the phone—"this is astounding."

I laugh. "As long as it pays for graduate school, that's all I care about." My smile fades as I think about the declined applications for funding I received earlier this week. I still have a few more requests outstanding, but the chances that I'll be awarded scholarship money dwindle by the day.

He studies me like I don't make any sense to him. "You look…*happy* in this video, Hannah. I haven't seen that much joy from one of your performances in a long time." He shakes his head. "Don't you enjoy this?"

I shift in my seat. "Of course." I shrug. "It's fun."

"That's all it is?" He gently pushes the phone toward me. I glance down at the video still playing. He steps back to answer another student's question, leaving me with the video.

I've watched my performances before. A couple times, they've ended up on the internet, but this one is different. Whoever captured this must have been close to the stage, because I'm there, front and center.

Maybe for the first time ever, I really watch the performance. I pretend that the girl on the screen isn't me. She's some other singer up on that stage.

And she looks…alive. Happy, even.

When the video is over, I turn the phone over to hide the screen. Pierce has gotten distracted with students asking about midterm scores, so he leaves me to my thoughts behind the piano. He wanders by, pocketing his phone as he starts class a few minutes late.

I play the songs he asks for, but my mind isn't on music theory. Instead, I think about that girl with all that energy and emotion, on that stage in New York.

Of course I know that I like singing. I don't think I let myself consider that I like it as much as the video suggests.

Class winds on until I'm packing up my things to leave. Dr. Pierce gets bombarded by students looking for extra credit, and I sneak out the back so I don't have to answer more questions.

In the lobby, I duck pedestrian traffic and dig out my phone. Skimming through the videos, I find one of me performing in the fall. It was for a charity holiday concert, and I played the piano. I look serene and happy, too, I guess, but it's different.

Closing the video, I drop down into one of the cushy seats in the lobby. Everyone's moving between classes, so they're not paying attention to me. I take a minute to think back on how I felt—first at the charity concert and then at the Zealots performance.

The experiences are completely different. When I play piano, especially classical piano, it's like the ocean. The energy of the music ebbs and flows through my fingers and out of the instrument. Singing, especially the kind of singing I've been doing is raw, full of my emotion.

What does that mean, though? And why do I feel like I need to choose between them? I can have both things, can't I?

I don't know. But I know that I love singing, and right now, it's paying the bills. I'm going to keep going with it until I can't anymore.

Ronnie Brandon hasn't returned my calls since I sang with the Zealots except to leave a rambling message about how Milo Parker thinks he's so high and mighty to yell at him about security. I don't have time for his hurt feelings, though.

I'm going to call Sebastian and ask him to put me in touch with Milo. I should have cut ties with Ronnie months ago. I don't know why I held on to him so long. Probably because I didn't want to admit how serious I am about my singing.

But I am serious. It's time to stop pretending I'm not.

Cord

"YOU TALKED WITH NEW Jersey." It surprises me that it's taken my dad this long to bring it up. He got into Pittsburgh last night and went twenty-four hours without saying anything. It might be a new record.

"I did."

"How did that go? Harry said that they're interested in signing you for defense." My father doesn't bother hiding his disapproval.

"Yes." I sip my iced tea. I knew we would have to address this. A part of me hoped that my father hadn't heard about the meeting, but that was foolish. He and Harry talk all the time.

"When I spoke with Harry, he said that he thought it would be a good fit for you." My father's shrewd gaze penetrates me. "Do you believe that as well?"

"I wouldn't have taken the meeting if I didn't." The response is too defensive, so I inhale a calming breath and try again. "After Linc got hurt in the fall, I enjoyed playing defense. It wasn't just about being captain for me. But they haven't offered anything yet."

"There's nothing wrong with being versatile. I just would hate for them to split your focus. It's hard for new players to find their place. I don't want you to get lost."

I'm not sure what that means, but I bite my tongue. I don't want to engage and drag this conversation out longer than necessary. When I don't respond, my father nods as if he's won the round. Everything with him is a competition, after all, and like me, he hates to lose. I continue to grit my teeth, waiting.

Luckily, at that moment, the waiter comes with our food, and we're one step closer to this dinner being over.

Reaching for my knife and fork, I dig into my steak. At least the food here is good.

When the waiter leaves, my father stares at me. "Harry told me that you're seeing someone new."

I swallow, the delicious food suddenly dry in my mouth. "Harry should shut his fucking mouth."

My father glances around us, glaring at me over his glass of wine. "Conrad, watch your mouth."

I roll my eyes at my father's use of my full name. No one is listening. There aren't eavesdroppers hiding in the trendy decor at Altius in Pittsburgh. In fact, from what I know about Pittsburgh, people here stay out of one another's personal business.

We eat in silence for a few minutes as tension fills the air between us. Finally, when I'm done, I set down my utensils and napkin. "Hannah isn't your business." I've been saying for the last year that my personal life is, well, personal, but it's been an uphill climb. It didn't matter as much until now. I know he worries about me. I'm an only child, and he doesn't have anyone else. But the attention is intrusive.

My father studies me. "Please. Tell me about her."

I sigh. "She's beautiful. Talented. A musician. She plays the piano and the guitar, but her voice is spectacular. She opened a couple of weeks ago for an up-and-coming rock band, the Dazed Zealots." I can't help the pride in my voice. "She's been accepted to graduate school next year."

"A singer?" He raises his brows.

I really hope that he'll give her a chance. But as I stare at him, I'm not sure he will, and I realize that I don't really care what he thinks of her. "I'd like you to be courteous to her tomorrow. That's all I'm asking."

"Of course. When haven't I been courteous to someone?" I don't even respond, only narrow my eyes at him. "I'm sure she's lovely. After all, I liked Rachel, and you picked her."

"She's nothing like Rachel." Hannah is my ex-girlfriend's polar opposite.

"Isn't she?" My father raises his brows. "Rachel is smart, beautiful, poised. Your new friend isn't any of those things?"

"She's those things." I shake my head at him, hating how he's trying to goad me. "She's just different than Rachel. She's genuine. Not fake. She'd never treat me the way Rachel did."

He folds his hands in front of him. "I think that was a misunderstanding."

"She slept with another guy, Dad," I grit out. "It was on the blogs, in the tabloids."

The look he gives me is almost piteous. "It was over the summertime. You hadn't seen her in a while. She was traveling. You were training. You're not married yet, and things can happen."

I narrow my eyes at him. "Things don't just happen. People do them to other people, and they hurt people who care about them." I force myself to take a deep breath. "I understand that things went bad with you and Mom, but that's not the life I want for myself. I don't want to always be wondering if someone is lying to me."

"This is a demanding life. You'll be on the road all the time. Do you think that is going to be easy?"

"Is that what you told Mom?" We don't talk about my parents' relationship, but if he's involving himself in mine, quid pro quo.

"I should never have thought I'd make her happy in the first place." For the first time in a long time, I see pain flash across my father's face. "I should have seen that there would be no way she'd be happy with the lifestyle. All the time away, all the time alone. She was miserable." He inhales a steadying breath. "She wanted a nine-to-five husband, someone home for dinner every night. Hell, someone in her bed every night. That's not what being a hockey player is like, son."

I soften my tone. "I'm really sorry that things ended for you guys. I know it was hard. But you're going to have to let me find my own way, Dad."

"I know."He narrows his eyes. "And if that means it's not with Rachel, that's fine. But you only just met this girl. How much do you know about her?"

"I know enough."

"Say you stay with her. She's going to graduate school while you head off to your professional career. Maybe it's in New Jersey, maybe not. You think that'll be easy on either of you? Or worse, if she's as talented as you say, then she'll be traveling as much or more than you will." He sighs. "Just…be careful with girls who aren't familiar with this life. I don't want to see you get hurt."

The conversation turns to other things. As we wait for the valet to bring the car, I check my phone. There's a missed call from Hannah. I want to hear her voice right away, but I wait until my father drops me off at the hotel and is pulling away to dial her back.

When she answers, I smile. “Hey, you.”

“Cord.” I love the way she says my name. “I realized after I called that you were at dinner with your dad.”

“No big deal. We’re finished.”

“How was it?”

“Fine.” I don’t really want to talk about it, so I change the subject. “I can’t wait to see you tomorrow.”

She’s driving out for the game tomorrow. With any luck, we’ll make it to the next round, and she can stay through the weekend. I tried to get her to come with me, but she insisted on staying to finish classes. I don’t believe for a moment that her grades would suffer, but I admire her dedication.

Her car, though… I tried to get her to take mine, but she said she didn’t feel comfortable driving it. I insisted that I didn’t feel comfortable with the reliability of hers. She threw back that I was the one who’d gotten it fixed in the first place, and I gave up the argument. But damn it, I would wrap her in bubble wrap if I could.

The next pause unsettles my stomach. “That’s why I need to talk to you.” She inhales. I can almost hear her worrying her lip. “The Zealots want me for another gig.”

“When? That’s great.” It’s only a matter of time before she’s a huge star. I don’t know what’s going to happen with my own career, but I have only faith in Hannah.

“It is. Thanks.” She pauses. “Except it’s really short notice. Friday night.”

“If we win…” Talking about winning makes me uncomfortable. If we win tomorrow night, then the final game will be on Saturday evening.

She exhales. “I know.”

I rub my face, my stomach already clenched. She’s not going to come. I can feel it.

The end of playoffs has loomed as the predetermined official end of our relationship, except neither of us has mentioned it. *Is this her way of telling me that she’s ready to call it quits now?* I might throw up.

She hurries on. “So I’m not going to be there Friday. I’ll be back on Saturday, after the concert. I’ll sleep and then be back in Pittsburgh.” She hurries on. “I know you don’t like my car, but I’m telling you, Cherry can make it. And I know you were hoping to take me sightseeing with your dad on Friday. Some inclined plane or something. But I really want to do this gig…”

Relief courses through me. She’s still coming. Thank God. I cut her off. “Absolutely not.”

She pauses. “You can’t tell me what to do.”

I give a side-eye that she doesn’t see, since she’s on the phone. “I mean, there’s no way you’re driving all that. I’m going to fly you out. And then back. And then back out.”

“What? No. That’s too much.”

I keep talking like she didn’t say anything. “I’m going to get you some plane tickets. You’ll fly here tomorrow. I’ll get you here, to the hotel. Then I’ll fly you back home on Friday. Saturday morning, assuming we win…”

“You will.” Her voice is full of certainty. It makes me smile.

“Assuming we win,” I repeat, “I’ll fly you back on Saturday.” It’s a lot of traveling for her, but I need her here.

“Cord…”

“I mean it. There’s no way you’re driving Cherry.” I can’t believe I’m calling her beat-ass car by the name she gave it.

"She's not making it across Pennsylvania twice. Even if she does, do you really want to do that to the poor old thing?" Things have gotten ridiculous. I don't care about the cost, and I don't care about the delay. I only want Hannah here, whatever it takes.

She laughs. "I mean, no…"

"That's right. Think of her, Marshall. It's better for Cherry this way." I'm playful, but under all that, I'm desperate. She can't miss the game, and there's no way I'm letting her do all that just to be here.

"Fine." She chuckles. "No, not fine. Thank you. I will drive, I swear. I only was worried you'd be upset…that I was driving…which is ridiculous. Because we're not really…" Her voice trails off.

This is a conversation that is too serious and too much for her. I know how I feel about her, but she's not there yet. "You want the plane ride or not, Marshall?" I ask, cutting off whatever overthinking she's probably doing right now.

"I do. Sign me up."

I laugh. "I'll text you details when I'm in my room." I stand there smiling like a lovesick fool, which is fair. "I'm serious, though. I'm excited to see you tomorrow, baby." It's as close to a declaration of affection as I'm sure she's ready for.

Finally, she says, "Me, too, Cord."

I close my eyes on the words. "Goodnight, baby girl."

"Goodnight," she says and disconnects.

I grin, pocket my phone, and head upstairs.

Hannah

THE FLIGHT CORD BOOKS for me gets in mid-afternoon. Since he's already at the rink, preparing for the game, his father offers to pick me up, so I don't have to wait for an Uber. When Cord called to tell me, I could almost feel his worry. I can count the things I know about his father on one hand. He was a professional hockey player. He and Rachel's dad are friends. He sounds overbearing. Beyond that, there's not much.

I didn't check bags, so as soon as I'm off the plane, I head toward the exit.

At the terminal, I immediately recognize Cord's father. He looks exactly how I expect Cord will look in thirty years. Tall, handsome with some gray hair and more wrinkles, but he has the same build. He's holding a sign with my name on it, so I head toward him, my hand out. "Mr. Spellman? I'm Hannah Marshall."

He smiles, but it's not Cord's smile. It's slicker and less genuine but still charming. "Hannah. It's nice to meet you. I've heard so much about you."

I'm not sure if that's true, but I nod. "You, too, sir."

"Please, call me Jon."

"All right." I have no intention of calling him that.

"I'm parked this way. Is that all you brought?" He eyes my carry-on duffel bag.

"Yes." *Should I have packed more? I'll be flying around, back and forth from home over the next couple of days. How much stuff do I need?*

He holds his hand out.

"Oh, I can carry it."

If I planned to argue, the stare he gives me would have changed my mind. I give him the bag, smothering my grin. I guess Cord got his need to carry everything from his father.

He motions me ahead of him, and again, the resemblance between them is uncanny. I march forward as if I know where I'm going, knowing that he will tell me when we get to the car.

Exactly like his son, he guides me through the parking garage, stopping behind what I assume is a rental. It's a Mercedes, but the plates say Pennsylvania, and he lives in Tennessee.

After he stows my bag in the trunk, he opens my door and coaxes me in. A few minutes later, we're on the highway.

"So, tell me, Hannah. How did you meet my son?"

I worry my lip with my teeth, thinking about Mikey Dischenski barfing in my car. "I'm the teaching assistant in his music class." That's not exactly a lie…

"He told me you're a musician."

"Yes." I resist the urge to call him "sir." "I play classical piano and guitar and dabble in a handful of other instruments."

He nods, his eyes still on the road. "And you sing. My son says you opened recently for a popular rock band."

"I did. I'm supposed to sing before their show tomorrow night as well, which is why Cord flew me here." I get the feeling he knows this already.

"I'm glad we could get you here. It would have been a shame for you to miss it." The "we" gives me pause.

"I wouldn't have missed it. I just would have been driving a lot."

We go through a tunnel, and I study him in the flashing from the running lights. I'm not naïve, and I've been watching people for a long time. He has something to say, so I wait for him to get to the point.

"You grew up in Chesterboro, didn't you?"

"Yes." I cock my head. "Did Cord tell you that?" I'm wondering how that would have come up in conversation.

"No, actually, he didn't." He pauses, gripping the steering wheel. "I had a friend look into you."

"A friend?"

He pauses and then continues, ignoring my question. "My son will be signing a contract with a national league team this summer. I needed to make sure you weren't looking for a free ride."

"Does Cord know you looked into me?" He hesitates, confirming what I suspect. Cord would be pissed. I cross my arms over my chest. "What did you learn?" I brace myself.

He stares out the windshield as we come out of the tunnel. "Your father managed a lumber yard. There were allegations of fraud and money laundering. He committed suicide." He stops, casting a glance at me as if needing confirmation. I nod stiffly, and he continues. "Your mother has had a few run-ins with the authorities. No other relatives."

My family history sounds bleak when he describes it. I didn't even know about my mother's record, but I'm not surprised. Still, it doesn't require a response, so I only nod.

"You're at Chesterboro on a scholarship and financial assistance. You'll graduate in May, magna cum laude with a double major in music and business. You work at a truck stop, on campus, and you sing." He waves his hand. "You're regularly behind on your bills, and you're two months late on your land lease."

"One month," I clarify. I've been a month late for as long as I can remember.

"Ah." He twists his hands on the steering wheel. "In a few months, my son will be in the NHL. He'll either sign on with New Jersey, or he'll sign somewhere else."

I understand the pride in his voice even while the full weight of what he's trying to say hits me in the stomach. "And you don't want anything to interfere with your son's future."

"Exactly." His mouth firms. "He's worked very hard for a very long time. I only hope you're aware of what's at stake for him. Now isn't the time for him to rock the boat."

"I understand." And I do. In fact, if I were an unbiased observer, his concerns would appear reasonable. After all the years supporting Cord, he doesn't want to watch a girl he's only just met derail him or bring any whiff of scandal at such a pivotal point in his career.

Didn't I think the same exact things when we agreed to our fake dating arrangement? I knew that I wasn't the kind of girl for him. That was why we agreed on the playoffs as our end date. He would go on to the NHL, I would go to grad school, and that would be it. Except the looming deadline just a few days from now fills me with dread.

Regardless, I knew all of this from the beginning. But for some reason, over the past week or so, it hasn't been at the front of my mind. This is a good reminder.

“You don’t have to worry, Mr. Spellman. I won’t do anything to hold Cord back.” I won’t. He deserves the best. But until Cord is ready to move on, I’m going to spend whatever time he is willing to give me with him, even if his father doesn’t approve.

“Thank you.” He smiles at me. “And Jon. Please.”

“Right.” I stare out the window for the rest of the trip to the hotel.

Hannah

OUR CHESTERBORO BULLDOGS BEAT their opponent, three to two. Even though it was a physical game, the Bulldogs stayed up the entire time and advanced to the finals easily. After the game, the excitement in the hotel is palpable.

The hockey team takes up an entire floor, so the place looks like a fraternity house party when we get off the elevator, except without the beer. There's no drinking this close to the end. Instead, the guys are bouncing off the walls, in various states of undress after or before showers. I can feel the energy. I'm thrilled for them. Cord asks if I want to stay for takeout, but I decline. He needs to be with his team, so I head back to my room. He promises to come visit after his shower and some food.

There's a McDonald's on the other side of the parking lot, so I run over there then take my food back to my room. I spend the next couple hours doing a few assignments that I need to turn in while I'm running around this week.

At close to eleven, there's a soft knock on my door. I close the lid on my computer with a smack and bound off the bed. I shouldn't be this eager to see Cord, but I am. The conversation with his dad earlier reminded me that our time is limited. Still, I can't help myself from relishing every moment with him.

I open the door, and he sweeps me up into a hug and spins me around. The door bangs shut behind him, and I laugh.

"We're in the finals, baby!" He buries his face in my neck, raining kisses there that light me on fire. By the time he sets me on my feet and drops his mouth to mine, I'm curling into him. The kiss doesn't go on forever, because he steps away, pumps his fist in the air, and whoops. I can only laugh. I'd expected him to be less excited by now, but he's still riding the high.

"Congratulations," I say. "I'm so proud of you." I mean it. He's worked hard, and it's fun to watch him achieve his goals.

He hugs me then plops on the bed, falling back. "What a rush."

I drop beside him and flop down, too, wiggling into his side. "I bet. You played great." He did. He had a power-play goal and two assists. On the ice, he is in his element. He shines, full of confidence. *Maybe that's how I look onstage…*

"Thanks." He lifts onto his elbow to stare down at me. "And thank you for being there."

"I wouldn't miss it for anything." It's true. I would have driven back and forth if I needed to. As far as I'm concerned, Cord is mine until he isn't.

He tucks a piece of my hair behind my ear. "I'm bummed you won't be here tomorrow. My dad was going to take us to the inclined planes."

I want to say that his father isn't going to be upset I'm not around, but I smile instead. "I'm sorry I'll miss it too. But I'll be on the way back to you on Saturday for the final game."

"I know." He leans forward and kisses me softly. "You're my good-luck charm."

It's cheesy and charming. I've never been anyone's good-luck anything. But like everything else in our relationship, I choose to believe it for that moment. Right now, with his lips on mine and my body curled against him, I feel lucky. So I fall into him, pulling him closer.

What starts as a lazy kiss becomes hasty undressing. We pull apart so I can tug his jersey over my head and he can drag his hoodie over his. Then we're back together, falling on the bed again.

I'm laughing, but then he's kissing me again, and then I'm sighing into his mouth. We're all touching and gasping. I can't taste him enough or feel enough of his skin. His scent is in my head, the sound of his groans in my ears. When he thrusts inside me, I sigh, running my hands along his back and shoulders, staring up at him. His hair falls over his forehead, and his eyes close as he starts our rhythm. I hold him closer with my legs, my heels digging into his back, not wanting to let him go.

Our movements become frantic, and his eyes find mine. Shifting his weight, his thumb finds my clit, and after a few of the softest, most aching rubs, I'm flying over the edge, crying out his name. He tilts his head back and plunges further inside me, shouting his own release.

When we're calm, he gathers me against him, and we curl up together.

Neither of us says anything for long minutes. Finally, I ask, "Do you need to get back to your room tonight?" It's late, well after midnight, but I'm not sure if he needs to check in with the coach or his team or something.

“No one will notice I’m gone tonight. I saw a few other guys sneaking out too. Everyone else is playing Xbox.” He grins. “I can stay until morning.”

The relief that courses through me is dangerous, but I can’t pretend I don’t want him here or away from me ever, to be honest. That’s a pain I’ll have to deal with later. Right now, though… “Then how about another shower?”

He winks at me. “I’m not sure the one I took after the game did a good enough job.”

“I should check,” I reply solemnly.

He grabs my hand and pulls me toward the bathroom without another word.

Cord

I DRIVE HANNAH TO the airport the next morning. She insists she can get an Uber if I have stuff to do, and I do—I'm missing breakfast with the team—but I refuse. It's bad enough that I'm going to be without her for the day and that I'll miss her show in New York tonight. I don't plan to miss out on whatever time I have with her.

I realize that if we're going to make this work, there are going to be a lot more times like this in the future. My father is right about that—we're going to be apart often. That makes me nervous. Or maybe it's only that being away from her feels so wrong. Either way, I realize I am going to need to get used to the idea but not right now.

It's about a twenty-five-minute drive, so we chat about what my plans are for the day—sightseeing with my father—and what hers are—a flight to Scranton then a bus to New York. She's playing a different venue this time, somewhere downtown. She tells me she's worried about the original songs she's worked on and plans to perform. I ask her to have someone film it so I can watch later. She says she will, squeezing my hand, her eyes so soft that I wonder if we can find somewhere private for a few minutes before her plane leaves.

Except we don't. I pull up to departures at the Pittsburgh airport and hit the hazards. She doesn't even complain anymore when I head to the trunk to get her bag then carry it as far as I can for her to the door. I haven't even set it down when she jumps into my arms, pulling me to her in the tightest hug.

"What's up, baby girl?" I ask, but my voice is husky. It's not often that she's the one who instigates public affection, and it touches me.

She squeezes me close then kisses my cheek before pulling back. Maybe I'm crazy, but I swear her eyes are watery. "I'll see you tomorrow."

"You're going to text me right before your flight leaves, right? Then again when it lands. Then again when you get to your place. Then again when you're on the train…" I make a winding motion with my finger. "Get the idea? I love to hear what you're doing. All the time, anytime."

"You're going to be busy, Cord," she laughs. "I'm not going to keep bugging you."

"I'm asking you." I pull her close, kissing her lips. "Please, baby. Tell me everything. Even the smallest, silliest things. I can't wait to hear about it." I kiss her again. Her hair is flying around her, so I smooth it down, cupping her face. "You're going to kill it tonight."

The words I want to tell her are right on my lips. I don't want to be away from her. I love her. I'm so proud. But instead, I just hold her gaze, hoping she can see and that sometime soon, I'll be able to say them and not scare her away.

"Thanks." She swallows. "I…" She stops whatever she's about to say, and I hold my breath. "That means a lot to me."

“No problem.” I step back, even though I don’t want to, and pull her jacket closer around her. It’s really chilly here. I guess Pittsburgh didn’t get the memo that it’s spring. “Now, get going. You don’t want to be rushing.”

“I’ll text you after I’m through security.”

“Hell, text me in the security line.”

She laughs. “You’ll be driving back.”

“I’ll be happy to read it when I get to the hotel.”

She shakes her head, gets up on tiptoes, and kisses me once more. We both know it’s the last one, so our lips linger. Finally, she pulls away, and I hand her her duffel. She waves as she walks away, and I smack her butt. “Safe flight, baby.”

I say it louder than I have to because I know she hates it. Sure enough, she turns back to glare at me. “Don’t call me baby.”

“You don’t mean that.” I wink at her.

She drops the glare, grinning. “You’re right. I don’t.”

I chuckle as she heads through the revolving door and away from me. I can’t help it—I watch her from the sidewalk as she walks toward check-in, and I don’t leave until she’s out of my sight.

I already miss her.

Hannah

BEFORE MY CONCERT, I go out to dinner with Sebastian, Libby, and Milo Parker. Since I fired Ronnie, I'm without a manager. While Ronnie might have been able to sign me with local places, he would never have the reach Milo has or the connections with record labels and producers. I officially sign my contract to be represented by him over dessert.

The concert is the best yet. The Zealots introduce me as Goldie, which I like. I get home just before dawn. After my flight earlier in the day and then the commute into the city, the concert, and the commute home, I'm exhausted and fall into bed.

I probably could have slept until eleven, when I need to head to the airport to catch my flight back to Pittsburgh. But my phone wakes me at seven o'clock. I don't answer it because I don't recognize the number. Whoever it is leaves a voicemail. Thinking it might be Cord from Pittsburgh and that he might be calling from the hotel for some reason, I yank my phone off the nightstand and listen to the message.

My mother's voice, full of tears, comes out of the speaker. "Sweetheart, I need your help. I'm in a lot of trouble. I got arrested, and I don't have the money for bail. I can't find anyone else to cover me. Please, come to the courthouse and help me out." She rattles off the address of a courthouse outside of Philadelphia. There is a pause on the line, and though it's been a long time since my mother sounded like herself, her next words give me a hit of nostalgia I didn't think I could feel anymore. "I know I've been messed up for some time, but this is the end. Please, I know I've let you down, but if you'll help me, I promise…" The message cuts off.

I sit up in bed and listen to the message again. Once it's finished, I can only stare at my phone, my groggy mind catching up.

Arrested? Not that I'm that surprised. Cord's father had insinuated she's had difficulty with the law. She's been lost for a long time, but I always assumed it was only drugs and alcohol.

This message gives me no details except the address of some justice center in Philadelphia, where I can post bail. If she's calling from jail, then I assume I won't be able to call her back. But driving all the way to Philadelphia is a no-go. It's at least two hours away, and I am supposed to catch a plane to Pittsburgh out of Wilkes-Barre Scranton at lunchtime.

A part of me wants to ignore the message, at least for the day. I could let her sit in jail and deal with the problem tomorrow. But shame licks on the tail of that reaction. She is my mother. I don't know what happened. Maybe it's a wrong-place-wrong-time situation. I don't know, so I can't abandon her when she needs help. Maybe she's being honest and this is the time she gets herself together. Either way, it's not too much to ask to bail her out.

Besides, if she called me, it was the last resort. She might hit me up for money sometimes, for rent, to buy food, or to pay for a fix, but never for bail money. She would've gone to someone else, if there was someone else, especially since this isn’t her first offense, and I didn't know anything about the other times.

I’m not sure I can help her, though, and still be there for Cord tonight. Because I won’t let him down. Not for my mom. Not for anything.

I check the time. Just after seven. If I can get to the courthouse by nine or nine-thirty, I should be able to get done by noon at the latest. If I can switch my flight to a little later or fly out of Philadelphia instead of Scranton, I should be able to do it all.

I fling the covers off and hop out of bed, wide awake. I let my computer start up as I grab a quick shower. When I’m back at my desk, I manage to exchange my flight for one a few hours later in Philadelphia, with the help of a pretty hefty fee. Then I quickly repack my stuff for the night, and I’m out the door by eight-thirty.

On my way to Philadelphia, I call Cord. It goes to voicemail, so I give him a vague excuse and apologize that I’ll be behind schedule. I don’t say much, and I definitely don’t talk about my mother. There’s no way for me to explain. I bet he’s never even imagined a reality where he’s bailing one of his parents out of jail.

I get to the criminal justice center at a quarter after eleven. It takes me many needed minutes to find where I need to go to post bail for my mother. Finally, I get to the person who can collect the bail. The number she gives me is astronomical.

“That’s so high.” I’m already mourning the hit to my savings. “Are you sure?”

“It says here that she’s being held on prostitution charges.”

"Prostitution," I repeat. That can't be. My mother…

"Her second offense. She's facing charges that could result in significant jail time and a hefty fine." The clerk behind the glass sounds bored. This sort of conversation is probably a daily occurrence for her. For me, it's devastating.

"I see." I really don't, but she doesn't need my sob story. "How can I pay for that?"

"We accept cash or cashier's check."

"Of course. Thank you."

I step away from the window and pull out my phone. I need to find a bank or a post office or something. Somewhere to get a cashier's check…

"Miss Marshall." My name surprises me, and I glance up. The man in front of me is nondescript. Average height, brown hair, glasses. But his eyes are sharp.

"Yes?" How does he know my name?

"I'm Calvin Weaver." He reaches into his pocket and removes a card, holding it out to me. "I'm a partner of the private investigations firm, Weaver and Taylor."

I take the card even as my mind is spinning. "A private investigator?"

"I've been employed to find out what I can about your mother."

Quickly, I pull apart the ways that a private investigator who knows my name could be here, looking into my mother. "Mr. Spellman."

Weaver nods. "He contracted my firm, yes. I wouldn't usually disclose that information, but he wished for me to speak with you if you showed up here."

"So you were following me?" *Isn't that against the law?*

"No. My partner was here last night, actually. He'd been following her when she got arrested. He made Mr. Spellman aware of your mother's predicament. I took over for him today." He buries his hands in his pockets and appears resigned to how unsavory that sounds. "Mr. Spellman said that if you showed up here, I should talk to you. It's not usually part of my job, but…" He shrugs.

I'd imagine Spellman offered him quite a bit of money to approach me. "So, what do you want?"

"Mr. Spellman would like me to tell you that he's willing to help your mother out of this." I snort, but he keeps going. "He is willing to speak with the judge on your mother's behalf."

"The judge?" I laugh. "How's he going to do that?"

"There are a few politicians he's willing to call. He believes that your mother doesn't belong in jail. Instead, he thinks that she would be better served with probation and an extended stay in a rehabilitation facility." He pulls a trifold pamphlet from his pocket and holds it out to me. "A rehabilitation facility in central Pennsylvania has agreed to hold a space for her." I take the brochure for Shooting Star Acres. A huge white Victorian with fields of grass behind it graces the front. A stream looks like it meanders past the facility. It's gorgeous.

"Is that so?" The possibility of rehab for Mom is more than I could ever ask. But when things sound too good to be true, there's usually a catch. "What does Mr. Spellman need in return? I assume he's not doing this out of the kindness of his heart."

"He asks that you leave his son alone. If you do, he's willing to give you a significant amount of money." He names a huge figure. It's enough to buy a house or pay for graduate school.

"Is this a joke?" There are numbers printed on the back of the paper, figures for outpatient and inpatient care. The one for a four-week stay at this place would wipe out the thousands of dollars that I've saved toward graduate school and then some.

"No."

I stare at the brochure in my hand.

"Just think of the possibilities, Miss Marshall. With that money, you could get your mom the help she needs and go to graduate school, like you've always wanted. We know you're struggling to find a way to finance it. This could change that for you." I glance up. Of course he knows all about me. It's his job. If his face held any contempt, I would have been able to work up anger or disgust. Instead, there's only sympathy. "You've worked really hard, Hannah. This could be the answer to all your problems."

Except it would mean the end of my relationship with Cord. "I don't need your pity." I hitch up my chin, hating how my eyes are burning.

"It's not pity." He sighs. "Why don't I give you a few minutes?"

I nod because I need him to get away from me. He starts to walk away before stopping to say, "Oh, and Spellman says there's no deal if you tell his son about any of this." He glances at the courthouse behind us, shakes his head, then heads toward the food cart on the corner.

I'm left to struggle with an ultimatum that could change everything.

How dare Cord's father involve himself in my life and make judgments about me and my family? What gives him the right to do this to me?

I crumble up the pamphlet in my hand and walk farther down the block, out of Weaver's sight. When I've got some breathing space, I sit on a wall behind the building.

Cord's father wants me out of his son's life. Apparently, he thinks that it's worth a significant amount of money. *Why couldn't he just glare at me or make passive-aggressive comments like normal people did when they didn't approve of who their kid was dating?*

Because Cord isn't just a normal guy, and this definitely proves that his dad doesn't think I'm good enough for him.

It's not up to him, though. If I've learned anything, it's that I need to fight to stand on my own, and I won't fold to someone else now. I've known that things aren't going to last with Cord. But it'll be our choice, not anyone else's.

I'm not the kind of person to be bought.

I tuck the pamphlet into my jacket pocket and set Mr. Weaver and Cord's obnoxious father aside.

Right now, my biggest concern is my mother. If I don't pay for her bail, she'll likely sit in jail until her trial, whenever that will be. I've read stories about people who find themselves and get their lives together in jail. But I don't see that happening with her, and I don't know what comes next. She might be a mess, but she's still mine.

I have the money to bail her out, but it puts a huge hit on my savings, and she'll still be facing fines and jail time. Fighting charges costs money for attorneys, money I won't have if I use it to bail her out. I might be able to find a public defender to take her case, but I don't know any.

Besides, if I get her out today, I don't trust that she won't skip out on me or relapse.

Shame sweeps through me at the uncharitable thoughts about my own mother, but I push it aside. People with money can afford to be idealistic. I need to be pragmatic.

For now, she's as safe as I can keep her—incarcerated. I head back inside.

The clerk tells me that her first hearing will be in a few days. I leave my contact information. I can call around on Monday to find legal help.

Back outside, I spot Mr. Weaver standing near a tree, eating a hot dog. I approach him, my hands in my pockets. "Please tell Mr. Spellman to mind his own business."

Weaver grins at me. "Will do. Not sure he's good at that, though."

"Obviously." I snort. I get the feeling that Mr. Weaver might not be that bad. He seems like a regular guy just trying to do his job.

I leave him there and head to the parking lot to get my car. Twenty bucks to park is a huge rip-off, but I didn't have time to find off-street parking.

It's only one o'clock. Plenty of time to get to the airport for my three o'clock flight.

Cord

AT TWO O'CLOCK, HANNAH calls me from the airport. Not wanting to be late, I'm already dressed and ready to get on the bus to go to the arena. Except I'm too early, so her call is the best kind of distraction.

"I'm about to get on a plane to come see you again," she says. "I'm so sorry that I delayed my flight, but something came up…"

She left me a message earlier, but it had been a rush. Something about an emergency and that she needed to push her flight back a few hours. I tried to get her back a few times, but she hadn't picked up. Her lack of response didn't help my nerves. But she promised she'd be here. I'm holding on to that.

"Don't apologize." Just hearing her voice has me smiling again. "Is everything okay now?"

"It's not. But it will be."

That sounds grim. I give her space to say more, but she doesn't. With nothing to go on, I offer a vague "That's good, then."

"Tell me how you are, though," she hurries on, obviously eager to change the subject. "Are you nervous? Excited? Calm?"

I glance down. I'm sitting on my bed in the room I share with Linc, dressed in as much of my gear as I can put on here. My feet, in hockey socks, are in my slides, and my leg is tapping, my giveaway nervous tic. "Totally cool here." I must not sound convincing, because she laughs.

"You are going to do great. You worked hard for this, and no matter what happens, you'll know you did your very best. I believe in you, and I'm so proud of how hard you worked to get here." The words seep into my chest, and any tension I'd been carrying eases. She continues, "I'm going to be there, cheering you on. As soon as they can get me off the ground here and into the air." The last part sounds impatient, and that makes me grin.

I close my eyes, inhaling a steady breath. "I can't wait to see you."

"I can't wait to see you too."

The bathroom door opens, and Linc comes out. He isn't playing because he still hasn't been cleared of his concussions, much to his frustration. Linc was drafted the year after me. He's a junior, but this was supposed to be his year to sign, to try his hand at the big show. The concussions this season have sidelined him. He hopes that next year, as a senior, he can get his career back on track. I hope so too.

He mouths Hannah's name, and I nod. "Hi, Hannah."

"Linc says hello."

"Hi, Linc," she says. "I'll let you go. They'll be boarding soon."

I don't want to say goodbye, but she's right. I need to get to the rink. Still, I stall hanging up. "Be safe."

"Good luck. I'll be there soon."

"Thanks." I disconnect, dropping the phone on the bed beside me.

"How was her concert last night?" Linc asks as he drops down on the bed beside me.

"Damn. I didn't ask."*Shit.* I pick up my phone, pulling up my search engine. "I'm sure it was great."

"Of course it was. She's insanely talented. I have no idea what she sees in you." He nudges my shoulder as we both stare at my phone, waiting to see if there are any videos of her gig last night. I search for the Dazed Zealots. What pops up makes my blood run cold.

The first hit is a tabloid with the clickbait title of, "Is Love in the Air for the Zealots' Sebastian Taylor?" The thumbnail is too small for me to see it clearly, so I click on it.

What pops up is a picture of Hannah and Sebastian. They're both smiling, and he has his arm around her. The color is high on her cheek. She looks gorgeous, as always. Jealousy slams through me. *What the hell is going on?*

"Is that Hannah with Sebastian Taylor?" Linc leans closer. "What the…" We pause as we read through the first part of the article, which talks about how they were seen at dinner last night, at some fancy restaurant in the city. Another picture shows them in different clothes. He's walking in front of her, and she's got her head down, trailing him.

He pushes the phone away, blowing out a disbelieving snort. "No way. Of course they were together last night. She opened for their concert. This article doesn't even give her a name. They make it sound like she's some random girl who showed up at their concert."

"I don't like that guy." I study the picture. "Hannah said he's just that kind of guy. Touchy-feely. But he likes her. I can tell."

I hate to admit how much that picture of them looks like she likes him as well.

"Fucking tabloid. Desperate for clicks."

"You're probably right." I can't take my eyes off that picture. This feels like the worst kind of déjàvu, except Hannah isn't Rachel. Not even close.

Linc stands and gives me a shot on the shoulder."Probably? I'm always right." He slides his feet into his sneakers. "Come on. It's bullshit. You have a game to get to."

Dutifully, I stand then pocket my phone. Following Linc out the door, I try to shake off the uneasy feeling in my stomach. The tabloids blow things out of proportion, and between my father and what happened with Rachel, I have more than enough experience. But in both of those cases, there was some truth to the pictures they posted. *Is there any truth to this?*

She didn't tell me that she was going out to dinner with the Zealots—not that she needs to clear her agenda with me, but we haven't had much time to talk with all the traveling she's been doing and all of the things involved with my playoffs.

Is this the real reason why Hannah is late today? Because there's something going on between her and Sebastian?

She still thinks ours is a fake relationship, and she hasn't shown any sign that she's willing to talk about that changing. But we're sleeping together. She isn't the type to have feelings for someone else and then sleep with me. *Is she?*

I should have said something sooner, convinced her that I want something exclusive with her, something real. I didn't want to push her too far, too fast. The last time I came anywhere close to it, she literally ran. *But did I lose my chance all together?*

As I step onto the bus, I shove all of my doubts aside for now. She is flying all over the place just to be here for me. That has to mean something.

Right now, I have a game to win.

Hannah

MY FLIGHT IS LATE.

We don't get off the ground in Philadelphia until almost four o'clock. Cord's game is scheduled to begin at seven, so I still have hope while I'm in the air that I'm going to make it.

Except because my flight was delayed taking off, there's a lot of air traffic to land. I don't hit the tarmac until six-thirty, and then we need to wait for an open gate.

I slide into the backseat of my Uber driver's Accord at almost exactly the time Cord's taking the ice.

I find the livestream of his game as we drive from the airport. Even in the first period, it's pretty clear that the momentum is with the other team. They score first. But right before the intermission, we tie it up. They're returning to the ice as I'm sitting in traffic outside the rink. By the time I get out of the car, their opponents score again. I rush through the arena, still keeping an eye on the game. I get to the concourse under the seats during the second intermission.

I'm supposed to sit with Cord's father, but after everything that's happened, I'd rather not. In fact, having a stomach flu sounds more appealing. Instead, I stand in a tunnel toward the top, where I can see the entire rink.

The CU Bulldogs tie the score. There's so much tension in the rink, it's hard not to pace. With three minutes left, though, their opponents get a breakaway and score.

The coach pulls Nate out of the Chesterboro goal, giving them one more skater. But no matter what they do, they can't seem to put the puck in the net. The time runs out, and our team loses three to two.

Cord and his teammates watch the other team celebrate, and the disappointment wafting off of them is unmistakable. I swing my duffel bag onto my shoulder and head toward the exit. I won't be able to see him here, so I order a car to get me back to the hotel. I'll wait for him there.

I stare at my phone, wanting to text him. *What can I say? What do you tell someone who got that close to a dream and watched it slip away?* So I end up with: *I'll be in my room. Just come up. I'm proud of you.*

I want a shower, but I don't want to miss Cord if he shows up, so I wash my face and sit, staring at my phone.

The day plays over in my head, from my mother's phone call, rushing to Philadelphia and Mr. Weaver, and ending with the plane ride from hell and Cord's heartbreaking loss. I need to see him, to hold him. All of this will be a lot better when he's here.

An hour goes by and then two. It's after eleven o'clock, and he hasn't texted. I don't know what to do. *Do I text again? Should I wait longer? Should I just go find him?*

What would a real worrying girlfriend do? I don't even know what that means anymore. All I do know is that I want to see him and make sure that he's okay. They've got to be back at the hotel by now.

I stand, smooth my hair, and head downstairs to the hockey floor.

When the elevator opens, it's a completely different atmosphere than it was the other night. The hallway is quiet. There are a few people sitting. A girl is talking to her guy, obviously soothing him. Three guys farther down seem to be sharing a bottle of something.

I stop in front of Cord and Linc's door. Inhaling, I knock. When there's no answer, I knock again.

The door opens finally, and Cord is there with a red plastic cup in his hand. "Hey," he says.

"Hi." I can't read his mood, and that leaves me in unfamiliar territory. Usually, he's an open book. "Can I come in?"

He steps aside to let me pass and closes the door behind me. The place is a mess, clothes everywhere. He puts down his cup and cleans off one of the beds.

"I didn't hear from you." It's an obvious statement, but I don't know what else to lead with.

"I didn't feel like chatting."

All right. Definitely not in the mood for company. Still, I'm worrying about him. "Where's Linc?"

"Said I wasn't good company. Went somewhere else."

Can't say I blame him. But I won't leave him here like this. He's hurting. "I wanted to make sure you got my message and that you're okay."

"I'm not okay, Hannah." He drops down onto his bed and buries his head in his hands. "We lost. We should have won that game, but we didn't."

"I saw." I hate seeing him like this. I squeeze his shoulder, my heart breaking for him.

“Did you?” He looks up at me. “You weren’t in your seat. I didn’t think you came.”

How could he think I would miss it? I knew how important it was for him. I was nervous for him, like I was playing the game. “I told you I was coming,” I offer softly as I sit beside him. “My flight got delayed out of Philadelphia. I landed here right around when the game started. I watched it on livestream until I got to the arena for the third.”

“Philadelphia?” He shakes his head. “I thought you were flying out of Scranton.”

I’m sure I told him I changed that. Maybe I didn’t in the middle of all the chaos. “It’s a really long story.”

“Is it?” He tilts his head, and I can smell the liquor on his breath. I wonder how much he’s had to drink. “Does it involve Sebastian Taylor?”

I cock my head, trying to follow this conversation. “Bash? What are you talking about?”

“Bash.” He snorts and snags his phone off the bed beside him. As soon as he opens the phone, he holds it out to me. “This is what I’m talking about.”

Some gossip rag is on the face, a picture of Bash with his arm around me at the top of the page. We must have been leaving the restaurant last night. “This is from Barone’s, last night.”

“That’s what it says.” He stands, reaching for his cup then downing a healthy amount.

It’s late, and I’m exhausted, so maybe that’s why it takes me a long second to get what he’s trying to say. “You think that something happened between Sebastian Taylor and me last night.”

“That’s you, isn’t it?”

"Of course." Obviously, but that's not the part that hurts. "We were at dinner."

"Is Sebastian the reason you were late today?"

The words hit like punches, and I inhale sharply, trying to get air in my lungs. Of all the things that have happened over the past twenty-four hours, this one shocks me the most. There are so many things racing through my head, but all I can latch on to is, "Do you think I slept with him last night?"

He holds my gaze, his eyes full of pain. He shakes his head and opens his mouth, but no words come out. I can only stare at him. After all the time we've spent together… I whisper, "I slept with you, just the night before this."

He exhales a shaky breath, and it dawns on me that maybe that isn't enough for him. I press my hand against my chest. It hurts so much, I'm surprised I'm not really wounded. I turn away, trying to sort this all out. It's hard to think around how betrayed I feel.

"You knew how important this game was to me. It was the playoffs. The final game." He puts his cup down with enough force that some of the contents slosh out. "Then you don't make it, and you're out with some rock star."

"I told you I tried to get here." I'm not sure whether I'm really angry or if I latch on to it to keep the tears away. "But something came up with…" I can't tell him about my mother, about Weaver, about his father's stupid ultimatum, even though I decided on the flight here that I should. But right now, when he's looking at me like this, the words stay trapped inside me. "I had an emergency. And yes. I know what this means to you. It's the reason we're together in the first place."

He flinches as if I slapped him. But it's a reminder for both of us that all of this was based on a lie. "But instead you made time for Sebastian Taylor."

Even though I don't know that he'll believe me, I try to explain. "I went out to dinner last night with Sebastian and Milo Parker. I officially signed on with him as my manager. It was a celebration. Sebastian is the one who went to bat with Milo for me. Milo and the Zealots want me to go on tour with them in the summer." I fold my arms around my stomach, hoping that it will hold me in. "Did you honestly think I'd be doing all of this flying around to be here with you and somehow plan a date in the middle?" I hate how broken my voice sounds. After all the time we've spent together, it's as if he doesn't know me at all.

Or maybe I don't really know him.

His eyes are glassy when he looks up. I know he's not completely sober, but he's sober enough to know what he's saying. "You let Sebastian help you. I offered to put you in touch with my agent, Harry, more than once. He's with one of the most reputable talent agencies in the world. Or I could have talked to my father. He knows celebrities, politicians… Why would you let Sebastian help you but not me?"

"I don't want to take anything from you or your dad," I spit out. His father, with all his special contacts and friends… "When this is over, I don't want to owe you anything." The words are so slippery, they're out faster than I can catch them. His mouth tightens. "Cord, that wasn't what I meant…"

"That's okay. I get it." His face is dark. "You don't need me to help you. Maybe you should have agreed to fake date Sebastian instead."

He can't mean that. But when he doesn't say anything else, I step back and away from him. I can barely hear my next words over the pounding of my heart. I knew that things with Cord couldn't last forever, but this wasn't how I expected it to go. I could argue more, try to convince him that he has nothing to worry about and that I want to be with only him.

But if it already hurts this badly, maybe it's better if I don't. With this pain lacing through me, I can't imagine how it would feel if this goes on longer and I fall even harder. "Playoffs are over. So there's no more reason for us to be faking anything." I clench my jaw, doing my best to hold my composure even though my eyes are burning. "This has been fun. I'll see myself out."

"Hannah…"

I leave, pulling the door closed behind me, so I don't have to watch the end of us on his face.

Back in my room, I stare at the walls. I haven't even opened my duffel, and it's almost midnight, but I need to get out of here.

I've been such an idiot. I told myself that I was prepared for when this ended. But I'm not. Not at all.

I drag out my phone, feeling numb. In a matter of minutes, I've booked a flight back to Philadelphia. I've got a real life to get back to.

Cord

IT'S DAWN WHEN LINC comes in, or at least I think it is. I closed the blackout drapes last night. I didn't want to see the sun.

I groan, regretting the alcohol. But after Hannah left, it had been the only thing that quieted the chaos in my head. Today, it's going to make me pay for that silence.

"You're here." He sounds like he hasn't slept. "I thought you'd be with Hannah."

I pull the covers over my head and close my eyes.

"Why aren't you with Hannah?" I hear him fall onto the bed beside me. "If I were you, I'd definitely be with Hannah. Alone sucks."

"I don't want to talk about it," I grumble.

"Fine. Because I don't want to hear about it." He snorts. "All your cuteness. It's disgusting to watch."

The words hit me in the middle of the chest. I lower the covers. "We broke up."

He shifts up on his elbows. "I'm sorry, what?"

"We broke up." I sit up, pulling a pillow behind my back. "Or she called off our fake dating." Only people in real relationships can break up, and it's clear she hasn't seen us like that.

"And you just let her?" He's incredulous. "Are you a complete moron?"

This is not the support I expected. "Shit, Linc, it's not like that."

"What the hell could it possibly be like?" He points at me. "You're crazy about her."

"She didn't make it to the game last night."

"Are you sure?" He narrows his eyes. "Why?"

"Her flight got delayed. She said she watched the first two periods livestream and then got there for the last period."

"So she did the best she could, it sounds like." He props his head up on his hand. "I thought she was on an early flight, though."

"She changed it. Flew out of Philadelphia instead of Scranton."

"Why did she do that?"

I still don't know. I was too wrapped up in everything else to push her on it. It said a whole lot about our "relationship" that I would even have to drag that information out of her. "She said she had an emergency. That's all I got."

"None of this sounds like reasons for a breakup. Sure, she might have missed some of the game, but she did what she could. Not just any girl would fly around for her guy."

I don't think I've ever felt like her guy. That's a huge part of the problem. I don't think she ever saw me like that either. "I brought up the picture of her and Sebastian Taylor."

"Jesus Christ…"

I glare at him. "I don't think it's unreasonable—"

"She flew everywhere over the past few days, and that was what you led with?" He shakes his head then lies down. "I'd break up with you too." He snorts, obviously disgusted with me.

I can only scowl. "You're an asshole."

"And you're stupid," he fires back. "She's not Rachel, you dumbass. You treated her like she was."

My irritation bleeds away, and I stare at him. *Was that what I did?* I know that they're different—almost polar opposites—but last night, I reacted like they were the same. I was tired, upset about the game. It's no excuse, but it's all I have. "Damn it."

"Exactly." He nods. "What was her emergency? Is everything all right?"

"She wouldn't say. But it made her have to fly out of Philadelphia."

"That's weird. It must have been a big deal if she missed it." He nods, convinced. "You should ask her."

"I don't think she's going to want to talk to me."

"Only one way to find out. Go find out." He drops back on his pillow, his hands behind his head.

I only stare at him, torn. After the things I said, she's probably pissed at me. "I don't know what to say."

"How about start with 'sorry I acted like a dumbass'? Go from there." He shakes his head. "If you haven't talked about Rachel, you should do that too. She deserves to know that it's your baggage she's dealing with and not hers. Now, leave me alone. I need some sleep."

I hop out of bed and search around for some pants. I brush my teeth quickly because I'm eager to get to her, to apologize and make sure she's okay. I head to the elevator while still throwing on a hoodie that is questionably clean.

On her floor, I bound out before the door opens all the way. Her door is already open, so I rush forward. Except it's housekeeping, not Hannah, inside.

"Excuse me. Where's the girl?" I ask as my stomach sinks.

"No girl. Housekeeping." The woman points at herself.

"I know. Where's the…" I peek over her shoulder. The room is completely empty. No bag, nothing.

I pull my phone out of my pocket and send her a text. *Hannah. I'm sorry. Can we talk?* I stand there in the hall, waiting for her response. There are no dots, nothing to indicate that she received my message or has any desire to get back. I blow out a breath and head back downstairs.

In my room, Linc looks up. "What are you doing back?"

"She's not there. Housekeeping was cleaning."

Linc's brows shoot up. "She's not there right now, or she's not there at all?"

I don't know, so I pick up the phone and dial down to the front desk. "Hello," I say to the chipper receptionist. "Could you put me through to Hannah Marshall?" I give them her room number.

"I'm sorry, sir. Ms. Marshall checked out late last night."

My eyes meet Linc's. "Thank you." I hang up. "She left last night."

"Did you try to call her?" He asks, sitting up.

"I texted." I pull out my phone, dialing her number. I wait, and it goes to voicemail. "Nothing."

"Damn. Sorry, man." He shakes his head. "We check out in a few hours, and we'll be home by this evening on the bus."

I nod. But I get the feeling that it's already too late.

The day is one of the longest of my life. Checkout is at eleven. We end up at a Denny's for lunch. By the time we're on the turnpike, headed home, it's one o'clock. If I had my car, I would be home in four or five hours, tops, but a bus is a different story. It's almost seven by the time we pull up to the rink.

I've texted Hannah a handful of times, but she's not answering, so I don't bother going into the locker room. Instead, I throw my bags into my trunk and head right for her house.

I pick my way over the potholes at Dreamland. But her house is dark, and her car isn't here. I stop, anyway, bounding up the porch and knocking on her door.

Nothing.

Burying my hands in my hair, I stare up at the dusky sky, worry eating at my gut. *Where the hell is she?*

Hannah

I BAIL OUT MY mother.

It's mid-afternoon on Sunday by the time she's released to me. She looks rough. Her hair is limp and greasy, and her face is still wearing the remnants of whatever makeup she had on when she was arrested.

There are no tearful hellos. In fact, neither of us says anything until we're on the highway, heading back toward Chesterboro.

"I wasn't sure you'd come," she offers, staring out the window. "If I were you, I'm not sure I would have come either."

"You're my mother." It's not "of course I'd come." I did consider leaving her in jail, where she couldn't get drugs or alcohol. "But this is it, Mom. I can't do this anymore."

"I know." She still doesn't look at me. "You've got graduate school. Just like you and your father always wanted." The words could have sounded bitter, but they don't. Only resigned.

"No." I shake my head. "I'm not going to graduate school. At least not now." My flight this morning took off in the dark. As I watched the sunrise out the window, I reevaluated a lot of things. Last night, leaving that hotel, I was angry. At Cord, at his father, at my mother…at all the things that had put me on this path. But at dawn, I decided that all those problems didn't have to be mine. My father's dream for me to go to graduate school doesn't need to stay mine.

What I want is to see what happens with my singing. Maybe I fail. But it's my turn to take control.

"But it's what you wanted." Her eyes widen as if she's panicked. "You can't give that up."

"I'm not sure whether it is what I wanted or what I always thought that Dad wanted for me." Music is something he and I shared. Though my mother liked it, she didn't have the desperate need to create it the way my father and I did. "I still plan to make music, but I'm going to do it a little differently than he wanted. I'm going to do it the way I want."

I can feel her gaze. Then she stares out the window ahead of us and doesn't say anything for long miles.

"I don't know what I want anymore." It's a quiet confession. When I glance at her, she's staring at her hands. "I haven't even thought about it in a long time."

Though the words anger me because she should have wanted to be my mother, I let all that wash over and through me. "I'm grown, Mom, with my own life. You should live your life too."

Her face turns to the window, but I see tears on her cheeks.

"It's time you figure out what you want next. What you want your life to look like, without me and without Dad's shadow." I shift so I can reach into my jacket pocket. The brochure from Shooting Star Acres is still there. I pull it out, flatten it the best I can, and hand it to her. "It's a lame name for a rehabilitation facility, but you've been admitted."

She looks at me, her tear-soaked face surprised.

"I have money, the money I was saving to go to graduate school. I'll be a little bit short, but after I sell the trailer, that should pay for the rest of it." I don't care that Cord's father offered me a fortune. I'm not taking a dime from him.

"Hannah, this"—she points at the listed costs on the pamphlet—"that's a lot of money."

"You can pay me back."

Her eyes widen.

"When you get on your feet. If you want to get back on your feet." I inhale, my fingers tightening on the steering wheel. "If you don't, I'm going to ask you to stay away from me until you do. I need a fresh start, and so do you." The words hurt. It's one of the hardest things I've needed to say. But I'm not helping her by being a crutch. She needs to want to do this on her own. "But if you do want to get on your feet, and if you do want to have a relationship with me, I promise I'll help you every step of the way."

We sit in silence for a few miles. I don't know if rehab will work. I don't know if the judge in her case will be lenient without Mr. Spellman's coaxing. I'm not even sure if she'll want to do it. But she's worth a shot, just like my dreams.

"What if I can't do it?" she asks, her voice small. "What if it doesn't work?"

I shrug. "Then it doesn't. But what do you have to lose?"

"Nothing," she says, straightening. "I don't have anything right now."

Even though I thought it would be impossible, my heart squeezes. "Exactly."

Her mouth firms. "You're right." She nods. "Let's do it."

I slow, pulling over to the side of the road and retrieving my phone from my purse.

"What are you doing?" She asks, alarmed.

I take the pamphlet from her, putting the address of the facility into my map app. "You said you want to go."

"I do."

"Well, what are we waiting for?"

She smiles, and for the first time in a long time, she reminds me of the mother I used to know. "You're right. What are we waiting for?"

We stop for late dinner at a cheap fast food place, and then I get my mother settled in at Shooting Stars. Cheesy name aside, the grounds really are beautiful. I don't know whether all rehab places look like this or if this is a particularly nice one, but if it passed Mr. Spellman's test, it's good enough for me. I get the feeling he's got high standards for everything, not just his son's girlfriends.

It's late by the time I leave her. I have no idea if this will work, but I'm at peace with it. Whatever happens next is her choice. I told her I would check in on her, but the house rules are no phone calls or visits for ten days while she works through detox.

I pay for a motel room Sunday night. I'm exhausted after getting barely any sleep last night then working through the day with my mother. I lie on the bed in a crummy roadside inn and stare at my phone.

Cord left a handful of texts and a voicemail. I've read them all, but I don't know how to respond. He says he's sorry, but I'm not sure what he's sorry for. He said he shouldn't have brought up Sebastian, that he hadn't meant it. Maybe not, but if it hadn't been Sebastian, it would have been something else—his father or his job, my job, being apart. We weren't going to last. Still, I need to hear his voice. I listen to his message so many times, I memorize it. I don't fall asleep until at least one o'clock.

But after I wake at five o'clock and can't go back to sleep, I get up, shower, and check out. My body hurts, and I feel like I'm moving through quicksand, but I'm sure that's just heartbreak. It'll dull with time.

That's what all the songs say, anyway.

Shooting Stars is a three-hour drive from Chesterboro, and I get to campus at just after nine. Dr. Pierce has office hours, and I need to talk with him.

I knock on his door, and he looks up, spinning his chair to see me better. "Hannah." He always smiles when he sees me, and it strikes me that Pierce has been the father for me that I haven't had these past years. "You're back. A shame about the hockey team, though, isn't it?" He takes off his reading glasses and shakes his head.

"It is, sir." I drop into the comfy chair in his office. I can't even count how many times I've sat here to go over things with him. "I needed to speak with you about something else, though."

"Sure, what can I do for you?"

"I was wondering if there was any way for me to complete the remainder of the term remotely." I wasn't sure about that when I was driving, but now that I've said the words, I am.

"Why would you want to?" He looks shocked.

"I'm going to be going on tour with the Dazed Zealots in a month or two. I'm going to be in New York to record an album." A zing of excitement flares through me. When I state it like that, I know it's the right choice.

He studies me. "I see." Turning to his computer, he pulls up my records. I'm only taking four classes this semester, and one of them is an independent study with him. Because there are only a few more weeks before finals, I bet I could just not come and still have good enough grades to graduate. But I don't want to leave my education like that.

He looks over my grades and my requirements, but I know he's seeing what I already know. I'm ready to leave. He pushes away from the screen and spins around to look me over. "We would need to speak with your other professors, but I don't see that there's a problem."

I exhale. "I'll return for any finals, if necessary." I can't imagine the trailer will be sold by then. "Thank you, Dr. Pierce. I'll be back for graduation, and when I'm on campus, I'll stop in to say hello."

"See that you do," he says. I stand, ready to go. "Miss Marshall?"

"Yes?" I stop at the door.

"Good luck. With everything." He pauses, but I can tell he has something else to say. "And also… Remember, sometimes you're running from things, and sometimes you're running toward things. It's always easier if you figure out which you're doing at which times."

I cock my head. I'm not sure whether he's talking about graduate school or the Zealots or something else. But no matter what he's trying to say, it's good advice all the way around. "Thank you. I'll keep that in mind."

He nods and stands, folding me into a hug that I didn't see coming. He pats my shoulder. "Now, get some sleep. You look tired. Oh, and send me a copy of that album, will you? I might be old, but I still appreciate good music."

"Will do." I laugh, though it sounds hollow to me, and wave before heading back to my car, feeling lighter. When I head back toward my house, though, I pass the hockey rink.

Cord.

I swallow the tears in my throat, desperate to push that ache aside. I miss him, his voice, his smile, and the way he lightens up every situation. I want to see him, hear him, hold him. Except that's stupid. More dependence on him will only make it worse later.

I'm not running from anything when it comes to him. I'm saving us both from more pain down the road.

Cord

I DON'T EVEN BOTHER to text Hannah more than once on Monday. She hasn't gotten back to me yet, so I'm not expecting anything. Any hope that I felt yesterday that I could get through to her or that she'd heard the apologies I'd left via text and voicemail dulled overnight. Still, I need to talk to her. I can't leave things like this.

So I'm navigating the potholes through Dreamland after lunch on Monday afternoon, hoping to catch her this time. If not, I'm not sure what I'm going to do.

Her car's in the drive, and though I'm nervous about what she'll say, I'm eager to see her. It feels like the past two days have been much longer.

When I knock on her door, she pulls it open slowly. "Hi, Cord."

That's it. That's all she says. Two days, no response, and all she can say is hello. "Hey," I offer then clear my throat. "Can I come in?"

She steps back, holding the door open. She doesn't get close to me, I notice. But that's not all I notice. There are boxes on the ground and a suitcase next to the washer and dryer in the hall. "What's going on?"

"I'm going to stay in New York, at the studio where I'm going to be recording."

"You're going to be recording an album?" This is huge news. "When did you decide this?"

"Milo mentioned it when he asked me to sign on for the Zealots tour this summer. He wanted me to have new material to distribute. I spoke with my adviser this morning. I'm good to go."

I look at her, and it's like I'm staring at a stranger. *How is this the same girl that I slept with just last week?* "So that's it. You're just going to leave school." She bites her lip, and it hurts as I ask, "Were you going to say goodbye?"

She swallows. "I think we said everything we need to say the other night."

That doesn't invite conversation, but I refuse to give up. "I disagree. I think I said a lot of stupid things, and then you ran away before I could apologize for being an asshole." I take a deep breath, softening my voice. "Which I want to do in person. Because I am sorry. I shouldn't have acted the way I did."

She goes to the sink, her back to me, so I continue.

"That wasn't about you. I don't know if I ever really explained why Rachel and I broke up." My hands are shaking, so I tuck them in my pockets. "Last summer, I saw a picture in the tabloids of her. She was with Tyler Laurence, a guy who played here last year and is now playing in Colorado. She slept with him, and they caught her coming out of his apartment." I hurry on. "I know it's not fair, but when I saw that picture of you with Sebastian, it was like revisiting that all over again."

"Sebastian is just a friend. I'm the opener for his band." She turns around, leaning against the sink. "I told you that in New

York, and I still mean it."

"I know," I step forward, closer to her. "I'm sorry, Hannah. So sorry. I let my own baggage get in the way, to cloud my reactions. Can you forgive me?"

"Of course." She smiles up at me, and I want to sweep her into my arms. But her next words stop me. "But it doesn't matter. It doesn't change anything between us." Her eyes are sad. "If it isn't Rachel, it's going to be something else. Our jobs, our families, being apart, and long distance. Our lives are different. We're too different. You need to see that."

"I don't. I have no idea what you're talking about."

"I'm going on tour, and you're going to a professional hockey team. You don't even know where. Even if we don't consider the geographical limitations, there's everything else. Your father doesn't like me." My eyebrows drop at that, and she shakes her head with a laugh. "Please. Trust me, I know that. And my family… my mom, me… We're a mess."

"I don't care about any of them or any of that. I know this started as something fake, but it's real for me. It's been real for me for a long time." I put my hands on her shoulders, almost crumbling from the feel of her. "And I know you're not convinced, but if you give us a chance, I know we can make this work."

Sure, there are a lot of obstacles, but I can't imagine repeating the last two days without her over and over with no end in sight. No matter how hard it is, it can't be any harder than that.

She exhales a shaky breath. "I know that you think it's going to work, and you want it to. But we aren't the same. Pretending like we are, that we belong together, will only make it harder in the end." She pushes away. "I spent this weekend bailing my mother out of jail on prostitution charges. That was why I was late to your game, Cord. Because I was at the justice center in Philadelphia, trying to figure out what to do with her."

"Hannah…" I run my fingers through my hair. "I didn't know…"

"I know you didn't know, but do you know who did know?" She hugs her arms to her chest. "Your father. Your father knew. Because he had a private investigator look into me. The guy approached me outside the justice center. He told me that your father would help my mother out, get her probation. He'd already secured a spot for her at a rehabilitation facility in central PA. And he promised he'd help pay for all of it. All I needed to do was leave you alone to your hockey life and not tell you anything about it."

"Oh my God." I go back over all the details of the weekend, her delayed flight, the way my father had insisted on picking her up. He'd wanted to talk to her, to warn her away. I've never felt starker anger or deeper betrayal in my whole life.

"He probably thought I wouldn't want to say anything anyway. Who would want to talk about having a prostitute for a mother?" She tilts her chin up. "But do you think that he would have pulled something like that on someone else? Someone more like you?" She shakes her head. "Because I don't."

This is a complete disaster. If I thought my chances of getting through to her were small before, this makes things even direr. Still, I grip her shoulders and try. "Hannah, I'm in love with you."

Her eyes flare.

"Please. I want to be with you, to hear your laugh, see you smile. I want to kiss your mouth and know everything about your day. My dad's an asshole, but I'm not him, and I don't care what he thinks or what anyone thinks. I only want to be with you. I've only wanted to be with you for almost as long as I've known you. We can do this. I know we can."

"No. That's what you think right now." She licks her lips, her eyes holding mine, and a tear spills onto her cheek. "But I think we'll only struggle with all this and grow apart, and when we end it later, it'll hurt even worse."

I rub my thumbs against her cheeks and search her eyes. But there's no opening there, nothing that I can see to tell her that is going to make anything easier or get through to her.

I already told her that I loved her. I don't know what else to say.

"You're a coward, Marshall," I whisper, and she closes her eyes, blocking me out. I force myself to drop my hands from her face, because the longer I touch her, the more I want to. "I thought you were a fighter, but you aren't."

More tears drip down her cheeks, and I turn away from them—from her. Just seeing them and knowing that she's tearing us apart like this because she isn't willing to give us a chance is shredding my gut.

Since I have nothing else left to say, I head for the door. Glancing back, I say, "Good luck. Wherever you go."

And then I leave her there, along with a chunk of my heart.

Hannah

September, four months later...

I OPEN FOR THE Zealots when they play to a sellout crowd at Madison Square Garden. MSG is the most surreal venue. So far, it's the largest that we have played, and we haven't ever sold out before.

I sing my songs, ride the wave of the crowd. It's magic. It's perfect. I'm made to do this.

When I step offstage after introducing the Zealots, I'm alone. I stare out at the sea of people rocking along to the Zealots songs. They released an album in August, and it's creeping up the charts. I'm so happy for their success. My first single is doing well too.

But no matter the success, no matter the happiness I feel from their success and mine, there's always something missing.

They have each other. They're a family, and though they've included me and taken me in as one of their own, I'm separate. Alone.

My mind slides to Cord, as it does a lot. I've watched his career. I can't stop myself. He signed with the Jaguars to play defense. All the talking heads say he's in the best shape of his life. I don't doubt it. He's driven and smart, destined for success.

His hard work got him called up last week. He'll be playing at the highest level in their exhibition game tomorrow night here, at Madison Square Garden, in the same space where I just sang.

I step away from the stage, return to my dressing room, and close the door behind me.

Leaning against the door, I stare up at the ceiling. It's quiet. It's worse this way. Because most of the time I'm busy. The sounds, people, and constant movement of my life distract me. But in these moments in between, I'm left to think about him.

I listen to the Zealots, waiting to come out after they're finished for the encore. We sing together, and the crowd is great. But something is missing.

Something is always missing.

We sing. We bow. The Zealots wave and smile for the cameras. When it's done and we're filing off the stage, I'm alone again. Empty, like before.

I pretend, though, as the Zealots hug, to feel the euphoria after a successful show. They don't pay much attention to me. I smile and find my way back to my dressing room in record time.

In the silence of my space, I turn the television to TSN. They have more hockey news than any of the domestic sports stations. I listen for any news about Cord and his Jersey Jaguars as I take off my makeup and the dress I wore to perform. It's late, almost midnight. I put on sweats and a T-shirt.

A knock on my door interrupts me. "Come in," I call.

Bash steps in. He takes me in, without makeup, watching TSN, and shakes his head. “Aw, Goldie Girl… Beating yourself up, I see.”

Over the past few months, Sebastian and I have become good friends. He knows some of what happened with Cord. His pity irritates me. “Shut up, Bash.”

He snorts, falling into the chair next to me, and I sigh, pulling my hair back into a ponytail.

“You should just call him.”

“I doubt he’d want to hear from me.”

“If I were him, I’d still want to hear from you.”

I shake my head. “It’s complicated.”

“It’s really not.” He glares at me. “Sure, things have changed. You aren’t the same girl you were then. But you’re miserable.”

“No, I’m not.”

“You hide it pretty well, but I can see. So can Libby.” He’s serious now. “Your album is great. You’re going to be a huge star. This should be one of the best times of your life, on the cusp of success. But it isn’t, and we hate seeing you sad.”

“I’m not sad.” I’m not. I have everything I’ve ever wanted. I love singing, and Milo thinks that I’ll be able to headline some of my own gigs after my album release in a couple months. I’ve become closer to the Zealots, even though I’m not technically part of their group and therefore don’t exactly fit. But they’re friends, something I’ve never had time for. Even my relationship with my mother has improved. After her time in rehab, she moved to New Jersey, closer to where I’m settled in New York. She’s starting back to school at the community college. She’s been sober since our car ride to Shooting Star. I couldn't be prouder of her. We're not exactly close, but we're working on it.

On the outside, everything is looking up for me.

Bash raises his brows.

"Fine. I think about him."

He shakes his head.

"A lot. I think about him a lot." I sigh. "I think about him all the time."

"He'll be here tomorrow night." I spin in my chair to look at him, and he raises his hands. "What? I know what's going on."

I laugh at him. "You're nosy."

"He's right here, Hannah." His eyes are so sympathetic that I look away. He steps behind me, placing his hands on my shoulders and meeting my eyes in the mirror. "Since you joined up with us, you've taken all sorts of risks with your music. I barely recognize the shy girl I met in the spring."

I smile. He's right—working with them has been inspiring.

"Don't you think you're worth a risk too?"

"I screwed up, Bash." I shake my head. "If I were him, I wouldn't take a chance on me."

"Well, he's not you." He pats my shoulder, and then he leaves me with my sports highlights.

I stare at myself in the mirror. *Is he right?* I don't know. It's been months, and maybe he's moved on. *I told him to move on, didn't I?* I shake my head and turn away, unable to meet my own eyes.

Cord was right—I'd been afraid. There, in that run-down trailer, with my savings depleted from paying for rehab for my mother, I didn't feel like I was worth anyone taking a chance on me. He had faith in us then. *But how does he feel now?*

Some things have changed, but a lot hasn't. I'll be on tour, and the hockey season is starting. There are things that will make it harder for us. But those are only excuses. I see that now. None of those obstacles matter if we're both committed to making it work.

I just wonder if it's too late.

Bash is right. There's only one way to find out. Pick up my phone and call Milo. He always answers, no matter what time. "Hey. I was wondering if you could do me a favor…"

Cord

LINC AND DECLAN STAY at my mom's in New Jersey the night before my first exhibition game. They've already started back to classes, but they both said they'd never miss it. I bust their stones, but I'm glad they came. I'm more nervous than I expect.

I've spent most of the summer with my mom. Usually, I split my time more evenly, but after everything that happened with Hannah, I haven't spoken with my dad. I don't know if I ever will. Maybe in time.

Mom treats us to breakfast at the diner in Menlo Park. They make the best pancakes I've ever had. She sips coffee and has an egg on toast while the rest of us tuck into more carbs than are healthy for anyone. She smiles at my buddies like they're her sons too. Back at her place, I pack up my stuff and head to the rink, promising that I'll meet them all after the game.

The game isn't until four, but I'm there early for an ice bath and to get my head together. I pull my car into a parking garage near Madison Square Garden. Most of my stuff will come with the team equipment managers, but I grab my personal bag and head down to the street.

September in New York is sweaty and oppressive. I breathe in the smell of too many cars and too many people and grin. Since I was a kid, it's been my dream to play here, at MSG. When I signed with the Jaguars, I wasn't expected to get here this fast, yet here I am.

I step inside. It smells like ice. My smile widens.

I ask for directions to the locker room and head the way they point me. The first strains of the national anthem split the air. They're probably doing a sound check. But when the singer begins, I stop, every muscle tightening.

Hannah.

I close my eyes, bracing myself. I haven't talked to her since that day in her trailer before she left Chesterboro, but her debut single has been on the radio. Every time I hear her, it hits me square in the chest.

But this isn't her single. This is the anthem, which means… she's here.

My feet are carrying me to the ice—toward her—before I can even stop.

As I step out of the tunnel and the rink opens up before me, I scan the boards, searching for her. Her voice is bigger here. Madison Square Garden is renowned for its acoustics. Though I try to rein in my anticipation—my excitement—I can't. It's as if my body knows she's close, that I'm near her.

I find her standing near the glass, a microphone in her hand.

She's singing, her eyes closed. She looks the same in so many ways. Her hair's the same length, and her mouth…I swallow.

But she's not as thin. Even from here, her face looks a bit fuller, and her hips, encased in dark denim, are more rounded than before. It looks great on her. There's color on her cheeks, and she's the picture of health. She's more beautiful than ever.

I hadn't expected she would hit me like this anymore—like a runaway truck—after so many months.

I hike my bag up on my shoulder, just watching her, unable to stop. Her eyes open, and she finds me as if her gaze is drawn to me too.

Her voice wavers the slightest bit, but she keeps going, holding our eye contact. As always, it's like electricity in my veins.

What's she doing here? Obviously, she's singing the anthem at today's game. But I refuse to think that has anything to do with me, even though my traitor brain wants it to. She performed here last night, with the Zealots, which I know because even though I've told myself it's over a million times, I can't stop following her career, rooting for her, and watching her like I'm doing now. It's as if I've been starving for her these past months, and now she's here. Pictures on the internet or in publicity photos just don't do her justice.

When she finishes singing, we stare at each other for a long moment. But I force myself to turn away. She's here for her job, and I'm here for mine. It's not until I'm heading back into the concourse that I can breathe again.

"Cord!" Her voice carries through the concourse tunnel, stopping me in my tracks. Footsteps echo, too fast to be walking. She's running up behind me, and then there's silence. I close my eyes, bracing myself to see her again.

Inhaling a steadying breath, I face her, attempting a smile. "Hi, Hannah."

Up close, she is perfection. My fingers tighten on the strap of my bag.

"Hi." She's breathing harder, from running. I take a few steps to her—I've always been drawn to her—before I stop myself.

She closes the distance, raising a hand as if she's going to touch me, and I stiffen because I don't think that I can survive it. She stops. "It's good to see you."

"You too." There's a pause, and since I've never been able to handle awkward silence, I say, "You're singing the anthem."

"Yeah." She waves toward the rink. "I've never done it before. Should be fun."

"You sound great."

"Thanks."

I nod. *God, this is painful.* I open my mouth, intending to cut this short and retreat to the locker room to hide.

But she interrupts me. "You got called up to play today." She rocks back on her heels.

Why is she extending this conversation? Maybe this isn't as torturous for her, but standing here making small talk is brutal for me. "Yeah. They think I'm ready."

"Congratulations."

"Thanks." I smack my lips, looking anywhere but at her. "Listen, I should get to the locker room to ice." I step back, putting space between us. "It was great seeing you. Really. Good luck tonight."

I don't even wait for her to say goodbye. I swear, I've spent the summer practically killing myself in the gym, on runs, working out to the point of exhaustion so that I am too tired to think of her. Even then, she shows up in my dreams. My career is about to take off—I can feel it—and I've never felt more confident. But when it comes to Hannah, all of that means nothing.

She calls after me, but I keep going toward the stairwell. I don't know my way around this rink, but usually, the locker rooms are on the first level.

"Cord," she says, following me into the staircase. "Wait, please."

On the landing, she's too close. "Hannah, come on. I'm trying to be a bigger person here, but this…" I wave my hand between us. "Let's not drag this out, okay?"

She steps closer. I flex my fingers, the need to hold her a physical ache. "No. I came to say something. I hope you'll let me say it."

I'm helpless to do anything but stare down at her, holding still to keep myself from doing something I'll regret like reaching for her.

"I was a complete idiot." She tucks a strand of hair that's come out of her ponytail behind her ear. "You were right. I was afraid. A coward. And I'm sorry. So sorry."

My eyes shift between hers. *What is she trying to say here?*

She continues, "I should have believed you when you said you wanted to give us a try. I just couldn't see why. Everything about me felt like such a mess. My whole life, I've been trying to be perfect, to be respectable. To be worthy…" She shakes her head, biting her lip. "And then you stood there, in the middle of my lowest time, and told me that you did care, that you loved me anyway, and I just…" Her eyes fill with tears. "I just couldn't believe it. And for that, I'm so sorry. I never meant to hurt you."

I swallow, my throat so tight that I can barely breathe.

"I asked Milo to see if he could get me in to sing here today. I thought if I could get near you, if I could talk to you. That maybe after the game, I'd be able to see you, to tell you…" Her voice fades.

"What do you have to tell me, Hannah?" I rasp out. I'm trying not to hope, but…

"That I love you." Her voice rings through the stairwell like she's using all the force in it. "I loved you when it should have been fake, and I've loved you ever since."

My bag falls to the ground, and I pull her into my arms. Whatever ponytail she'd been wearing doesn't stand a chance as I bury my hands in her hair and cover her mouth with mine.

I kiss her with all the raw pain and emotion I've been carrying around these past months. I rub my thumbs on her cheeks, trying to clear away the tears, but they keep coming, so I keep kissing her until we're both breathless. It's savage and rough, but she returns the kiss, her fingers digging into my back and pulling at the hair at the back of my head.

When I pull away, I drop my face into her neck, breathing her in, and wrap my arms around her. The feeling of her in my arms again is straight out of my dreams, and I close my eyes, afraid that if I don't hold her tight, she'll disappear.

"Please," she says, her face in my chest. "Please, will you give me another chance? I know it's going to be hard, maybe even harder than we ever thought. But I've been miserable without you."

I offer a silent prayer to whatever gods made this possible. "I've missed you so fucking much." My voice is coarse, so thick I'm afraid she can't hear it. "I love you too."

She exhales, and it's shaky. "Still?"

"I can't imagine ever stopping."

She takes my face in her hands, and her kiss is fierce. Then she says words that I never would have expected to be magical, but they are: "I have a private dressing room."

"Hell yes," I respond. It's not the most romantic thing I could have said, but I think it gets the job done because she grabs my hand. I barely have enough time to pick up my bag before she's dragging me out of the staircase and we're rushing through the concourse, looking for an elevator.

We make out like adolescents on the elevator. Then the door dings, and she pulls me down a hallway and into a room.

Closing the door behind us, she slides the lock home. I dump my bag right inside the door, and she throws herself into my arms. I catch her, hiking her legs up around my waist. I drop my mouth to hers and guide us to the sofa, lowering her then following her down.

Not once do we hesitate. The time apart means nothing now. I'm reverent, my hands shaking. After all this time, I never would have expected that I would have her against me again, that she would be willing to give us a chance.

Our clothes are off in a matter of seconds. Her skin against mine is like coming home. I can't touch her enough or kiss enough of her skin, and she is as desperate. When I push inside her, we pause and lie still, holding one another, breathing. I meet her eyes, and she sweeps the hair off my forehead, cupping my face in her hands.

"I love you," she says, and the words sing through my chest.

We hold each other's gazes as we move, and when we find our ends, we fall over the edge together, clinging to one another. It's the hottest, most emotional experience I've ever had.

In the aftermath, we curl up on the couch, our arms around each other. We don't say anything for a long time.

Finally, though, she breaks the silent spell. "What time do you need to be in the locker room?"

I exhale. "Fifteen minutes ago, probably."

She laughs, but I force myself to loosen my grip. We shift to sit, and I slide her onto my lap, hesitant to let her go. She presses a kiss to my cheek. "I love you so much. It took me so long to say the words, but now that I have, I want to keep saying them all the time."

"I love hearing them, baby." I catch her mouth with mine.

When I pull back, she cups my cheek. "I know that I have things to make up for to prove to you that I'm serious about giving us a chance. I promise you, though. If you are still willing, I'm ready."

"Baby girl, I have never been happier to hear anything in my life."

We kiss again, and I can't get enough of her. When we pull back, she's studying me. "Then I have one thing to ask you for now."

"What's that?"

"Do girls still wear their guys' jerseys to their games at this level?"

My face splits into a grin, and there's so much happiness inside me, I feel like I can't hold it all. I wink at her. "My girl does."

Hannah

THE BACKGROUND MUSIC WAFTS through my headphones. Eyes closed, I sing the lyrics I wrote to go along with the melody, swaying to the beat.

Recording in the studio is so much different than singing live. It's quiet and cozy. I feel alone, though Miles and my producer, Jeff, are sitting in the booth in front of me, listening.

Still, I'm almost alone, and that makes the experience of singing here personal. I'm glad, too, because this song is probably the most intimate thing I've ever written. It's the song I wrote for Cord months ago, when I was certain that we didn't stand a chance.

It's a song about longing and loss, about making mistakes and having regrets. It's all the pain I carried the time we were apart.

As I wind through the last refrain, I open my eyes, not surprised to find my cheeks wet. So far, I haven't been able to sing it without crying. The track is going to be on my debut album, so I'm sure I'm going to have to sing it roughly a billion times in the future, if Miles is right and the tour dates he has planned all pan out. I'll need to figure out how to do that without turning into a blubbering mess.

I swipe at my cheeks, desperate to get my emotions under control. My gaze falls on the booth, and I wonder if Miles and Jeff noticed. Except they aren't who I see through the booth window.

Cord.

I haven't seen him in a week, thanks to a string of games on the West Coast. He wasn't supposed to get home until later this afternoon, but he's here now, standing in the booth behind Miles and Jeff.

Unceremoniously, I fling off my expensive headphones, dodge around the sparse furniture in the room, and rush out the soundproof door. He must have been running to me, too, because we meet in the doorway of the sound booth, and I jump into his arms. He catches me then spins me around as he buries his face in my neck.

I laugh, holding him close. "You're home early."

"Just a few hours. I caught an earlier flight. When the jetlag catches up, I'm sure I'll crash, but I needed to see you." He lowers me to my feet but keeps his arms around me. "I missed you."

"Are you up for dinner with my mom tonight?" She has the night off, and I offered to take her out. She'll finish her data-entry certification courses this week, and I wanted to celebrate.

"Sure." Then, more softly in my ear, he whispers, "And later, if you're up for it."

"Hard yes." I draw him close, and his mouth covers mine. Like always, the kiss consumes me. I doubt I'll ever get used to how his lips feel on mine.

A throat clearing interrupts us, and Jeff's amused voice cuts in. "You guys are disgustingly cute, but we only have the studio for another half an hour."

We laugh, pulling apart. “No problem, Jeff,” I say. “How was that take of ‘Cry by Myself’?”

“I want one more today. Just to be certain.”

“Of course.” I nod. Squeezing Cord’s hand, I smile up into his gray eyes. “Mind hanging out while we finish up?”

He runs his thumb along my jaw. “Nowhere I would rather be.”

I go on my tiptoes and kiss his cheek before hurrying out the door and back into the studio. Tucking the headphones back on my ears, I say into the microphone. “From the top, then, Jeff?”

He nods and gives me a thumbs-up.

This time, I sing for Cord.

The past month has been more amazing than anything I could have imagined when I wrote these words. Our times apart have been difficult, and they won’t get easier. My touring is going to kick into high gear after New Year’s, and Cord’s been sent up to the Jaguars, moving forward. We’re going to be busy, but we’re both determined to work through it all. I’ve never been so sure of something in my life.

Though Cord has read the lyrics, this is the first time he’s heard the song performed. As I finish, he mouths, “I love you.” I don’t know whether he said it out loud or not, but I nod and mouth the words back, so the sound doesn’t catch on the recording.

After singing his song this time, happiness is the reason for the tears on my cheeks.

Acknowledgments

First, thank you to all the readers who are giving my hockey boys a chance. It's only because of you that I get to do what I love. Thank you.

A special thank you to my amazing husband and kids. You guys are always cheering me on, propping me up when I need support, and telling me to get back to work when I'm slacking off. I love you all.

This series wouldn't be what it is if it hadn't been for Jessica Ruddick's insight, pompom shaking, tough love, and general brilliance. Love you, girl. Also, thank you to Kate Birdsall and the work of everyone at Red Adept Editing. You keep my commas in the right spots.

Finally, thank you to my early readers…Jean, Aubree, Brook, Nikki, and Tracy. You guys are amazing. XOXO

About the Author

Josie Blake writes college-set, hockey romance with sass and emotion. She also writes award-winning romantic suspense and scifi thrillers as Marnee Blake.

Originally from a small town in western Pennsylvania, she now battles traffic in southern New Jersey where she lives with her hero husband and their happily-ever-after: two very energetic sons. When she isn't writing, she can be found next to a hockey rink or swimming pool, cooking up something sweet, or hiding from encroaching dust bunnies with a book. She loves to hear from readers so please feel free to drop her a note or visit her website at josieblake.com. Connect with her on Instagram at instagram.com/josieblakeauthor, or on Facebook at Facebook.com/JosieBlakeAuthor